WE
CAN
NEVER
LEAVE

Also by H.E. Edgmon

THE OUROBOROS DUOLOGY

Godly Heathens

Merciless Saviors

THE WITCH KING SERIES

The Witch King

The Fae Keeper

WE
CAN
NEVER
LEAVE

A NOVEL

H.E. Edgmon

WEDNESDAY BOOKS
NEW YORK

First published in the United States by Wednesday Books, an imprint of St. Martin's Publishing Group

WE CAN NEVER LEAVE. Copyright © 2025 by H.E. Edgmon. All rights reserved. Printed in the United States of America. For information, address St. Martin's Publishing Group, 120 Broadway, New York, NY 10271.

www.wednesdaybooks.com

The Library of Congress Cataloging-in-Publication Data is available upon request.

ISBN 978-1-250-85365-3 (hardcover)
ISBN 978-1-250-85366-0 (ebook)

Our books may be purchased in bulk for promotional, educational, or business use. Please contact your local bookseller or the Macmillan Corporate and Premium Sales Department at 1-800-221-7945, extension 5442, or by email at MacmillanSpecialMarkets@macmillan.com.

First Edition: 2025

10 9 8 7 6 5 4 3 2 1

In equal measure, this book is dedicated to those who can never go home and those who can never leave.

Author's Note

All of my books are incredibly important to me, each of them a love letter to traumatized teens, a promise that there's light flickering in the distance—but there's something really special about *We Can Never Leave*.

I wrote this book largely inspired by growing up in evangelism in the very Deep South, the sort of culture where snake-handling and speaking in tongues were normalized parts of the everyday churchgoing experience. I fictionalized that time in my life by writing about the Caravan, a secret traveling group of magical people who stay hidden from human society, engaging in their own questionable—and sometimes deadly—practices in the shadows. The main characters of this story are five teenagers living in the Caravan, each of them with their own secrets and trust issues because of the things they've experienced within it, who one day wake up to discover that all of the people they know have disappeared. They're the only ones left. And with no ability to trust the outside world—or one another—they struggle to figure out what really happened.

The characters are very different from one another, but their scars take similar shapes. Through them, I hope to help readers confront what happens to kids when they grow up in homes that aren't safe—a home completely isolated from the outside world, with no touchstone of normalcy and therefore no ability to see just how messed up things are where they came from. These characters don't know how to be in relationship with one another, don't know how to listen to their own instincts, and are left with no idea how to navigate life without the rest of the Caravan, even if the way their life was going before wasn't something they were happy with. And each of these characters will have a very different ending, holding true to the book's dedication—that this is a story meant both for those who can never go home again and those who never get to leave in the first place.

I hope you enjoy. If you can stomach it.

WE
CAN
NEVER
LEAVE

Chapter 1

Bird

The night the unthinkable happened, Bird woke to the sound of fevered laughter and their own desperate gasps for air. As their dreams brushed against reality, they could've sworn they were choking, their own wild heart trying to clamber up their throat and into their mouth.

As dreams do, the sensation faded, and Bird was left with only the laughter outside their bedroom window and a pit in their stomach. They threw away the age-softened blanket and tugged their legs to their chest, pressing their sweat-damp forehead to their knees in a bid to recalibrate to the waking world and their body. Cool air, heavy with a stale residue of incense and the all-natural deodorant that clung to their soft palate, nipped at their ears and stamped gooseflesh across their skin. Fingers, toes, thick with pins and needles. Heartbeat, *there you are, you*, drumming beneath their temples. Bird had never been a stranger to nightmares, though these unsettling dreams had become increasingly unrelenting in recent months.

Perhaps that was no surprise, considering how unsettling their everyday had become in tandem.

In fact, for that very reason, *bedroom window* was hardly an apt description for the divide between their bed and the revelers outside. When Bird finally lifted their head, it was to squint at the tiny panel of cloudy glass embedded at the rear of their mother's camper. Beneath it, their twin-sized cot with its inch-thick foam mattress had been propped open—the same cot Bird had slept in for most of their childhood, and a place they'd once planned to never sleep again. At least this time they'd been generously allowed something resembling a wall—a faded old bedsheet strung up from the ceiling to act as a curtain between their corner and the rest of the makeshift home. If Bird didn't know better, they'd think its threadbare state a personal slight—the pettiest of little revenges for daring to leave in the first place. But the fact that they could still see every twinkling fairy light and abandoned candle on the other side wouldn't have been flagged as a problem to their mother, even if she had noticed.

They pressed their knuckles into their eyes as if to rub away the dogged tendrils of sleep or the steadily encroaching headache. When someone gave a delirious shriek from the campground and sent a spike of pain through Bird's eardrums and into their limbic system, they accepted defeat. They fumbled in the dark for their phone before their fingers tightened around cool metal and tugged it free of its charger. Air hissed through their teeth at the burning light of the home screen, eyes struggling to adjust.

11:43 P.M. Nearly midnight, and the lunar festivities refused to be quelled. Bird couldn't even remember if it was a *new* moon or a *full* moon they were dancing under. In either case, it would do no good to try and convince anyone to keep the volume down. If they so much as asked, Bird would only be teased for being a stick-in-the-mud.

Resentment, like acrid smoke, lapped at the inside of their mouth and tasted their eyeteeth. Returning to their role as the Caravan's insipid court jester was as unwanted as returning to their sad old cot.

With a groan, they threw back the curtain and stomped into the dark of the camper. Of course they were alone, their mother's nest of a hammock abandoned over the pull-out kitchen table, fringed blanket edges teasing the Formica. Holly Stieber would be nowhere else but at the center of whatever was happening outside.

More familiar resentment, an old bruise that might've healed if Bird had ever learned to stop pressing on it.

The outside air was chilled, autumnal and sharp, and Bird doubled back for shoes and a mantle the first time they ventured into it. On the second attempt, their sandals met brown grass, their fingers twisting in the woven tapestry draped over their shoulders, and Bird—who was being *very* brave— ventured toward the smell of the Caravan's hopes and dreams going up in flames.

It was, in fact, a new moon being celebrated. New moons, new beginnings. Marking a cosmic rebirth, they were nights when the universe begged all creatures to make their desires known. And just by doing so, they might wish them into existence.

The ritual happening at the campground was one Bird had grown up watching every month for nearly their entire life. Members of the Caravan scrawled their wishes on scraps of paper and threw them into the flames, their smoke signals decorating the sky like prayers wafting to the ears of a nameless, omniscient god. And all night, they danced, barefoot and drunk and brimming with hope for what was sure to come in the aftermath of the night's magic.

Nothing ever came, and there was nothing listening. Bird had figured that out a long time ago.

But that *is* what a stick-in-the-mud would say.

No one noticed when Bird's cloaked shadow joined the edges of the party, too busy enjoying themselves. That was for the best. Bird didn't need—or want, really—to be seen here; they were only here to watch. Golden eyes flicking through flame-shrouded bodies, they searched the crowd until they found their mother.

The sight of her made Bird's stomach gurgle, their hands curling even tighter into the tapestry weave. Holly was practically nude, unsurprisingly, and her bare skin was lathered in oils and powders made of dried, crushed herbs. Her hips rolled and her head swayed, both with such frantic conviction that it made her levitate, looking less like a dance and more like a situation that warranted an ambulance. *If* the Caravan were made up of the sort of people who ever called an ambulance.

Not far behind Holly were her parents, Bird's grandparents, Basil and Cassandra. The couple sat on the steps of their own RV, watching the gathered crowd. Elders in the Caravan, Bird's grandparents had been around nearly since the community's inception. Neither had been born into it—instead, like so many of their people, they'd been found. Now they continued the work that had brought them safety and community, traveling the country to find others who needed them. Others who were . . . different.

Bird's eyes fluttered over their grandmother's forehead, to

the curled snakes making a crown around her skull. As they watched, another snake head appeared, peeking through the dark coils of her hair—then another, and another. Cassandra whispered something to her husband, her own forked tongue flicking into the air between them. Basil's wings, soft tawny feathers turned monstrous by a trick of the firelight, twitched behind them, curling his wife closer.

Different, yes.

Not everyone in the Caravan was as easily identifiable as Basil and Cassandra. Holly had inherited pieces of both her parents but—though she did *literally* levitate—could pass as human when it suited her. It'd certainly suited her when she'd met Bird's father, a very average and normal human himself. And Bird, for their part, may as well have been 100 percent free-range grass-fed *Homo sapiens*. At least on the surface.

Their appearance had served them well three years ago, when they'd decided to leave the Caravan, never intending to return. For three years they'd managed to live with their dad in the world of humans, chasing a life they thought they might be able to build there. Of course, they'd failed. In the end, everything fell apart before it had the chance to come together, and Bird was forced to run back home and beg for a place to stay and their inch-thick mattress. Forced to bite their tongue until they tasted copper and accept their mother's sympathetic grace.

It didn't matter what they looked like. They would never be human. And more, *this* would always be the firelit hole they'd crawled out of.

Someone had warned them of that, once, before they'd run away. But Bird hadn't listened to him.

Their eyes searched the crowd for another face, hungrily seeking a familiar set of antlers.

Where are you, Hugo? What wishes are you throwing in the fire tonight?

What would a boy without hope demand of the universe, anyway?

Before they managed to locate the bony branches of their splintered other half's brow, Bird's gaze stuttered on an ominous red glow from within their grandparents' RV. Their eyes skittered quickly away but doubled back again, locking with the cardinal blood-moon stare that burned even from behind glass.

On the other side of the window, Eamon, a shadow in the shape of a boy, watched them. The newest addition to their Caravan, Eamon had been picked up and collected into the fold only days before Bird's own return. Like so many who'd come before him, he had no memory of who he was or where he'd come from. The nature of his power was unclear. He was staying with Bird's grandparents until he'd found his footing.

Or perhaps until he'd killed them all in their sleep. Bird did *not* get a good feeling from the guy.

Only those red, red eyes and the sharp planes of his face could be made out, illuminated by the glow of the fire between them. Interesting, how his eyes could so closely match the shade of popping ember venturing to warm the bleak October midnight, while the weight of them could feel like ice on Bird's skin.

For the second time since waking, they felt their throat tighten. The chasm of that stare was too deep to wade into, singing a kind of primal warning that made Bird want to bolt for the camper and bury themself beneath every timeworn scrap of fabric they could find. For someone who seemingly knew nothing, Eamon certainly stared at them as if he knew everything he needed to know. It was as if he could see right through them—a particularly terrifying thought, since no one really knew what he was or wasn't capable of.

Least of all himself. Or so he said.

He looked at Bird as if he knew everything they kept tucked behind their teeth. As if he knew exactly what dreams had been haunting them, and which ones they would throw into the fire tonight if they dared to throw any at all.

Bird broke his stare, turning away from the window.

If that were the case, Eamon would benefit from keeping his eyes on his own page. The things Bird didn't say went unspoken for a reason.

Some prayers were better left unanswered.

Chapter 1

Hugo

The last thing Hugo sees before claws dig into his arms and drag him into consciousness is the light filtering through the trees, decorating his somnolent limbo in dappled specters. The first thing he sees on the other side are the wild eyes of ichor that he would know anywhere, in any shade of life or in death itself.

"Get the fuck off me." He peels the frantic hands from his shoulders and shoves Bird out of his bed. The memory of their fingertips at his clavicle makes him want to set himself on fire, like cauterizing an open wound. "What the hell is your problem?"

"Where is everyone?" The rasp in Bird's voice has warped into an accusatory rattle, less honeyed and more hornet than usual.

Hugo blinks sleep from his eyes and stares at them with undisguised irritation. The light from outside his tent is still the hazy blue of early morning, and his skin summons a layer of gooseflesh at the bite of cold beyond his den of blankets. It can't be long after sunrise. There is something deeply wrong with Bird that they would wake him at such an hour, and more still that they'd have the indecency to allow the dawn light to turn the frizz of their curls into a whimsical, misty halo.

Of course, there is something deeply wrong with Bird anyway.

"Who is *everyone*?" he asks around a mouthful of a yawn, disguising the tectonic strength of his pounding heart by reaching up to palm at the back of his neck. He tries, and fails, to not feel a quiver of satisfaction at their wince as he cracks the first few vertebrae into submission.

"Everyone." Bird's arm flourishes behind them, motioning to the unzipped tent flap they must've crawled through. "Hugo—*everyone* is gone."

Well, that can't be right. He frowns, considering the obviously misguided worry on their face, before glancing over at the other side of the tent. Felix's bed, a perfect mirror of Hugo's except for the addition of his brother's army of books and stuffed animals, is empty.

Hugo doesn't remember standing, but he bodies Bird out of his path to get outside, the movement intentionally, paradoxically careless.

The memory of the night before is evident in the campground. Smoke still clings to the air, desperate to survive its confrontation with morning dew. The damp, trampled grass around the extinguished firepit is littered with discarded bottles and clothes and singed tears of paper, wishes and castaways crying careless echoes of the new moon frenzy still churning on only hours ago.

When a gentle wind brushes against the spindly stretch

of trees, Hugo tilts his head back to watch the falling yellow leaves that come to meet him. The growing pink-laced sunlight of morning glows, steady and unshakable, from behind the half-bare bone-white branches, painting life in streaks along the stark, toothy cut of whatever Rockies they've nested beneath this time. A memory tugs at the back of Hugo's mind, something about the monsters in his dreams, but it's too far away for him to get his hands around it.

It's quiet. There is no one outside but the two of them.

"Everyone must be sleeping," he offers, forcing his tone to wear a mask of condescension, even as his heart forgets the choreography of his pulse.

"The campers are empty. The tents, too. There are sleeping bags but no one's sleeping in them." Bird steps close enough to his back that he can feel the heat of their breath burn at his nape. "It's just us and—"

Hugo has already stormed off before Bird has the opportunity to finish their thought.

"Felix!"

Panic tastes like sulfur and the malty beers he'd filched the night before from the cooler in the back of his dad's truck; feels like the floor of his chest falling open and beckoning him to drop through it while his devils make their escape. Nothing bad is allowed to happen to Felix.

You see, the world is not good. He knows that much. Hugo hasn't shown his face in the human world outside the Caravan. He hasn't ever been—and won't ever be—allowed to experience it for himself. But he understands enough to know it is *not good*, and he has for a long time.

There is nothing truly good in the world because nothing is actually fair. If it were, he might get to live in the real world himself. Instead, everything everywhere is tainted by greed and cruelty and a series of cosmic jokes.

Justice isn't real and it never has been, and anyone convinced of the existence of fate or karma or the triumph of good over evil is probably actually evil and trying to sell something. Like his parents. Like most of the adults in the Caravan. And maybe he isn't exactly evil himself, but Hugo still isn't *good*, and neither is anyone he's ever known.

Not even his beloved little brother. Sure, maybe there was a time when Hugo thought Felix was different. But he knows better now. Everything, and everyone, is ugly at their core.

And none of that means anything. Hugo doesn't care about being good. What he cares about is keeping his brother safe—the rest of the wide and worthless world can rot for all it matters.

His throat burns. "FELIX!"

"No one has seen him."

Another voice trails its talons down the shell of Hugo's ear, making him shudder. He wheels toward it and finds Calliope Guerra watching him from the steps of her camper. The venomous wolf-girl watches him with heavy-lidded amber eyes through short, choppy hanks of dirty black hair, her pointed ears sticking through the tangles.

Bird steps into his periphery. Hugo tries and fails to avoid noticing how they cross their arms. "Like I was saying. It's just us, Cal, and Eamon. As far as I can tell, there's no one else left in camp."

"Did anyone bother to try calling?" Hugo demands, shoving his hands in the pockets of his sweats like he might find his phone. It isn't there, of course. He moves to double back to his tent, but Bird holds up their palms to stop him. He comes up short, inches from enduring their touch for a second time in a single morning. Every scrap of his flesh is needles.

"Hugo . . . no one can answer their phone."

"Why?"

It's been years since Hugo was this close to Bird. Other than their wake-up call minutes earlier, which only halfway counts when the moment was fogged by sleep, he hasn't been close enough to touch them since the two of them were fifteen and even stupider than they are now. Back before Hugo knew trust was a trick and the world was just a board game for a bored god.

He can see it on their face like he's reading a dog-eared paperback, the way they don't want to answer his question. The way their eyes bounce over his shoulder, front teeth tracing the cracks in their dry lips. Finally, Bird admits, "Everyone's phones are still here."

Hugo's stomach detaches from his body like a hot-air balloon lifting from the ground.

"No, that's . . ." It can't be true, because that would mean something really, deeply wrong, that something unthinkably fucked up had happened while he was fast asleep and none the wiser. That under his watch, or lack thereof, his brother disappeared from his bedroll a mere arm's reach away. "Why would they just leave them?"

"Because they did not have a choice."

Christ. Has Eamon been here this whole time? Hugo realizes now that the boy is leaning against someone else's RV, arms a barricade across his chest, red eyes burning holes into Hugo's face like lit cigarettes trying to extinguish themselves. But he can't have been here this whole time. Hugo is grotesquely aware of that freak, has been since he showed up from whatever hell he escaped from, and he would've noticed him before now.

No, Eamon probably just materialized from shadow or smoke or whatever the fuck he does when he's lurking around like some kind of omen.

And like the harbinger he is, Eamon adds, "Something very bad happened here."

Hugo wheels toward the woods, soul already plunging ahead of his body into the spindly cage of white-barked trees. "FELIX!"

"Your brother's gone," Cal calls out. "You're wasting your time."

"Shut up," Bird snaps. "What, do you think that's going to help?"

"I don't care about helping. I need him to focus so we can figure out what's going on."

"You are such a bitch."

"FELIX!"

"He is obviously with the others." Eamon isn't trying to be heard, but his voice scrapes against Hugo's eardrums anyway, unable to be tuned out. "If any of them are still alive."

Hugo spins on his heel, turning from the forest to face the others again. "I will cut your goddamned heart out, you sick—"

"Huey?"

A voice as careful and quiet as the practiced edge of a sharpened razor presses against Hugo's throat. Slowly, he turns back to the trees.

Felix has stumbled out of the tangled underbrush and into the campground. His inhuman ears, tan and soft with fur like a deer, droop down over his pale face, obscuring one of his eyes entirely. From the other, he rubs the remnants of sleep, blinking the verdant, spring-green mosaic awake.

"What's going on?" he mumbles around a stifled yawn.

Hugo's mind doesn't know how to grapple with the slap-dash cocktail of adrenaline and fear and relief that tips into his veins like a faithless transfusion. His body does, though, and it doesn't hesitate to storm forward and slam his fist into his little brother's face.

Chapter 2

Cal

There are bruises forming on the delicate apple of Felix's cheek and the mountainous ridges of Hugo's knuckles, but it's the younger Beránek brother apologizing. Over and over again. It was amusing the first half-dozen times, but now?

"I'm *sorry*," Felix begs, like an unbaptized baby pleading at the doorstep of the Catholic god.

That *is* Catholicism, right? The one where babies have to be baptized or burn in Hell forever? Cal's life has been a long stretch of too much alone time with nothing to do, and most of the books kept around in the Caravan are theological ones. Something to do with their desire to understand where they all came from—like maybe if they read every holy book in existence, they'll eventually find the missing puzzle piece that explains who they are and what they're supposed to be doing here. Cal must've read hundreds of them by now.

She still doesn't know shit.

Felix apologizes yet again. She rolls her eyes and turns away from the brothers. Like everyone else in the Caravan, she's seen more than enough of their toxic codependency on display. She doesn't need to watch another episode of their disturbing marionette act.

Besides, there's a much bigger problem than whatever traumatic family dynamic the two of them are working through.

She checks her phone again—still no calls back from anyone she tried to get in touch with, but she knew that would be the case. Everyone's phones are still here, after all, along with all their clothes and journals and spell jars and everything else that belonged to anyone. It's all still here. And even if it weren't, no one ever calls her back anyway.

One fang presses into the inside of her mouth until a sour mixture of blood and venom leaks onto her tongue.

"Is it possible they left of their own free will?" Eamon's voice is as unsettling as everything else about him. In fact, it sounds less like a voice at all and more like someone put flint and ash in a blender, then tried to teach that blender to speak.

Predictably, Hugo dismisses himself from whatever fraught exchange he's in the middle of to level an accusation at their newcomer. "That's a really convenient suggestion from someone who might've had a hand in the alternative."

"Why," Eamon drawls in more of a monotone than usual, "would I choose to be left alone with you?"

"I don't know. I don't know *anything about you*. No one does."

"Yeah, dumbass, including him," Cal scoffs, crossing her arms over her chest. She has no real interest in defending Eamon—on the contrary, she doesn't think Hugo is entirely wrong to suspect him—but the blame for his own ignorance doesn't sit right with her.

"Why would anyone just up and leave like this?" Bird asks,

fingers yanking through their long, bouncy hair. "Without their stuff? Without telling us?"

"Maybe none of them like you very much," Eamon offers, though he's still looking at Hugo.

"Hey." Felix frowns . . . and, notably, doesn't actually argue with Eamon's assessment.

Not to wish she'd been caught up in the Rapture or whatever, but there is something so profoundly humiliating about being stuck here alone with the other misfit toys, and it makes Cal's teeth hurt. It only makes the sting worse that Eamon's cruel suggestion isn't far off. If anyone was going to be abandoned by everyone who'd ever known them, it *would* be the five of them, and her perhaps the most.

For starters, Cal is unwantable and unlovable and unknowable and she will die alone and she has felt the truth of that carved into her bones since she was too small to spell her own name. And that's that.

She's not the only one with issues, though. Eamon is creepy, and Hugo is annoying, and Felix is pathetic, and Bird is . . .

Well. Hold up, actually, because no one would go ghost without Bird. The day their mom fetched them from that Podunk airport and drove them back to the Caravan after three years away set off a celebration that never really ended. Last night's new moon party was the biggest and loudest and longest Cal had ever witnessed.

No, if the prodigal child has been abandoned at the campsite with the outcasts, something terrible *really* must have happened.

"Maybe Basil and Cassandra rented a party bus and packed up everyone else real quiet-like," she drawls. "Wouldn't be the first time the grown-ups around here pulled some fucked-up trick on the kids."

Everyone, involuntarily, looks at Hugo, who, suddenly on the spot, has to pick someone to glare at. He chooses Eamon.

Cal hikes her thumb in Bird's direction without looking. "Just sayin'. Princess here would never get left behind for realsies."

"*Princess*," Bird hisses, "is incongruent with my gender. Try rubbing two brain cells together to form a single creative thought, Calliope."

The correction is noted and carefully filed away for later. Cal still flashes fangs at them.

"The alternative is that something happened *against* their will." Eamon somehow manages to make even the prospect of a mass kidnapping sound dull.

"But—" Felix shakes his head, ears flopping about like one of his stuffies. "If something horrible happened, why would we still be here? Why everyone else and not us?"

The others exchange glances, no one wanting to offer up a possibility. They all know there's no answer that doesn't send them down some deeply fucked-up rabbit hole, because the very baseline of their existence is already a daily shitshow. Cal has spent a tremendous amount of her life feeling like Alice lost in Wonderland. Personally, she has no desire to make that feeling worse.

"Maybe we got lucky," Hugo finally suggests.

For a breath, no one says anything. Cal thinks that's fine. No one really needs to say what they're thinking right now, probably.

Except, apparently, Eamon does. "When I first arrived here,

I did not think it was possible you were as stupid as you look. Yet every day, you have endeavored to prove me wrong."

Bird pinches the bridge of their nose. "For crying out loud, you're not helping."

For the first time since Cal's known him, Eamon looks something adjacent to admonished. Of *course* he would care about the perfect little Birdie's opinion of him more than he cared about anyone else's. Cal can stand up for him all she wants when Hugo's being an ass, but she can never hold a candle to the sun personified.

Her shoulders tense until she can feel them at her ears, hands balled into fists shaking beside her thighs.

Whatever.

"What would you like us to do?" she demands, tossing her hand demonstratively at the rest of the empty, abandoned campsite. It may as well be a graveyard of vehicles and garbage, ringed by forest that stretches on and upward for miles before barren, rocky cliffs, already capped with snow, bludgeon it into submission. "See if we can find their footprints in the woods? See if we can catch their scent and follow the trail? Please, enlighten me, how you expect us to do anything right now."

Bird looks like they're thinking of hitting her. Cal wishes they would.

"You really haven't changed at all since I left, have you?" they ask.

"Not one bit," Cal agrees.

Eamon slips quietly from the group, headed in the direction of the golden-capped forest.

Are you part hound dog, shadow?

"Screw this." Hugo rolls his eyes and turns to go back to his tent. "We're not just gonna sit around here and stick our heads up our asses. Felix, c'mon. We're leaving."

"Leaving?" Felix pales but trots after his brother, on his heels like the loyal puppy he is. "Why would we do that? What if everyone comes back? Where are we gonna go?"

"We'll figure it out once we're on the way there," Hugo huffs.

"Do you really think it's a good idea to split up right now?" Bird calls at their backs. Both brothers freeze.

Felix's head whips back and forth between Bird and Hugo, opaline green eyes growing frenzied. "You—Huey, you can't seriously mean we're going to leave, just you and me, right? You meant everyone when you said we were leaving, didn't you?"

"Of course he didn't." Cal watches the way Hugo reaches up to twist his hands around the base of his antlers, massaging them at the root where they sprout directly from his skull, and a smug ember stirs in her chest.

Most people in the Caravan couldn't pass for human. But Hugo has always been the most obvious animal—in more ways than one, as far as Cal's concerned. His parents should've put him in obedience classes. He'd probably be way less fucking irritating with a muzzle.

"He's going to storm off half-cocked into the open and get both of you killed." Cal continues her warning as Felix's eyes grow wider and wider and the flush drains from his cheeks, like crawling vines overtaking the brick wall of his face until all that's left is the still-darkening bruise from his brother's fist. "It's hunting season in Colorado, you know."

"Hu—"

Hugo spins toward Cal, jabbing a finger in her direction.

"You, of all people, have no right to talk about me getting anyone killed."

Felix gasps.

Bird groans something under their breath.

But Cal doesn't need or want them to be offended on her behalf. She's heard worse. She's *thought* worse about herself plenty of times. There's nothing this insignificant little creep, angry at his own enormous inadequacy, could say to actually hurt her. Words can't hold that kind of power over her, especially not Hugo's. Besides, "As far as we know, I'm the only one here who *does* have the right to speak on it."

An uncomfortable silence swells until it fills all the space between the four of them. Good. Cal refuses to break Hugo's stare. Eventually, he looks away, and the smug ember snarls into a soothing little flame.

He opens his shitty little mouth to try and hurt her feelings anyway, but Eamon emerges from the woods at the same time. The red-eyed boy says nothing and looks at no one. Just stomps toward a pickup truck on the outskirts of camp—the old two-tone Ford that belongs to Basil, Bird's granddad.

When he flings open the driver's-side door, Bird calls out, "Hey! What the hell are you doing?"

Eamon tilts his shorn head to glare at them through the window. "I *saw* what is in the woods. I am getting far away from you people."

In the wake of skidding tires and crunching gravel, the clearing is stiller and quieter than Cal ever thought possible.

The silence is a far cry from relief.

Before

Cassandra spent the ages of two to eight hidden behind the walls of an old plantation home in the Deep South, watching her family live their lives through the crumbled plaster between the lath and the pinpricks in the wallpaper, leaving traces of herself only in the long sheds of snakeskin discarded in the crawl space. If her father heard crying, he simply assumed it was one of his other children. If her brothers or sisters heard the scampering of her quiet footsteps inside their rooms at night, they chalked it up to trapped squirrels, when they felt brave, or to the old house being haunted, when they didn't. The house *was* haunted, of course. Cassandra was just the youngest of its many ghosts.

Her mother was the only one in the family who knew Cassandra was with them. She would visit her once a day, hunched and hurried in the carved-out corner at the back of her wardrobe, to bring her daughter food and water, and sometimes thrice-mended clothes or forgotten toys passed down from Cassandra's older siblings.

In the beginning, Cassandra would beg to be let free of

the walls. She could not understand why she was no longer allowed to be with the others. She was lonely, starved for attention, and confused. In response to her pleas, her mother would guilt her viciously, reminding her that she was hidden to keep her safe.

Safe from whom, exactly, was never entirely clear, but Cassandra came to suspect she did not only mean from the wider world. The way in which her mother would whisper, half prayer, half tremulous fear, while touching the tips of her shaking fingers to her daughter's face, told of deep danger within the walls of the house.

"No one can know you're still here," she'd say, a litany. "No one can know what I've done."

By the age of seven, Cassandra had long learned to stop begging. She made friends with the mice and the occasional bird who tucked itself into her walls, making her own hidden world and fashioning dolls from splintered beams so she might have a toy no one else had played with.

But she'd also grown more clever. She'd discovered she could slip free of the walls during the night and wander the rest of the house. Every evening, she would sit two feet away from the family's dinner table, watching them eat their fill from pretty, painted plates and talk about their day. When the housekeeper took the dishes away and her family made their way upstairs, Cassandra would follow. She would sit behind her younger sister's bed and listen to her mother and father read her bedtime stories. She would lie there, resting her eyes and pretending the wall studs were a headboard, inches away from where her baby sister's breathing was growing slow and even, until she heard the housekeeper leave through the front door, and the last of the lights flicked off. And then she would begin to play.

As quiet as any phantom, Cassandra would push open the loose board at the corner of her sister's room. She would crawl along the floor, keeping her belly low to the ground like a true serpent, in case the little girl stirred and opened her eyes. Balanced on the tips of her toes and fingers, she would creep to the bedroom door and let herself out.

In the kitchen, she would splay open the refrigerator and devour the leftovers. In the living room, she would turn the radio dial for hours just to puppet the late-night voices and music crackling through the speaker. Often, she would visit the rooms of her older siblings, trying on the clothes that would eventually be hers and playing with the toys too beloved to ever go missing. And sometimes, indulgently, she would curl up at the foot of her parents' bed and let herself sleep for stolen minutes, imagining she could feel the warmth of their arms curled around her.

One night, she allowed herself to open a window and sneak outside. The prickling severity of fresh air in her throat was painful—no, vivid. Alive. She swung on the swing set in the backyard until she could imagine she was flying somewhere far away, until she felt as if she were up there with the stars.

Still, no matter what she did the night before, Cassandra was always careful to put everything in its place just so and be back in the wall by morning.

Unfortunately, there was no way she could have been careful enough.

Her brother, Peter, was the one to spot her. One night, she let herself into the kitchen, stomach already growling for the ambrosia and tuna casserole in the fridge. But she wasn't alone. Peter stood at the sink, faucet on, a cup held beneath the water.

He stared at her.

She stared at him.

He screamed.

She turned and fled back into the walls as quickly as she could.

The damage was already done. Peter woke up the entire house, screaming that he'd seen her. It took hours for their parents to calm him down enough to send him back to bed, hours of assuring him it was just his imagination or some sad waking nightmare. But a bell can never be unrung. Her siblings began to notice the way the house shifted and breathed at night, things never put back in the precise spot and angle they'd been left in. Her father started asking questions of her mother, probing questions that grew from curiosity to denouncement in their tone and language.

Finally, one day, when her father was at work, and the older children were at school, and her baby sister had gone down for a nap in her beautiful, lacy nursery, Cassandra's mother called her out of the walls. She had never done so in daylight. In the foyer, there was a man and woman dressed in dark, thick fabrics, hoods pulled over their heads despite the cloying summer heat. Her mother said Cassandra was going to live with them. They were her people now. They would keep her safe.

At first, Cassandra wanted to protest. She didn't want to leave her home, or her family. Even if she could only live alongside them and not *with* them, she wanted to be in that house.

But the woman pulled down the hood of her cloak and revealed a row of tiny little horns across her forehead. In a voice soft and even, she promised, "If you come and live with us, Cassandra, you will never have to hide in your home ever again."

The hive of snakes that had replaced Cassandra's hair hissed with curiosity, flicking their tongues into the air to scent the stranger. Nervous, but already swelling with a new hope, she pressed her small hand into the woman's. And together, with her mother weeping like a mourner in the open doorway, they said goodbye to her old life.

Years later, when Cassandra was halfway through her teens, the Caravan's leader had a problem.

"There's a boy—one of us, but entirely feral. I'm not sure how long ago he showed up without his memory, but it wasn't *people* who found him. Nothing we've tried so far can convince him to come with us."

They told her the boy was about her age and even more skittish than she was when she first showed up. She offered to go and see him. *Maybe like will call to like*, she thought.

He was living in the iron bones of an abandoned greenhouse, plopped down in several empty acres that were once someone's homestead. Overrun by ivy vines and sprawling wild basil, the greenhouse was a death trap of peeling lead-filled paint and broken glass and an echo of used-to-bes. Wind whistled over the few sharp teeth of glass still clinging to the iron, while the skeleton gave out great groans and sighs of exhaustion. Cassandra silently thanked the Caravan for her fancy hiking boots as she crunched over rusted metal that was maybe once gardening tools, pushing past the curtain of greenery to get inside the rib cage of the conservatory.

And within, she froze, eyes bugging wide. She'd been warned

it wasn't people who'd found him, but she hadn't been told what that meant. All at once, it became obvious.

Pigeons—*hundreds* of pigeons—were gathered in every nook and crevice, gnarled nests built from scraps of dead plants and abandoned tools. An entire flock of little heads, silver and iridescent and beautiful, twisted toward her. It must've been more than a thousand red eyes that stared her down then.

Everything was very quiet and very, very still.

Until, finally, Cassandra gathered up the courage to speak. Her voice did not echo in the metal decay, not with the abundance of plush feathers and greenery determined to swallow the bones whole. "I'm not here to hurt anyone."

The pigeons chittered and cooed in response, shifting this way and that with understandable skepticism.

"I was looking for the boy. He isn't one of your flock—but he might be one of mine." She jutted out her chin. "You know who I'm talking about."

"Who says I'm not one of them?" rasped a voice directly behind her, hot breath hugging the shell of her ear.

Cassandra jolted around so quickly it made the pigeons squawk and tousle in irritation. A few of them flapped their wings, whipping from one corner of the nest to another. Bits of down rained, unhurried, in a timeless, breathless flutter.

In fairness to the boy, he very well may have looked more like a pigeon than he looked like her. At least insofar as the wings are concerned—massive golden wings jutted up and out from his bare back, looming over them both. Her gaze dipped over the soft feathers that trailed all the way down to his— Oh.

Well, he was quite naked. She flushed when she realized it, eyes darting back to his face.

He scowled, unimpressed. It made her feel dreadfully

immature. Something deep in her belly begged her to flee back into the walls.

"What's your name?" she asked, instead of running. "Mine's Cassandra."

"I haven't got a name."

"Oh. Well." She sniffed, straightening to her full height, casting her eyes about for something to go off. She smiled when she found it. "Maybe we could call you Basil."

Chapter 3

Eamon

"What would you like us to do? See if we can find their footprints in the woods? See if we can catch their scent and follow the trail?"

Well . . . yeah, okay.

Eamon makes his way toward the tree line, ignoring the arguing at his back until it disappears, buffered and tucked away by the underbrush beneath the cover of aspen and pine.

Aspen, right, and pine? Are those the names of these trees? Yes. He's certain of that. He makes a note to wonder, later, how he knew that the pines are towering evergreen individuals, and that the aspen are all one great being, watching him tread through their vast body from all sides. He reminds himself to question at some point how he is able to identify the way they appear to be watching him with literal eyes because they have pruned themselves without hands or blades, leaving dark, uncanny scars that stare out in all directions. Eventually, he will have time to ask how he knows it is the aspens that stand white like great bleached bones because instead of bark, they wear their bare skin, and that, like people, the outermost layers of their flesh are dead.

The silence of the woods is stark. Only his boots, crackling through yellow and orange leaves, and his breathing make any noise at all. It is the kind of silence that would make others uncomfortable. Despite the supposed newness of his existence, Eamon feels comfortable making that assumption, because he has watched these *others*. The Caravan is full—when it *is* full—of people who love noise. Music, laughter, screaming of many kinds. It is always something. It is always loud.

But Eamon appreciates the quiet. There is something familiar about the solitude that comes in fleeting moments like this, reminding him of a moment that he can no longer actually remember, the echo of a memory of a memory that is no longer his. If he were to close his eyes and stand very still, Eamon might even believe he were dead. A grim thought, perhaps, but one that feels true nonetheless.

And why? What has he forgotten? What stands just out of his reach, just beyond the veil of solitude? More questions to ponder later.

It is somewhat an exercise in futility, his pondering. The list does not often shorten.

There is no immediately recognizable disturbance in the woods; no collection of footprints leading away from the campsite, no signs of a confrontation that would explain the disappearances of the others. Eamon is not entirely sure what he is looking for, but he would know it if he saw it.

It does not even briefly occur to him that he could have asked for help from the others. They do not want to help him any more than he would like their help.

Eamon knows there is an expectation of gratitude placed

on him. He was *found* by the Caravan, after all. He was rescued, saved—although from what, specifically, no one is actually sure.

As far as anyone else knows, Eamon was just like so many others who have been picked up by the Caravan over the many years of its existence. With no memory of his life before, and obvious, if ambiguous, signs that he was not entirely human—his red eyes being the most obvious among them—he needed to be brought into their fold before isolation or exposure put his safety on the line. In this version of events, they preemptively protected him from himself, shielding him from his own likely inability to survive in the so-called human world. Obviously he was meant to be grateful for that protection.

He might have been grateful for it, if all of that were true. What the Caravan remains ignorant to is that Eamon is not *entirely* without memories of his life before being found. And what he *can* remember serves as a warning: These people are not to be trusted.

Whatever happened to the others last night was likely no more than exactly what they deserved. If Eamon were truly being looked out for by some benevolent protector, Hugo would have been exiled with the rest of them. He supposes there's still time to see that transpire.

In any case, it does not hurt to search for evidence of the night's offenses. Whatever he finds will be for his eyes alone.

What he finds, however, is not footprints or signs of a struggle or a meandering trail of identifiable personal items like breadcrumbs leading back to camp. He notices the black grass blades first. There is a patch of earth off the worn path, nestled between lichen-covered stone and bundles of forgotten white limbs, where prey has probably hidden in the long grass for longer than people have existed here. But this patch is wrong. It is a far cry from the emerald green of its neighboring blades and bushes, its texture too heavy and still. This spot has turned to an oily pitch. It is so dark, in fact, that it could be a hole in the Earth itself, a chasm opened wide like a portal to nowhere.

Eamon considers the gaping nothing, standing very still for a moment. It would be foolish to get any closer. If there is something truly wrong with the Earth here, he does not want to touch it.

And yet, as if by compulsion, he moves forward anyway. Inching closer, he crouches next to the tainted ground. Examining it from a nearer distance does not make it appear less dark, and certainly not less ominous. What it does allow for is his noticing the ring of mushrooms surrounding the zone, a perfect circle of fungi, each of their bright red caps decorated in white spots.

That is . . . odd.

Or perhaps it is not. Eamon knows very little about most everything—and if that is not the case, then Eamon simply cannot remember knowing very much about anything. He has no idea if a ring of mushrooms in this perfect a circle is normal or something that should unsettle him. He *does* know perfect circles are natural anomalies. He also knows mushrooms are an exception to many norms. He does not know how he knows either of these things, and the details begin to break down like interrupted fractals the further he gets from the initial clips of knowledge. It really is just simpler to say he does not know things when poking at facts gets him nothing but pounding temples.

It does unsettle him, for the record. For whatever reason,

be it some forgotten knowledge or his anxieties running unchecked, something about the scene makes him nauseous.

It does not help that he is fairly certain the mushrooms are talking.

What was a nearly silent wood a few instants earlier is now slightly less so. Eamon has to strain to hear it, focusing hard and quieting his breathing. It is almost believable that he had known this would be here if he went looking, because he had to have gone looking at all in order to find it—the sound of whispering, words indistinguishable but somehow still there, hovering in the air like idling cars waiting for the green light of a breeze through the last remaining aspen leaves to carry them home.

It cannot possibly be coming from the mushrooms, though. Eamon may not know many things, but that much seems easy to be decisive on. Mushrooms cannot talk unless they are the kind he has seen Caravan members drink in tea. Even then, the rambled recounts of finally feeling one with the Earth require a mouthpiece to deliver them and they do not ring entirely true.

Yet there he is, kneeling in the dirt, pressing his ear as close to the red caps as he can without letting them touch his skin.

The murmuring grows closer, louder, but not yet decipherable as language. He could still convince himself he was imagining things, could still leave this place and tell himself he had invented whispers where there were only the quiet calls of insects underground and hushes of high-up pine needles in symphony.

Instead, Eamon holds his breath and waits. Even the beating of his heart is too loud, pounding in his eardrums. He seals his lips and holds air in his chest, waiting patiently as his lungs begin to burn and his vision begins to swim, until his pulse begins to slow . . . slow . . .

And there, in the stolen silence between heartbeats, he finally understands what the mushrooms are saying.

WE DIDN'T MEAN TO KILL ANYONE PLEASE FORGIVE US WE DIDN'T MEAN TO KILL ANYONE PLEASE FOR-GIVE US WE DIDN'T MEAN TO KILL ANYONE PLEASE FORGIVE US WE **D**IDN'T MEAN **TO** KILL ANY**O**NE PLEASE FORGIVE US WE DIDN'**T** MEAN TO KILL ANY-ONE PLEASE **FORGIVE** US WE DIDN'T **ME**AN TO KILL ANYONE PLEASE FORGIVE US WE DIDN'T MEAN TO KILL ANYONE PLEASE FORGIVE US WE DIDN'T MEAN TO KILL ANYONE PLEASE FORGIVE US WE DIDN'T MEAN TO KILL ANYONE PLEASE FORGIVE US WE DIDN'T MEAN TO KILL ANYONE PLEASE FORGIVE US WE DIDN'T MEAN TO KILL ANYONE PLEASE FORGIVE US WE DIDN'T MEAN TO KILL **A**NYONE PLEASE FOR-GIVE US WE DIDN'T **M**EAN TO KILL ANYONE PLEASE FOR**G**IVE US WE DIDN'T MEAN **TO** KILL ANYONE PLEASE FORG**I**VE US WE DID**N**'T MEAN TO KILL ANY-ONE PLEASE FOR**G**IVE US WE DIDN'T MEAN TO KILL ANYONE PLEASE FORGIVE US WE DIDN'T MEAN **TO KILL** ANYONE PLEASE FORGIVE US WE DIDN'T MEAN TO KILL ANYONE PLEASE FORGIVE US WE DIDN'T MEAN TO KILL **A**NYONE PLEASE FOR**G**IVE US WE DIDN'T ME**A**N TO K**I**LL ANYO**N**E PLEASE FORGIVE US WE DIDN'T MEAN TO KILL ANYONE PLEASE FORGIVE US WE DIDN'T MEAN TO KILL ANYONE PLEASE FOR-GIVE US WE DIDN'T MEAN TO KILL ANYONE PLEASE FORGIVE US WE DIDN'T MEAN TO KILL ANYONE PLEASE FORGIVE US

Chapter 4

Felix

You have to understand, Felix had an extraordinary childhood.

Everyone else who grew up in the Caravan can say the same. Extraordinary, peculiar, queer—in one way, if pointedly not the other. It doesn't matter, for most of them, that it's the only life they've ever known. A thing can be the only thing you've ever known, and you can still know, somehow, it isn't *normal*.

For example, Felix's earliest memories are secrets. The first lesson he learned, really learned, was that playing pretend was the best way to keep himself and everyone else safe. After all, the world is terrifying; it's huge and loud and unkind and it just wasn't made for people like him. Keeping secrets meant being protected.

And things that weren't secret were still *complicated*, more often than not. Like how Felix loves his parents, really loves them so much, but still knows they're not very nice people. And how he genuinely wants them to be happy, but he's always also hoped someday they would disappear. Those wants have never felt mutually exclusive. If the world was not perfect but perhaps kinder, Felix's parents and their happiness could exist somewhere far away from him and his brother.

This certainly wasn't the way he'd imagined their disappearance happening. But there's a part of him blaming himself anyway. As if all his wanting could make a thing happen.

And maybe it could. You know, his parents hadn't had many good ideas between them, but Felix always thought their best by far was how something didn't need to be seen in order to exist. Faith, they always claimed, was the strongest force in the world. In fact, it was so strong sometimes just believing in a thing was enough to make it true.

He's always believed that, too. Maybe not in the same way his parents do, because he doesn't believe in all the same stories as them. Their faith, as far as Felix can tell, seems largely grounded in fiction. His is rooted in what is tangible and beloved by him. He *believes* everything is going to be okay, that somehow all of this is going to work out and make sense someday, so he knows it will.

His magic is not divorced from his faith. Like so many people in the Caravan, his family doesn't understand what they're capable of—not really, not fully. His parents were once robbed of any memory of their origin, and now understand neither themselves nor their children. For some people, that could be limiting. For others, including Hugo—*oh, Hugo*—it's infuriating. But for Felix, it's okay. It's more than okay—it's a gift, because it means he can do anything. If he has faith he can do it, he can. Simple.

Maybe that makes Felix a miracle worker.

Anyway, that isn't really the point.

Like I said, you have to understand Felix had an extraordinary childhood. Extraordinary childhoods usually result in extraordinary people, in one way or another. Felix is *another*.

He knows how he seems from the outside. He knows people infantilize him. They see his cartoonish towers of childish books and collection of comforting toys, or the glitter clinging to his eyelids and fingertips and strands of white-blond hair, or they hear the pitched-up, melodic lilt in his voice, and suddenly they think they know something they don't. They think growing up the way he did, with parents who weren't very nice, in a community that wasn't very safe, must've broken his brain a little. They see a teenager turned to a time capsule; a forever little boy longing for the safety he never really had.

Felix isn't broken, though. He isn't trapped in his extraordinary childhood the way people think he is—the way even *Hugo* thinks he is.

He just knows how important good things are. Good things are rare, and special, and need to be protected when so much of the world is scary. Faith is so perfectly augmented by things soft and pillowy and pretty and *fun*. Felix isn't broken. He's just wholly unashamed to cling to things that make him happy.

His friends make him happy—when they aren't trying to kill or abandon each other.

And with all of that in mind, you understand why he's struggling to find the words to fix things between Cal and Hugo. That's what's already in motion when Eamon appears from out of the trees and announces, "I *saw* what is in the woods. I am getting far away from you people."

Felix makes a noise like a kicked dog, panic shooting through him and landing in his hands. He wrings them together as if to massage it away. "You can't leave!"

Everyone is so *cruel* to Eamon all the time, and it isn't fair.

He's weird, sure, but no weirder than the rest of them, and he really doesn't know anything about anything. He has no idea where he came from and the things that had to happen for him to get here. Felix doesn't think he's scary. Felix wants to be his friend, and Felix believes Eamon will let him—with enough time and faith.

"Just let him go," Hugo snarls. He really does behave as though he has a wolf's teeth in lieu of a young buck's antlers. "Safer for us if he gets the hell out of here, anyway."

Of course Hugo would believe that. It makes Felix's chest hurt.

"I do not think it's a good idea for us to split up," Bird warns, shaking their head.

"That," Hugo snaps, and Felix knows he's going to say it before he does, even though he really, really wishes he wouldn't, "is rich, coming from *you*."

"If you're going to spend the rest of your life bitching about being dumped when you were fifteen, please do us all a favor and just martyr yourself already." Cal rolls her eyes. But to Eamon she says, "What the hell did you see in the woods?"

"What I *saw*," Eamon says, "was only the beginning."

"Probably his own shadow," Hugo sneers, all bark just *longing* to bite.

"*Please*," Felix presses, taking a step toward the truck, a step closer to where Eamon is hovering. He offers his hands, palms up. "I know you're scared. And I'm scared, too. But you should stay. You don't have anything to fear from the people here."

Not anymore, anyway.

Eamon's crimson eyes dart between the other faces over Felix's shoulder. One side of his mouth curls up, lips exposing his teeth in a grimace. "You cannot speak for everyone."

"Yes, I can," Felix insists, taking another step forward. "Because I love them and I trust them and I have faith that we *all* want everything to be okay. We can figure this out, Eamon. Together."

Eamon is still for a moment, considering it, the limbo sustained just long enough to get Felix's hopes up. But then he sighs and grips the driver's-side door of Basil's truck and, hiking himself up and into the cab, says, "Good luck with that."

The truck door slams behind him. The engine turns and turns and rumbles to life. And then the almost-stranger peels out of the campground as fast as he can get away.

"Good." Hugo's voice bats against the back of Felix's neck, closer than he expected. "Now we can come up with a real plan."

"What do you think he saw in the woods?" Bird wonders out loud, eyeing the bright, homogenous grove of trees in which Eamon disappeared and reappeared.

"I'll check it out," Cal offers, already heading in that direction. When Bird moves to follow her, she glances at them and snaps, "I don't need help. I don't want you near me any more than Eamon did."

"What if he saw something *really* bad? There could be something awful in there," Bird demands.

"Then it will still be a welcome reprieve from looking at your fucking face."

Cal stomps off into the forest and Bird stares after her with their mouth hanging wide open and Hugo laughs like a knife kissing a rod of sharpening steel.

Felix doesn't think any of this is funny. He takes a deep breath and doesn't let himself cry, and he pretends—*believes*—Eamon is going to come back to them.

Chapter 5

Bird

Perhaps time does not exist in the cavernous white-barked wood. Perhaps here, in this valley of evergreen and rust and photosynthetic white bark, nestled in the serrated shadow of a mountain and its never-ending chain of cousins, time chooses to step lightly, mindful not to disturb the sylvan dreamscape. That is the only guess Bird can summon for the way daylight seems to drip away with the sway of the trees, and the uncomfortable quiet in the wake of last night's ceaseless din and detritus, empty hours disappearing until twilight reemerges in their nearly empty campsite.

Knowing the cold will creep closer no matter how few bodies it has on which to feed, Bird starts a fire. Somehow, the act is both grounding and absurd. There is a familiar ritual in gathering wood, stacking kindling, scraping matches, spitting curse words at the infantile humors of the first smoky flickers. Bird's hands are no stranger to flame. And yet, given everything that has transpired since morning, given that the bed of ash on which the flames dance so recently belonged to a pyre of celebration that's gone cold and dead, it seems offensive, even, to go about with such a mundane task. How bizarre that in the wake of unthinkable tragedy, people are still forced to eat, sleep, brush their teeth, and find shelter from the cold.

Once, in the years before they'd left and returned, Hugo might've laughed to find them fiddling with kindling. His fingers would've coaxed the sticks from Bird's hand with a gentleness lost to time, rough, smoke-hewn calluses no heavier than feathers across Bird's pale skin. And Bird would have protested, of course, because despite the soft press to their sternum at his care, their insistence that they had the knowledge and skill to do it themself would've necessitated an argument. Hugo simply would've held the kindling out of reach, leaving them to grab hopelessly past his golden locks and skyward antlers as he aimed as if to shoot a pistol and started a roaring fire like it was nothing.

They haven't seen him start a campfire since they returned. Not for anyone. Not even Felix.

And so Bird gets soot and splinters all in the folds of their soft white fingers, and just like they always insisted, they summon the flames themself. Like moths bound against their will, the others are compelled to the warmth of the fire.

Felix joins them first, sitting a few feet to their left. Firelight makes his already inhuman features seem even more so, juxtaposing the vivid greenery of his eyes with the downy white of his ears. The freckles on his round cheeks usually remind Bird of a fawn's spotted coat. But in the trickery of the dancing blaze, they could be storied constellations just beginning to emerge in a pink-swathed dusk.

Bird cannot remember the day Felix was born. Not actually. He isn't that much younger than them. But they've heard the story so many times, it feels as if they do. In this false memory, this corroded film reel projected on a smokescreen by their own unbiddable mind, Daphne Beránek disappears into the woods, nine months pregnant with not one baby but two. The deer-woman of the Caravan leaves her elder son with her husband for four agonizingly long days. When she returns, she cradles one child in her arms.

The other walks on four legs, stumbling behind her.

Like his brother, Felix carries remnants of an animal in his appearance, but he is *not* an animal. The same cannot be said for their sister. Sometimes, in Bird's imagination, Charlotte Beránek is entirely doe, indistinguishable from the natural fauna of the woods. Other times, she is entirely doe but for her face, which bears the uncanny features of a newborn human.

In the Caravan, this is not seen as something to be afraid of. On the contrary, Charlotte's birth is celebrated by everyone who meets her. Daphne and her husband, Nevin, are like gods, the miracle of their union capable of creating life unlike anything seen before it. Charlotte is truly special. Charlotte is a gift.

And the Caravan can think of no better way to show their appreciation for this gift than to consume it, to disperse the unprecedented good fortune throughout the entire community. The fawn is butchered before shedding her spotted coat. A feast is held in Charlotte's name.

Daphne and Nevin are such proud parents.

Bird forces their throat to swallow around a lump that's formed behind their tongue. They do not let themself think that it feels like a tiny hoof trying to kick open the hinge of their jaw. It is impossible to look at Felix a moment longer. And so, instead, when Hugo joins them from directly across the fire, they look to him instead.

If it weren't for the antlers, Hugo would look more human than his little brother. With them, there is nothing human about him at all. Tonight, they are made more imposing by the fire casting its dancing shadows, elongating his bone-carved crown until it looms over the entirety of the campsite, sharp and ubiquitous in one stroke.

Were Bird anyone else, it's entirely possible the sight could inspire a thrill of intimidation. Unfortunately—or fortunately, Bird hasn't decided and doesn't know when or if they ever will—every single thing about Hugo is so intimately familiar that there is no world where they ever look at him and feel the ghost of a threat. Even wearing his new cloak of rage, he will never pose a danger to them.

They could carve a perfect replica of his antlers with a dull knife and their eyes plucked out. They could write poetry to predict his words before he says them, and they could turn those poems into songs set to the beat of his pulse. Starving and delirious and they would still know him by his sweat between their teeth, the salt of him as well worn into Bird's DNA as their own blood.

They could spend the rest of their lives pretending to hate each other, and it would never be enough to unwrite what was written between them. For all their nights of overthinking, Bird does not know if this is a good or bad thing.

What they *do* know is that sometimes they wonder if Hugo is their soulmate. Maybe fate decided a long time ago that they were meant to end up together. They can never linger on that knowledge, because *that* thought makes them want to die.

But with the fire staged between them, Bird can imagine Hugo is the one burning at the stake.

"If you're going to spend the rest of your life bitching about

being dumped when you were fifteen, please do us all a favor and just martyr yourself already."

Calliope's words from earlier come back in a taunting whisper, the memory skirting across the top of Bird's skullcap. They *hated* hearing those words. In the first place, nothing that happened between Bird and Hugo is any of Calliope's concern. Nothing Bird has ever done has been that girl's concern. But that isn't the only issue.

Because it's also not true. Bird did not break up with Hugo. And as much as they hated Calliope saying what she did, it shone a spotlight into a newly uncovered blind spot, and now they have to know—was the mistake hers? Or is that the version of events Hugo has convinced people of in their absence?

They can't ask now. But someday, eventually, maybe, if he ever stops growling when he looks at them. If they ever decide whether this thing between them is good or bad.

Calliope herself is the last to join their circle, sinking into a crouch at Bird's right. She's positioned, with laughably obvious intention, almost exactly halfway between Hugo and them, clearly not wanting to be any closer to either. She doesn't look at anyone, just braces her forearms over her knees and holds her palms open toward the fire, warming her hands. The flicker makes a cave painting of her tendons and muscles.

Bird *knows* they can't really remember the day Felix was born, but they aren't convinced they can't remember Calliope showing up. They would've only been two years old at the time. It isn't impossible to believe the roots of the memory are real, even if a miraged bouquet of poisonous flowers have bloomed over them in the years since.

The Caravan's purpose is simple. They travel around the country, seeking out nonhumans and tucking them into the safety of their ranks. There are many theories on where these people come from. Some say they fell out of mysterious, magical pocket worlds and into this one, with no memory of their planet or life from before. Others think it's more likely they used to be human, until something happened to them—some awakening that activated their magic and wiped the slate of their memory clean. As far as Bird knows, no one actually has a real answer. And, if they are being uncomfortably honest about their opinion, no one ever will.

Calliope was the youngest of their kind to ever be found alone. She was abandoned at the sticky indoor playground at some fast-food chain in Texas. When authorities handed her over to social services, they noted she seemed to have a full set of teeth, molars and all, despite being barely old enough to toddle around. Her canine teeth were of particular interest, sharper and longer than the rest of them. And her ears were awfully strange, huge and pointed and batty as they were.

After decades of doing what they do, the Caravan has a loyal whisper Network that extends far beyond those who travel with them. After all, some people look more human than others. And those who *look* human can live among them, if they so choose—and they can contact the Caravan at the first stirrings of a dumped baby girl with the features of an animal.

In Bird's memory, they are hiding behind the corner of their mother's camper, trying not to be seen. It's late and they're supposed to be asleep in their camp cot bed, but the heat near the Gulf sticks around on summer nights, glued to the air by saltwater and sweat. It's still roasting inside the camper, no matter how dark it gets out, and a soaked, miserable stretch of tossing and turning in nothing but underwear does no one any good. Besides, Bird heard their grandparents talking about the baby that was on her way. They want to catch a glimpse of her.

And they do, just barely. One of the elders is holding a bundle wrapped up in a pink blanket, patting it absentmindedly while the grown-ups talk among themselves. There's a whole group of them gathered around a picnic table, standing beneath the singular bulb strung up to illuminate the campsite du jour. Their shadows heave like the brown Gulf shore break, stretching and shortening dizzyingly as the bulb rocks in the breeze. The nighttime bugs are screaming so loud that Bird can't hear a word anyone is saying, but that's okay. They don't care what they're saying. They just want to see the baby.

The bundle wiggles and shifts. A mop of wild brown hair appears, followed by two beguiling brown eyes, deep and wet like freshly tilled earth, so big they take up most of the girl's face. Bird's heart thunders a little faster. They take a step forward, trying so very hard to be careful and sneaky.

But they are still only two, and their body is too new to know how to tread with featherlight precision. Those brown eyes lock on them and widen. Bird freezes. The little girl tilts her head, watching them with interest. Slowly, Bird raises their fingers to wave.

The motion catches the attention of their mother, standing with the rest of the grown-ups beneath the light. Holly turns and plants her hands on her hips and shouts a flippant warning at her insolent toddler to *get that tiny hiney back to bed.* The sudden raised voice from behind her startles the baby girl, her body jerking like she'd stuck her finger in an outlet. And then she screams, shrill and shrieky and so loud it makes Bird's eardrums crackle in their head.

They turn to run back inside. Before they reach the camper's door, there's more screaming—screams of adults this time, sounds grown-ups aren't supposed to make, joining the wailing new baby.

Though they've never said it out loud, Bird knows there is a good chance every awful thing that happened that night is their fault. They wonder, sometimes, if Calliope knows that, too, or if she was too small to remember seeing Bird's face in the dark moments before the blood came. It seems impossible. But it would explain why Calliope has hated them ever since. Bird could never begrudge her for that, not really.

Somehow, Calliope doesn't look all that different than she did the first time Bird laid eyes on her. Her black-brown eyes are still deep like fertile soil and too big for her head, made bigger by the framing of her long eyelashes. Her dark eyebrows are thick and severe and messy, matching the badly chopped nest of her hair. Everything about her is a warning— the sleeves ripped from her dirty T-shirt, the knife-shaped earring dangling from one ear, the calluses on her hands and the bruises on her arms.

Bird doesn't know what the warning is. They only know they're heeding it.

"What do we do now?" Felix is the first to speak. He wraps his arms around himself, resting his chin on his knees, watching the fire dance.

Bird takes a deep breath. Smoke smudges their lungs on the way out. "Port Haven."

Across the way, Hugo jolts his head up to raise an eyebrow at them. "Seriously?"

"What's Port Haven?" Calliope demands, eyes narrowed as she glances between Hugo and Bird.

Bird gnaws on the chapped skin of their lip, reaching for a shred of credibility and praying their tongue answers the call. "Back when my mom was a teenager, the Caravan passed through a city on the coast of Washington called Port Haven. There was a lot going on at the time—a bunch of people didn't want to keep moving from place to place. It was causing some tension. And it all reached a boiling point. A chunk of the Caravan decided to stay behind. Put down roots, for once. My grandparents basically pretended they'd never existed. But—" Bird shrugs—"my mom had friends that stayed behind. So, she kept in touch. She even visited a few times. As far as I know, the community is still there. It's even bigger now. If anyone might know what happened here, that seems like as good a place to start as any."

And even if they don't know anything, somewhere where the view from your front door stays the same every day seems like a nice place to start over.

Before

"Who's your favorite Pokémon?"

The question came out of nowhere, startling Bird out of their textbook. They had a free hour in the middle of their schedule every day, a block of time meant for lunch that they always spent holed up in the library. Somehow, their dad had managed to convince the school to let them in as a sophomore, despite their only proof of prior education effectively being "*I pinkie promise I was homeschooled and definitely not in a cult.*" This was fine. Bird was smart, and a fast learner, and they knew they could do this.

But they also felt like they were lying to everyone all the time. In all of their classes, there was this perpetual undercurrent of misunderstanding that they just had to pretend wasn't there. They knew they were missing half the rungs in the ladder, and no matter how good they were at reaching ahead, they couldn't quite find their footing. So, yeah, they had a standing date with the library every day, desperately trying to build their foundation before everyone working on the roof realized they didn't have one.

The subject of the day was biology. Earlier in class, a boy at the neighboring desk with a crooked grin had informed them that his dad was out of town, and did they want to make a Punnett square at his place after school? Bird hadn't known what that meant but *had* picked up on him being a douche and a creep and was able to play their confusion off as disdain. Here they were, a couple hours later, scowling at something called genotypes and wishing their body could survive a cycle in the dishwasher. *The mitochondria is the powerhouse of the cell*, they chanted in their head like some warped mindfulness mantra, trying not to think about how disgusted they apparently should have acted when told they'd be dissecting frogs next week.

That's where their head was when someone's voice interrupted their reading, the sound cottony through their veil of hyperfocus. Hoping like hell no one had noticed what they were looking at, Bird slammed their book closed and blinked up at the speaker.

"Oh, hey, Megan." Bird tucked a curl behind their ear. "Um. What'd you say?"

Megan Blackwell was not popular—or maybe she was. Bird was struggling with figuring out all the ins and outs of the social dynamics in a public high school. *Popular* seemed to mean a very specific thing that had nothing to do with the dictionary definition of popularity. Being popular wasn't so much about how many people knew you or liked you, and instead was about how much . . . social clout you had to trade on? Which came from things like . . . Instagram followers, maybe? Or having your own car? It seemed to mostly have to do with being conventionally attractive, cishet, and neurotypical—or good at masking. Bird didn't really understand the situation there.

To that end, Megan didn't qualify for popular status. She wasn't necessarily conventionally attractive—she had acne, and her hair was kind of fried from being bleached and dyed a few too many times, and she wore the same cardigan and scribbled-on Converse every day—and the bi pride pins on her backpack indicated she didn't meet the threshold for cishetness, either. Maybe she was neurotypical, and Bird certainly wasn't qualified to say she wasn't . . . *but*. She sure did love to talk about horses and anime.

If it was based on the actual definition of popularity, though, Megan was extremely popular. Everyone in school knew her, and most of them liked her. She always had a boyfriend, sometimes multiple. She went to every party, joined a ton of clubs. And she was nice. She'd even made herself some kind of unofficial welcome committee when Bird transferred in. At a school with a few thousand kids in Ventura County, California, it would've been easy for them to go unnoticed. Megan hadn't wanted that to happen.

And Bird really wanted to be her friend. They were just struggling to figure out how, the same way they were struggling to understand the basics of sophomore level biology. Missing rungs in a ladder. Sometimes it felt like they had nothing more than two bare poles.

"Pokémon," Megan repeated. "Who's your favorite? I'm taking a survey for a project in AP Psych. I needed a reference I figured everyone would be familiar with, so it was Pokémon or Marvel, and I like Pokémon better. My favorite's Rapidash."

"Um . . ." Bird felt their cheeks beginning to heat. Their eyes burned, and they blinked, trying to make that stop before it got worse. "Um, I don't know. I'm sorry."

"C'mon, it's really not that deep. Like, who do you think

looks the coolest?" Megan chuckled. "I know not everyone knows *all* the Pokémon. But if you just tell me what they look like, I probably know their name."

Bird swallowed. Unfortunately, Megan wasn't a scumbag, and even if she was, Bird couldn't throw it back in her face to escape scrutiny. Not if they wanted her to actually like them. So . . . "Um. I don't . . . I don't know what Pokémon is."

Megan tilted her head. "Huh?"

"I've never heard of it."

"What the hell do you mean?" It doesn't come from Megan, but from another library table a few feet over. A boy in thick glasses and a dark hoodie had been pulled out of his book by their conversation. "Everyone has heard of Pokémon."

What would the two of them think if they knew Bird also had no idea what a Marvel was?

"You know, like . . ." Megan frowned, giving a tiny shake of her head. "Like Pikachu? Like . . . Poké Balls?"

"Oh." Bird nodded, blinking rapidly, silently cursing themself if they dared to start crying right now. They kept nodding, too fast and for way too long of a pause. "Totally. I remember now. Yeah, Poké Balls is my favorite one."

As soon as they said the words, they realized it was the wrong answer. Megan blinked at them, even more confused, and the guy at the other table laughed out loud.

"Dude . . . what planet did you come from?" he demanded.

"Um . . . I just . . . I was homeschooled . . ." Bird's vision started to go wobbly, stomach gurgling, head fuzzy. Around the edges, everything started to feel a little numb.

"By *aliens?*" the guy asked.

Bird imagined they were anywhere else but that library. For

a moment, their view was superimposed with thick, gnarled live oak branches, and bile tickled their throat.

"Hey," Megan mumbled, putting a hand on their shoulder. Bird's flesh screamed at the touch, and they, very irrationally and definitively, decided the only solution was to saw off the entire limb. But, oh, Megan was talking, and people who wanted to be friends were supposed to listen to each other. "Was it, like, one of those religious things? Were you not allowed to have a TV or . . . or wear pants?"

"I gotta go." Their voice came out mortifyingly gummy and monotone. Bird pushed their chair back and scrambled to their feet, snatching up their backpack and tossing it over their shoulder. "Sorry, I just, um. I have to go."

They felt eyes follow them all the way out of the library. If they kept walking out of the building and off campus, into traffic and preferably in front of a fast-moving garbage truck with a faulty brake pedal, they were pretty certain they'd still feel the eyes all over their skin while the coroner noted their time of death. They couldn't pinpoint which one had made them feel worse—the random boy's cutting mockery or Megan Blackwell's pity.

In the end, maybe the distinction didn't matter. It still felt like shit.

Had they made a horrible mistake?

Chapter 6

Cal

When Cal dreams, the warm skin beneath her hands is familiar in a way it will never be when she's awake.

That night, in a sun-soaked somewhere that only exists in her mind, she drags her palms over yielding flesh. Her nails follow the same path and leave scores of white scratch marks behind them, claims to her territory. Her fangs ghost against the throat of her favorite unreality, and the warm body beneath hers does not flinch away.

"Tell me what you want me to do to you," she insists. In this dream, Cal feels no remorse for demanding exactly what she wants. And from who she wants it.

A tremble threads down every inch where skin meets, a clandestine seam pulling them together. In a breathless whisper, the fantasy answers, "You know what I want."

Cal does. The dream wants the same thing every time they meet, and Cal is always eager to give it. But she still wants to hear the words. Maybe she needs to.

. . .

From outside the camper, sunlight punches through her bedroom window, slicing a line over Cal's face. More asleep than not, she groans, rolling to give her back to the light.

She doesn't want this to end. Not yet.

"Maybe I do," the dream of Cal teases. Her body rolls down into the fevered embrace of the illusion beneath her. "Maybe I just want you to beg me."

"Please."

Her lip quirks. One fang pokes out against her mouth. "Please what?"

For the others at the campsite, the day is beginning. Through the fog of sleep and taboo desperation, Cal can just barely make out the sounds of morning. People are talking. There might be breakfast being made.

She needs all of it to go quiet, just for a moment longer. She needs this—just for a moment longer.

"Please, please, please, please," the imagined lover whispers, voice hoarse.

Want drips between them like liquid fire. It threatens to burn Cal to cinder at her core.

"Please *what?*" she growls, the teasing edge of her tone sharpened to something else entirely. Her nails dig into the shuddering hips beneath her thighs until they buck to meet her.

The answer comes as it always does.

"Please kill me."

When Cal's eyes blink open in bed, the dying screams of someone she'll never really touch echo off the walls of her skull. The phantom taste of copper floods her mouth, so distinct and vivid she has to run her tongue against her teeth to check for blood. Nothing.

Of course there's nothing. It was just a dream. It always is.

Shame bubbles in her gut at the way her thighs saw together. Even knowing the way the dream always ends, she can't seem to control her body's reactions to the rest of it. She rolls over onto her back, sheets sticking with sweat to her skin until she peels them away and tosses them to the floor.

Guilt is a terrible and useless emotion. It has ruined any part of her already grim life that might've been spared if she could only tune it out. And yet here she is, still bound to it.

Well . . . mostly bound.

Cal's fingers tiptoe through puddled droplets of her own sweat, carving a path down her belly and past the hem of her underwear.

She is not a parishioner in the pews of the churches whose holy books she knows better than their pastors. There is no penance for the sins she has committed, and no forgiveness for the *thing* she is. Whatever she does or does not do, the weight of her guilt cannot be set aside.

She may as well enjoy what she can.

Before

"I really like your boots."

Cal jumped at the sudden proximity of a stranger's voice, her eyes snapping up from where they'd been studying the cover of an old Chicks CD. It was one of a few dozen in the bins crammed between the roller skates and the paperback romance novels at the back of the weird, claustrophobic little thrift store she'd popped into.

The voice belonged to a girl with bubblegum pink hair and October eyes who was decked out in green corduroy overalls and a big jean jacket with more patches and pins than Cal's Nalgene had stickers. Her cheeks went bright red when Cal just stared, paralyzed, and she danced a step back.

"Sorry. I have, like, no sense of personal space. My mom's been saying I've needed to get better at body boundaries since I was, like, two."

Cal blinked. "Um . . ."

"Wow, I'm making just, like, the best impression, aren't I? Let's start over." The girl cleared her throat, then again, cheeks still aflame, and gives a little shake of her pink head as if to physically shuck away the intense awkwardness of the moment. Her earrings—long and dangly, with a planet at the end of one and a shooting star on the other—jingled when she did. Then she gave Cal a cute little wave, her pretty, plump lips quirking up in both corners.

Oh *fuck*, she has *dimples*.

"I'm Thalia. I come in here, like, every day, 'cause there is nothing else to do in this town, and I've never seen anyone who looks as cool as you. And I wanted to tell you that I liked your boots."

"Thank you," Cal hurried to get out when the other girl paused to take a breath. She glanced down at her shoes. There was nothing remarkable about them. Just a pair of old, thoroughly worn all-black Doc Martens that she'd found in a dumpster outside a high-rise apartment building a year ago. "I got them out of the trash."

Now, why the hell did she say that? She hadn't meant to say that. Not to some random girl at some random thrift store in Arkansas. She opened her mouth to try and retcon the statement, but—

"Oh my god, that's so cool." Thalia laughed, twirling a strand of her bubblegum hair around one finger. "It's insane, the kind of shit rich people will just throw away, isn't it? Like, those are vintage, right? Like, made in England?"

"Um . . ." Cal struggled to remember if she'd seen that on the tag. They certainly were high mileage, though. "I think so?"

"Yeah. People are wild. They probably paid, like, four hundred dollars for those or something." Thalia shoved one hand in the pocket of her overalls, then waved the other in a semicircle beside her head. "So, you, uh, come here often?"

"No." Cal frowned, glancing around the poorly lit store. Save for the towering piles of stuff, it was almost empty, the only living things inside were the two of them and the old guy asleep behind the counter—and his even older hound dog, snoring on the floor at his feet. A sign on the counter said his name was Buckets, and that he hunted shoplifters for sport. Cal could just make out his long, floppy ears spread out on the ground. She'd chosen this store specifically because it was nothing special. She didn't think anyone would look at her closely, let alone twice, and she definitely hadn't assumed anyone might try and talk to her.

People didn't, usually. One of the nicer things Cal's been told about herself is that she has intimidating vibes.

Self-conscious, she tugs nervously at the edge of her beanie, hoping her pointed ears have the courtesy to stay properly hidden. "Uh, my family's just passing through town. I needed a break from them, so."

"Why would you possibly be passing through Bentonville, Arkansas?" Thalia laughed. "Are y'all really big fans of Walmart?"

Cal chuckled with a knowing nod, as if she understood the joke, then said, "Uh, no. We're on our way to the Ozarks. We're, um . . . going camping."

"Oh god, that's even worse." Thalia put her hand on Cal's arm, fingertips gently brushing the bare skin of her elbow, her thumb pressing lightly at the pulse point in the bend. "Blink twice if you need to be rescued. I cannot *imagine* having to go camping with my family."

And Cal totally would have come up with some clever response to that if her brain hadn't short-circuited at the feel of another's girl hand on her body. She stared down at it, silent, desperately trying to rub two brain cells together but unable to do anything but focus on the warmth and softness of Thalia's palm.

How long had it been since another person had touched Cal in any way? Long enough ago that she couldn't remember who it was or when. The sudden reminder of what it felt like to not be completely alone and detached in the world made her want to scream.

Thalia's hand fell away, the blood bursting back into her cheeks. "Sorry—I'm sorry. Body boundaries, I know."

"No, it's—I liked it." Cal heard the implications of the words only after she'd already put them out there in the air between them, and there was really nothing she could do at that point to suck them back in. She flushed but didn't try and fix it.

"Oh. Well." Thalia straightened and grinned, and Cal caught the sharp end of it when she finally managed to raise her eyes from the branded spot on her arm where she'd been touched. "In that case, I guess I will admit I thought it was more than just your *boots* that looked nice. Absolutely devastated to learn you don't live here—not surprised, though. This town could only *dream* of cooking you up."

Cal couldn't help herself. She grinned in response—and watched Thalia's eyes latch on to one sharp canine tooth. The other girl's head tilted with a spark of curiosity.

Her mouth snapped closed. Fuck.

Cal breathed in deep through her nose, readying to offer an explanation, but Thalia, once again, cut her off.

"Duuuuude." She leaned in close, eyes narrowed. "Open your mouth again?"

When Cal didn't, Thalia frowned and met her eyes. Whatever she saw there made her flush again.

"I'm sorry—I know, body boundaries, yeah, I just—that was such a weird thing to say, I'm sorry, I just—like, your teeth? Are those real?"

She didn't sound afraid, or even concerned. She sounded . . . Cal wasn't sure, actually. The closest thing her mind could summon to the other girl's tone was interest, maybe even excitement. But that couldn't have been right.

"Um. Yeah."

"They're like . . . fangs."

"Yeah, it's, um . . ." Fuck. What explanation was there, really?

She was going to get her ass handed to her by Cassandra and Basil for going out in public and fraternizing with humans. Cal's features were easier to hide than other people's, but that didn't mean she could *pass*, not really.

"It's fucking cool is what it is," Thalia finished for her, when Cal's words just drifted off into nothing. "You were just born like that?"

Cal blinked.

Maybe it *could've* been right. Thalia *was* excited.

Slowly, she opened her mouth a little wider, flashing the sharpened edges of her teeth so the other girl could examine them. "Um . . . not exactly."

"Oh, so you, like, had a dentist do it or something?"

"Well, no. I mean, I wasn't born like that, 'cause, uh, I didn't have any teeth when I was born."

"You—" Thalia pulled her head back and narrowed her eyes at Cal. After a moment, she grinned wide enough that it split her face in two. "Oh, you're an asshole, too, huh? Easy, now, I might just go and fall in love with you."

Cal laughed, shaking her head. "That'd be a bold choice on your part."

"And very sad for your family, because I do *not* want to go camping, and I *would* be keeping you here."

And for a moment, Cal let herself imagine a world where that were possible. She imagined herself meeting a girl at a thrift store and flirting over the dusty CD bin and then, instead of going their separate ways, going for coffee. Then going back to the girl's place, meeting her cat and her plants and her friends. She imagined sleeping in her bed under a string of fairy lights, and Thalia's fingers touching the tips of her ears, and no one being afraid.

It was a fun fiction to entertain, but the aftertaste sure was bitter.

"I should get going," Cal said, dropping the CD back into the chaos. "My family is probably ready to hit the road, actually."

"Wait, um—" Thalia bit her lip. "I'm sorry—I know I have, like, no social skills. Um, is it totally weird if I ask for your number? We could text! I could entertain you while you camp."

Cal swallowed. "Sorry. I don't think so."

She brushed past Thalia, shoving her hands in the pockets of her jacket and leaving as quickly as she could.

The fantasy of sticking around was dreamy, but it wasn't the whole story. The aftertaste came from the final tragic chapter.

Because eventually, Thalia would probably want to kiss her. And Cal would have to tell her no. And if she asked why, if she pressed, Cal would have to tell her she could never be kissed.

And if Thalia kept pressing, Cal would have to tell her the truth about her sharp teeth and the blood they'd tasted and how she promised herself she would never, ever do it again. How she would never, ever give herself the chance.

And when she did, Thalia's interest and excitement would give way to panic and fear.

And Cal would be even more alone than she already was.

Chapter 7

Hugo

"So!" Felix claps his hands together, a greasy plate once towering with bacon balanced on his thigh. With the morning's crawling start and a half-assed attempt at feigning normalcy with breakfast foods now behind them, the day—and its looming journey—can begin in earnest. "Whose car are we taking?"

"Ours, obviously," Hugo answers, at the exact same moment that Bird says, "My mom's?" and Cal replies, "I'll drive."

Hugo glares at Cal, which is how he knows Cal glares at Bird. And Bird, if the scorching weight on his face is any indication, glares at him, but he doesn't look at them to confirm as much. He spends most of his time lately trying very hard *not* to look at them. It makes everything so much easier—when he's successful.

"You are not driving," he tells Cal instead, not even bothering to respond to Bird's suggestion.

Even if he didn't hate them—and he hates them, he absolutely hates them, that much is true—it doesn't make any sense to take Holly's piece of shit old camper. Bird hasn't been around in three years. Bird didn't learn to drive with the rest of them. Bird doesn't know how to function in any capacity beyond exalted perpetual child, let alone what route to take or what to do about a flat tire or whether their camper even takes diesel or regular. They lost their chance to make adult choices on the road. Humoring them just to let them feel like they're part of the conversation would be pointless.

"Of course I'm driving." Cal turns her head slowly, peeling her eyes away from Bird to glower at him, instead. "Why would I not drive?"

"Why *would you* drive?"

"Why do you assume you're the default driver?"

"Oh, okay. I see where this is going." Hugo scoffs. "Do not make this a sexism thing."

Felix coughs. "Um. I can drive."

Everyone pretends, very politely but not at all convincingly, that they do not hear him.

"Interesting. See, I'm not making anything a sexism thing," Cal retorts, crossing her arms over her chest. "You're the one who's thinking about misogyny, apparently. I just asked a question."

"Yeah, a bad faith question, asshole. You were trying to bait me. I'm not stupid."

"Not stupid, huh? See, now who's trying to bait who?"

Hugo takes a step toward her. He isn't entirely sure what he would do if he got his hands on her, or if that's even what he wants in the first place. His body moves completely disconnected from his mind, pushed forward by a surge of irritation and adrenaline that stings in his veins as it goes down. By the time he realizes he's moving at all, he's stopped himself.

When he imagines *actually* hurting Cal, the thought makes him want to throw up. A macabre canvas of ivory and scarlet flashes in his mind's eye before he suppresses it. It is part memory, part reverie, and entirely intrusive in its persistence.

Later, when he's alone, he'll have no choice but to sink back to that place. He never escapes it. It's always there, waiting for him. For now, he doesn't have time to look at it.

Someday, his head's going to have to be faster than the rest of him, because he can't be *this* forever, can he? But what's it going to take to get there? If he were anyone else, anyone normal, he'd have reached his breaking point a while ago. How much more blood will be spilled before Hugo can convince the animal of his own mind that there isn't actually a target on its head, and it doesn't have to kill to survive?

"Huey?"

Felix's lyrical little voice is so close it could be plucked like a stray hair from between his antlers. It's enough to rattle Hugo out of his thoughts, and he jolts, looking to his brother.

"Hm?"

"You okay?"

"Uh—" Oh. He must've just been standing there for a moment too long. Just standing there, staring at Cal, and lost in thoughts about bloodshed and murder and how he's fairly certain he was born for no greater purpose than to hurt those around him.

Well, that must have been unsettling for her, hm? Maybe she'll learn something from it.

Ha.

He rolls his eyes, sweeping the moment away. If one refuses to look at a thing, it doesn't exist—so long as one keeps one's starry eyes away. But if one refuses to look at a thing for long enough that others begin to forget . . . then it may as well have never existed in the first place.

Hugo has never had the privilege of not looking at a thing, but goddamn has he gotten good at pretending.

"Fuck you, Cal."

"No thanks." She smirks.

"Tell me," he says, stepping back this time instead of forward, loading words like bullets into the chamber of his mouth. "Does all your cleverness make it easier to swallow the fact that no one has ever *really* wanted you here?"

There. It's gone as quickly as it comes. If he hadn't been watching so intently, so greedy in his anticipation, he would've missed it. But there, right there, on Cal's face. At the corners of her eyes, sweeping down the bridge of her nose toward her upper lip, skittering into her cheeks like heat lightning. For the briefest flicker of a nearly wasted moment, Hugo can see the endless horizon of her grief.

If he sawed off his antlers right here and now, he'd still never pass as human. Not with this relentless prey drive of his. Like sites storied with atrocity, he must reek of danger to everyone who enters his orbit. The air smells of wounded game, and the beast in his chest howls for an easy kill. It takes everything Hugo has to remain perfectly still, instead.

There is something so very wrong with him.

"*Hugo,*" Felix snaps. He needn't say anything else—one word, embellished with barbed wire lace, conveys all the disappointment it needs to.

Bird's voice floats over his head, just out of reach. "That was—"

"Yes." Cal shoves her hands in her pockets.

"What?" Oh, *fight* is so much more satisfying than *flight* or *freeze.* Hugo tilts his head at her, raising an eyebrow. The beast gives a low growl from behind his sternum. "Yes what?"

Whatever vulnerable thing briefly showed its soft belly on Cal's face has donned its infallible apathetic armor. She does not rise to his bait, and she won't—not tonight, anyway. "Yes, being clever makes it easier. You should consider it as an option." From one pocket, she pulls free her keys, spinning the carabiner around her index finger. It ought to be innocuous, a key ring, but through a ludicrous collection of keychains, she's made it a guerrilla weapon. Tense but resolved, Cal turns and heads in the direction of her RV. "Get your shit together and get on board. Or don't. I'm leaving in an hour, with or without any of you."

The door slams behind her, leaving the quiet of the campground in her wake. And Hugo's body trembles, aching for a fight it didn't get to have.

"You—" Bird begins again, but this time Hugo is the one to cut them off.

"Fuck off." It hurts when he finally allows his eyes to fall on their face, like he's fully palming a hot pan. But of course it does. It does every time. "You don't get to have an opinion about anything I do or don't do. Not ever again. So fuck off."

He storms into his tent to pretend to pack the last of his things, knocking things about for a few minutes to give the appearance of action and let some of his pique out in private. For a while, he expects Felix to follow after him. But the tent flap never moves. Hugo is abandoned, left to rot with his thoughts.

For the rest of their last hour at the campsite, he lies face down in his bed. He closes his eyes and he breathes deep, imagining he could fall asleep like this, though he knows he won't.

And he tries not to think about golden eyes full of accusation. He tries not to think about still-warm blood and freshly dug earth making their marriage bed on his hands. He certainly does not think about the sound of a child's screams and the taste of his own vomit.

He tells himself if he tries hard enough, he can be reborn as something new before anyone else has to know he has only ever been a monster.

Before

"Where do you think we come from?" The little girl who would grow up to be Bird asked, lying on their belly beneath the gnarled limbs of an ancient live oak tree in a field somewhere in rural Texas. The knotty branches stretched out like protective arms overhead, thick and wise and heavy as stone. Each one sheltered them from the towering legion of storm clouds steadily rolling from the East, their bottoms feathery with falling rain, a bruised swath of cumulonimbus steadily feasting at the edge of otherwise endless blue.

Hugo lay on his back at their side, a dozen tiny acorns digging constellations around his spine. The picnic blanket beneath them had been made by a member of the Caravan and gifted to him a few months earlier, on his eleventh birthday. A collection of different scraps of colorful fabric, held together with golden metal clasps and zigzagging thread, it reminded him of what it felt like to be home. The mayhem of trying to fit mismatched pieces together, the satisfaction of watching them eventually blend into one chaotic, cohesive thing. His fingertips toyed absentmindedly with a jingling pile of gold embellishments by his hip.

"Um . . . our parents?" he suggested, unsure what exactly his best friend was trying to ask him.

They rolled their eyes but snickered gently, clearly finding his misunderstanding more charming than annoying. Hugo loved that particular facet. He would, on occasion, feign misunderstanding in hopes he might catch a glimmer of their adoration. "No," they tell him. "I mean, where do you think we all came from? Before we were here. You know . . . are we human? Did we used to be?"

Ah. That question. The *how and why was I put on this Earth and what am I supposed to do now* question. Hugo didn't spend a lot of time thinking about questions like that, but he knew a lot of other people did. That was kind of the Caravan's whole thing, trying to figure out an answer to that question.

So, he knew his other half wasn't really looking for an answer. He knew they knew he didn't know anything about anything. They were just looking for his opinion. His feeling, whatever it was—it held some sort of precious value to them, no matter that it was without worth in the grand scheme of things. He rubbed the gold pieces attached to the blanket between his thumb and finger, stroking the metal until it heated under his touch. Then he let it drop.

"I guess I think that . . . we fell out of the sky."

Their eyes widen, and they push themself up a little higher on their elbows, perching over him so they can look down into his face.

Hugo swallowed, staring up at the golden-flecked eyes he knew better than his own. The air was beginning to feel charged, petrichor knocking politely at his nose.

"Like aliens?" they asked, voice a hushed whisper, as if this was top secret information the two of them were sharing.

He doesn't laugh, because he knows they would get their feelings hurt. He does smile, though, because he finds their misunderstanding just as charming as they find his, and he can't help it. Aliens weren't exactly what he meant. But, well, okay. Maybe. "Um . . . I guess? Just . . . not from here. I think we're from somewhere else."

They mulled that over, nibbling at their lower lip. Hugo couldn't help himself. He watched their teeth work at their mouth, unyielding white pushing against soft, pillowy pink, and he swallowed.

Lately, he'd been having a lot of thoughts about his best friend that hadn't always been there. Or maybe they'd just gotten louder. It was a lot to think about, and most often, when he tried to look directly at it, those thoughts melted into a million grains of sand.

"You don't feel like you're from . . . here." They waved their hand at nothing specific, catching the sky, the canyons in the tree bark, a neighboring fire ant mound. "Like, this whole world?"

"Not really." Hugo shrugged. He didn't think saying that was too much of a reach, not for people like them. "Do you?"

They frowned, pushing at the corner of their mouth with their thumb, expression all pinched and thoughtful. They were so cute. It made his bones hurt the same way a growth spurt did. "No, I guess not. I guess . . . the only place that feels like it could ever be home is wherever you and me are together."

He could've cried, but he didn't. Instead, he reached up and twirled one of their curls around his finger, stroking along the silken length, watching the sunlight thread it with a brassy shine. He thought about kissing them and blushed. He did not actually kiss them.

"Yeah. Wherever we came from, you and I are from the same place."

"Totally," they agreed, nodding empathetically. "Maybe we used to be part of the same constellation."

"Maybe that's where your light comes from."

"And your fire!" They flushed when they realized they'd yelled, biting at their lip again, bone pressing into pink until it gave way to white. "Sorry."

"It's okay." He smiled. Hand still in their hair, his knuckles brushed their cheek.

Their lips parted.

His stomach turned with nerves, anticipating something— something that was right there, on the cusp of happening. He was as much a storm cloud as the approaching gray, his chest staticky with what was surely soon to be lightning the moment the ground gave permission to strike.

"Hey, guys!"

Both of them jumped at the interruption, Hugo's hand flying away as if he'd been caught doing something dirty. Felix ambled over, dropping down onto their blanket, rolling onto his side so he could face the other two.

"What are you doing?" He grinned, oblivious to what might've happened if he hadn't shown up.

What might've happened, though? Hugo couldn't be sure. Maybe all of this was just in his head. Maybe they didn't feel the same way. Maybe the ground hadn't realized the storm was even coming.

"The only place that feels like it could ever be home is wherever you and me are together."

He memorized that line, replaying it over and over again until it was etched into something irrevocable in his body, until it became a promise that laid a foundation that would hold up his forever home, no matter what shape its renovations took, no matter how many times it was leveled and rebuilt. There would always be the two of them. There was no other option.

When the rain finally started, the girl that would become a Bird was telling Felix about the stars. Both boys listened, hanging on to their every word.

None of them noticed that the rain didn't dare to touch them. They didn't question they were safe there, with each other.

Chapter 8

Felix

I'm sure by now you're very concerned about our cast of characters here. That's perfectly reasonable—you should be concerned. What have the traumatized teenagers in this book *done*? What horrible secrets are each of them white knuckling, convinced their lives would be destroyed if anyone else were permitted to hold the truth of them? I suppose, one way or another, we'll find out soon enough. I don't think it would be a very good story if we didn't. And if it makes you feel any better, you aren't the only one who's worried. Felix is practically beside himself. He was already being eaten up by guilt of his own, convinced that his own wishful thinking was enough to manifest the disappearance of the entire Caravan. He blames himself for the confusion and fear taking vicious bites out of those he loves, an unforgivable thing for a boy who loves as strongly as he does. And now the friends he cherishes are leaving him, too.

Sure, only Eamon has walked out on them so far, but it isn't a secret no one wants to be together here. How much longer will it be before Cal decides she's had enough and takes off on her own? How much tension can Bird stomach before they take flight—again, and maybe for good this time?

Felix can't even let himself wonder whether or not his brother could survive being abandoned by Bird a second time. He doesn't *want* to wonder at that answer, at least in part because he already suspects what it is.

No, Bird cannot leave again.

The interior of Cal's RV is stubbornly, rustically warm, a surprisingly inviting home for a girl who spits at the mere thought of letting anyone in. The seats have been reupholstered with a painstakingly curated mismatch of fabrics. She's crammed knickknacks and trinkets into every wood-paneled cubby, dangled suncatchers from the ceiling, plastered every inch of the mini fridge with magnets and then screwed sheet metal on the neighboring cabinet so as to collect more. She's filled the RV with as much *stuff* as something meant to stay in motion could possibly hold. The whole thing must jingle with the road's every curve and pothole. Whether the sound is comforting or maddening is something they're all about to find out.

It's quiet as Cal turns on the ignition and begins to pull her RV away from their campground, leaving the quiet, dark graveyard of vehicles in the rearview. It feels *wrong* to leave this place, the last place they saw their families, even if it has to be done. Felix stares out the window for a long moment, watching the last vapors of smoke drifting off the doused campfire where they made breakfast for the last time.

In all his sixteen years, Felix has never gone on the road without his parents. It's strange, the way he doesn't really want them here and still feels like he could cry at their absence.

Maybe it would be easier if he at least knew they were okay where they are.

But then, maybe it wouldn't be. Some questions are easier to carry when they aren't weighed down by the burden of their answers.

Besides, he has important work to do here, right where he is, with the people he actually wants to be around. He's lucky for that.

Turning away from the window, he glances to Hugo. His brother is sitting at the little kitchenette corner bench, hunched over the pine table, eyebrows tightly pressed together over his nose, mouth set in a firm, stony line. He stares at his hands, knuckles curled taut around the neck of a beer bottle.

Felix recognizes the label. Hugo must have taken it from their dad's stash before they loaded into Cal's RV. Of all the mementos to pause and grab, all the little things to remind them of their parents, of course that would be Hugo's choice.

It's not that Felix thinks his brother drinks too much, exactly. And it's really not that Felix is trying to be some kind of stick in the mud or morality police. He doesn't have a *problem* with alcohol. He doesn't really have a problem with anything that feels good, in a world that doesn't feel good at all more often than not—actually, reaching for things that feel good is kind of Felix's whole schtick. It's just . . . he's pretty sure Hugo only does it so he doesn't have to think, and even a thing that isn't a problem can become a problem if someone is doing it for the wrong reason. Right?

I don't know if that'll make any sense to you. Sorry if it doesn't. I'm just here to tell the story. No one is paying me to write a D.A.R.E. campaign.

Cal is glaring out the front windshield, hands like vises

around the steering wheel, her shoulders set as if someone poured concrete down her spine. A swinging pendulum fashioned from something's wire-wrapped jawbone hangs from her rearview mirror and shines a spotlight on her unnatural stiffness. The road in front of them is beautiful. A rocky mountainside reaches high to their left, and a thick row of trees streaks by in a blur on their right, the whole world painted in green and yellow, orange and red, with a pigeon blue sky peeking through anywhere it can stretch to reach for them. But—even though her eyes do not stray from the road once—it doesn't seem like Cal *sees it* at all.

Whatever she's seeing, Felix thinks it's more in her head than right in front of her. He can sympathize with that. The sort of lives they've lived, it only makes sense to disappear into their own heads.

Reader, did you know it's a fairly common trauma response to sit in a car and stare out the window and imagine someone running next to you? Kids trapped in cars with their parents for long stretches of time, feeling uncomfortable or even unsafe, nowhere to hide and nothing to distract them, are prone to inventing these unknown protectors. Felix has spent an enormous chunk of his life doing exactly that. It wouldn't surprise him if that was what Cal was doing now, dissociating herself some guardian angel that might protect her from the tension in the RV.

Of the three, Bird looks the least like they would throttle Felix for trying to talk to them. Perched in the lofted space above Cal's bed, nested between vintage storage trunks and half a dozen throw pillows, they've got their knees curled to their chest, eyes turned to watch the yellow-leafed trees pass out the window.

Bird really is exceptionally beautiful. Felix doesn't have much interest in things like kissing, but he could understand how someone might look at Bird and want to kiss them. Their soft chestnut curls falling just beneath their chin, bordering their round, bronze cheeks like the opulent frames he's seen in museum movie scenes. Mesmerizing golden eyes set over a button nose set over a full pink mouth.

But they look sad. That mouth is quirked down at the corners, pinched at the center. Those eyes are heavy-lidded and wet and far away. Perhaps Bird is too troubled for even a fantasy savior sprinting in the treetops to lift their spirits.

Felix sits on the windowsill seat across from the bed and its overhead loft, tilting his head so he can look at them.

"I like your new name." He knows to be patient. When Bird finally realizes he's talking to them and looks in his direction, he smiles. "I've been meaning to tell you that for a few days, but things kept happening and I never got a chance. It really suits you, though."

For a second, it looks like Bird isn't sure what to do with that compliment. Like maybe it's the first time they've ever heard it. Or maybe they just never expected to hear it from someone in the Caravan.

It's kind of strange, the way his parents and the other adults have always handled things like . . . well, things like Bird. Gender and sexuality and anything adjacent to that. For all Felix and Hugo and the rest of them were sheltered by necessity, unable to go out and be seen in the human world, it's not like they grew up not knowing it was out there. Felix got his first cell phone when he was twelve, with full access to the internet and everything. Nothing was ever exactly hidden.

It's more like most of the adults in his life—and Bird's life, and all of their lives—were convinced things like *that* were human matters that didn't actually concern them. Racism, sexism, homophobia, and transphobia, all of those things were bad, sure, anyone in the Caravan would agree with that. But all of those things were human issues.

No one in the Caravan had ever been *trans* before Bird, who had come back from their three-year stint living with their human father with a new name and new pronouns. Felix wonders if they'd been afraid of how they might be received, and wonders if that fear was unfounded. After all, nothing bad really happened.

Though . . . they also hadn't been back that long. And who knows what people might've said—or done—when the shiny glow of their return began to fade. When they weren't as vigilant about calling each other out for an incorrect pronoun or kindly, firmly reminding old habits to remake themselves. When they got comfortable, and they weren't still trying to tiptoe around Bird's feelings for fear of scaring them away again.

Personally, between you and me, I'm getting the impression most people in the Caravan would not have *actually* continued to pretend to respect Bird's identity. This whole thing is reeking of a religious cult. Have you picked up on that yet?

"Thanks," Bird finally says.

"How'd you pick it?"

"Um." They run their fingers through their hair, fluffing their coils. "I don't know. I guess I just wanted something that felt—"

"Flighty?" Hugo offers, voice gravelly with disuse and barely checked anger, and Felix's stomach drops.

Bird's cheeks pale. They narrow their eyes, tilting their chin to stare down at the back of Hugo's head.

For his part, he pretends he doesn't feel their eyes on him and takes another slow swig of his beer.

"Huey, enough," Felix mumbles. To Bird, he says, "I'm sorry."

"It's o—"

"Why are you apologizing?" Hugo turns around, leveling Felix with a hard, cold look. "No one has done anything to them, especially not either of us. If anyone should be sorry, it's them."

"I am not going to listen to this all the way to Washington," Cal calls over her shoulder, still not taking her eyes off the road. "Figure your shit out or get out and walk!"

"You are not being fair." Felix is very careful to keep his voice even and calm, holding his hands out, palms up, fingers splayed wide as if demonstrating there's no weapon. As if trying to win over a dog with its teeth already bared. He doesn't want this to be a fight. He hates fighting with his brother. "You can choose to be nice, you know."

"Are you fucking kidding me?" Hugo lifts his eyebrows, his voice rising one decibel louder. "Why are you taking their side?"

"I'm not—I'm not taking anyone's side." Felix can feel the moment starting to spiral out of his control. He knows he needs to get this back on track.

Hugo is a good person.

Or, okay, maybe he isn't a *good person*, but he's *good* and he's *Felix's person*, and that's all that matters. It's just that also, sometimes, he can be cruel. And it isn't like Felix doesn't understand why. Sometimes being cruel is the only thing Hugo can be. Sometimes Hugo being cruel is the only reason either of them get to stay safe. He's been backed into a corner enough times that he *had* to learn how to bite the open, gentle hand appealing to him, and that wasn't his fault.

It's just sometimes, like now, he doesn't always know when he's being actually backed into a corner and when the corner is all in his head. That isn't his fault! It just . . . is.

"I can't believe this." Hugo's thumbnail drags against the paper label on the sweating beer bottle, peeling away a strip of it. "You're really gonna turn on me, too? Just like everyone else?"

"Grow up, Hugo." Bird rolls their eyes. "How much longer do you think this angsty bad-boy shit is going to be cute?"

Felix can see it happening before it actually does. Maybe it's because Hugo is his brother and their blood speaks the same language, a language no one else left alive in the world can ever understand. Maybe it's because of Felix's magic, the miracle of believing in a thing making it true, and he believes he knows what Hugo's doing, so he does. Or maybe it's all just happening in Felix's head.

You get to be the judge of that.

In any case, Felix watches his brother rise from the table with a smoky ring of magic billowing out in a perfect circle around his body, like the ash cloud around the mouth of a volcano. He watches that smoke envelope Bird, making them gag and cough and choke, the burning, windblown embers burrowing deep, deep into their skin in hissing, smoldering flecks until they scream and claw at their cheeks to make it stop. He watches Hugo curl his hand around the neck of the beer bottle and swing it out in an arc toward Bird's already disintegrating face.

He watches all of that happen in the span of time it takes Hugo to rise from the table at all. Smoky magic is just beginning to appear in wisps from the folds of his clothes. Felix knows he can't let this scene keep playing.

"Stop, stop, stop, please, stop." He flings himself from the windowsill and presses his flattened palms against Hugo's chest. In this moment, he is a shield between his brother and the person *everyone* knows his brother is in love with.

Even if Felix didn't care about Bird as much as he does, he cares about Hugo more than anything or anyone. And he knows Hugo would never actually forgive himself if he let the dark corners in his own broken brain convince him to bite down on their jugular.

Hugo stares down at him, raising a brow at the splay of Felix's fingers against his ribs. Felix doesn't need words to know he's being dared to do . . . something. Hugo has always believed him capable of anything. But Hugo conceptualizes power in capacity for violence, where Felix would rather hang the stars.

Certain, now, that his brother at least won't fly off the handle, Felix drops his hands, wringing them against his belly. Hugo huffs a single, humorless laugh through his nose, so deeply and visibly disappointed.

That's okay. Felix understands disappointment. All things considered, it's one of the more tolerable flavors of grief.

Before

The night was mild, the Caravan was quiet, and the boy with a forest fire where his heart should be had never been more afraid in his very long thirteen years of life—because tonight was the night he would tell his North Star he was in love with them.

In the middle of nowhere, New Mexico, there was no civilization for miles and miles and miles. The desert sky, uninterrupted by mountains or trees, undiluted by the polluted hands of humanity's so-called advancements, seemed to last forever. It stretched around the nothing like an old blanket fort billowing over children's heads, a patchwork of cerulean and jade that made teal where they mingled, embellished by a billion strings of fairy lights strung up in all directions.

For the last week, their roving community was parked here among the sage and sand, and they would linger here for a short while longer. There was a family living in the nearest city, one of the many branches of the Caravan's sprawling Network. They were camping with them now, spending the last and next few days catching up Cassandra and Basil on things they'd seen, possibilities they'd uncovered since their last communication—whatever that meant, Hugo was not sure and did not particularly care.

In all other instances he could recall, he had enjoyed the presence of the Network in their encampment. The members of the Caravan were aware of their methodology being . . . unique, aware their rituals and rites might turn the stomach of the unsuspecting foreigner who found themself sitting suddenly in the warm belly of their sacred traditions. And so, for the sake of peacekeeping, the more extreme of their practices were put on moratorium for these visits.

Not to mention how the adults were just less likely to be complete fucking assholes in general when other people were around and watching them parent.

But this visit was different, for one humiliating reason— Gabriel.

Gabriel was the oldest son of the Networkers, one year older than them with a shaved head and two deep dimples and eyes of pewter that couldn't seem to remove themselves from Bird. For three days now, he'd been regaling them with stories about his life in the outside world, making them laugh and gasp and lean in closer and closer like a toy directed by some invisible string.

It made Hugo want to bite him.

Bird had never looked at *him* that way. And of course they hadn't. He had no stories to tell them. Every memory, every scar, every ugly inch of Hugo inside and out, Bird was already well acquainted with. He could offer them no novelty or adventure, only everything he had or would ever get his hands on and the promise that he, like a stray dog brought in from the cold and collared, would never leave them.

It was pathetic, he knew, but it was all he had. And it was what he'd planned to give them tonight.

Of course, that was before Bird *stood him up.*

More than fifteen minutes of solitude passed in the shadow of their agreed-upon rendezvous point, a plateau of stacked red rocks that made him feel like he could reach up and run his fingers over the stars. With every minute he was forced to sit there in silence with no sign of Bird, Hugo imagined plucking another one from the sky and macerating it between his teeth. It felt like universes died, were reborn, and died again, all in the stretch of those minutes.

Finally, his best friend emerged, backlit by the distant glow of the Caravan's campers, a shadow bounding closer with a skip in its step.

"Hey." They grinned, their keenly drawn features finally coming into view as they hoisted themself up onto the platform alongside him. Hugo pretended not to stop breathing when he saw them, just the way he always did.

"You're late," he pointed out immediately, knees at his chest and expression undoubtedly, embarrassingly petulant.

He didn't need to ask why. The why was obvious. *Gabriel.* Bird must've gotten wrapped up with their new obsession. They must have lost time sitting there listening to the older boy talk about how he was in human high school this year but had to take his classes on the computer for some reason—for the dozenth time.

"I know, right? It took me forever to find the good blanket." Flopping onto their backside next to him, their arm brushing his skin like a tattoo gun leaving a permanent mark, they dragged the canvas bag he'd only just realized they were holding between their legs. From it, Bird fished out their favorite quilt and spread it over both their thighs. "I thought it might get cold."

The constellations wedged between his teeth disintegrated into stardust and tumbled free from his parted lips. A desert breeze carried them away like dandelion seeds, each glittering speck off to grant the wish of a new world somewhere else.

Any festering ire was gone in the span of time it took for Bird to tuck their head against his shoulder, nuzzling their cheek into his collar and casting their honeycomb eyes to the sky. Maybe it was only his imagination, but Hugo would've sworn he could see the whole of the galaxy reflected in Bird's stare.

Even if they *didn't* come from the same faraway planet, he would've found a way to launch himself into their orbit someday. He knew that much.

"So," they asked, breath warm and enigmatically dangerous against his neck. "What did you wanna talk about?"

Hugo wanted *this* the way he had never wanted another thing in his entire very long very short life. Only now that it was time to make his want known, he didn't know if he could. What would be worse—to never say a word, to love his best friend from as close a distance as they would let him, to always have them and always want for more? Or to admit his feelings and risk their rejection—to have even the fantasy of what might've been ripped away from him, no longer allowed the rapture of possibility even in his fantasies?

Being Bird's best friend was his second-most important job and the one he loved doing more than anything. He couldn't put that on the line. Not for a what-if.

"Um." Hugo coughed, quietly, smoke filling his lungs as he smothered the flame in his chest. "It's nothing, actually. I don't even remember what I wanted. Sorry."

"Oh." Bird's disappointment somehow stretched the word into an extra syllable, pulling it through their teeth like saltwater taffy. "It's okay."

They sat there beneath the stars, ribcages pressed at the seam as if they came together to make the single spine of a book. Hugo wondered, if this were a story, what would it be about? Who would the hero be?

"Hey, Hugo?"

"Mm?" he asked, tilting his face down, careful not to knock the top of their head with his antlers.

Bird surged forward and slotted their mouth against his, their skin already beginning to glow that familiar, incandescent glow that put every other star in the sky to shame.

Hugo kissed them back. And the boy who had never known what it meant to be wanted without also being wrecked resigned himself to burn and burn and burn forever.

Chapter 9

Bird

Change is not a hunter Bird has ever tried to flee from; what point would there be to such an effort, when nothing is as inevitable as the constantly turning wheel of time? With every tick of a clock, an innumerable tally of transformations have already occurred, most undetectable to the naked eye.

Broken down to its simplest parts, everything about their existence is cyclical. The organic matter that allows them to be alive at all has already been here for millions of years. Nothing about Bird is *new*. They are just a collection of atoms picked up from stars and trees and oceans, ancient and unkillable gods of Earth, who all decided to come together and take the shape of a person for a while. Bird's life began at one pantheon's slumber, and their death will mark the start of a hundred thousand new beginnings.

And they *know* all of this to be true, and that is the most romantic thing in the world. After growing up with their mother and her wild eyes and her clueless belief in an endless nothing, there is very little as satisfying as Bird's power to find real magic in science.

Nothing stays the same, but nothing ever really disappears, either. Everyone Bird knows has always been here, and will always be here, even if they look different. Even their mother, wherever she is now, whatever has happened to her, still *has* to be here. If Bird were to be still and listen, they might be able to feel her nearby, in the beating of a beetle's wings or sap sticking to the bark of a fir tree.

Bird has no interest in being still and listening—though they wish Holly well, wherever she might have ended up.

In any case, it remains true that change is inescapable, and Bird has spent most of their life excitedly running toward it. That things might evolve has never once frightened them. Instead, the idea things might be stifled, frozen in place, that their life may not change at all, has always been the worry caught in their throat. Their atoms have almost surely been insects before; they almost surely will be again. Bird hopes, fervently, none of their future bug selves will ever find themselves fossilized in amber.

Perhaps there is no way to know that anything will be good; perhaps it would make more sense to fear an unknowable future. But any change would mean things were not like *this* anymore. And Bird's childhood was marked by much of the feeling of *this*. It was the sort of childhood, they have now come to terms with, that made one eager for it to end.

This obvious change between Hugo and Felix, however, is curiously alarming. For those two, Bird will make an exception in their love of change, in favor of wondering, *What the hell is going on?*

In the aftermath of the almost-fight, the something-brutal-that-nearly-happened-but-didn't, Felix disappears into the tiny Emily Dickinson–themed bathroom, locking himself behind a paper-thin door to escape the prying eyes of the others. Bird wonders if he'll cry alone in the dark and feels a pang of sympathy. How many times did they do the same, cramped on the postage stamp of floor in the water closet of their mother's camper? Desperate to find a single scrap of space they could carve out to fall apart, without knowing the same people who'd brought them to the edge were probably listening on the other side of a dinky sheet of metal?

Growing up in the Caravan was not without its bright spots. But most things that happened to Bird there are things they will spend the rest of their life healing from.

"*What* is going on with you two?" they demand, keeping their voice low in the willfully naive hope it will prevent poor Felix from overhearing them. "I've never seen you act like this."

"You haven't been around to see *anything* in a long time," Hugo reminds them, because of course he does. Because he's incapable of letting himself miss a single sliver of opportunity to bring up how they abandoned him. Even if that isn't what happened.

"What, you're telling me this is your new normal?" Bird brushes right past the accusation, refusing to take the bait and give Hugo the argument he's looking for. All this new shade of him wants is a bloody, drawn-out fight. Even if Bird was willing to give it to him, it wouldn't lead either of them anywhere they want to go. "Even when you were a dick to everyone else, you looked out for Felix. So what, you've become even more of an asshole than you used to be? Now you can't even bring yourself to go easy on your little brother?"

Something resembling an *answer* flits across Hugo's face, a shadow of some unspoken secret. Bird tries to follow after it, their eyes hungrily tracing the familiar hills and valleys of his face. But Hugo's faster, and the secret is gone long before Bird can sink their talons in and lift it away.

He's still got the empty beer bottle by his side, clutching the neck, knuckles white like he's trying to strangle it and eyes lost in the middle distance, fixed on something he won't let anybody see. "You have no idea what you're talking about. What goes on between Felix and me is none of your business."

"Fuck that," Calliope croons from her spot in the driver's seat, and if Felix hadn't been able to hear them before, he certainly can now. When Bird glances up, their eyes meet Calliope's in the rearview mirror. Heady browns pin them down for the briefest moment before darting responsibly back to the road. "When the two of you keep acting like dipshits for everyone to see," Calliope tells the asphalt, "it *becomes* everyone's business. And anyway, Bird's right for the first time in their life."

"If you tried to say something nice about me without adding an insult at the end, do you think you might go into anaphylactic shock?" Bird sighs, hands folding around their hip bones.

Calliope pretends she can't hear them. "This shit between the two of you? It's new. You used to walk around with your hands outstretched like you might catch him if he fell. Now you're the one who's gonna shove him."

"Fuck both of you," Hugo drawls, stepping away from Bird and shaking his head. He wears something bizarrely close to a smile, an uncanny valley display of mirthless amusement at some dark joke only he is privy to. "Neither of you know fuck all about anything. Least of all how I feel about my brother."

"So, tell us," Bird presses, their tone treading terribly close to a beg, even as they know he won't.

Because Calliope's right. Hugo used to have Felix up on the grandest and sturdiest of pedestals. They're fairly certain when they were kids, Hugo thought the sun only rose in the morning because Felix was afraid of the dark. And Bird knows that because Bird was right there with them, fingers intertwined with Hugo's, catching fireflies and making shadow puppets under the moon.

And then things between Bird and Hugo changed. And clearly, he couldn't handle it.

Just as expected, rather than answering, Hugo stomps to the back of the RV, flinging himself down on Calliope's bed like a petulant toddler. He turns his back on all of them, ignoring her shouts from the front to *get his goddamn shoes off the duvet*, a silent, simmering storm. Self-contained, but only just.

If something has changed between him and Felix, it stands to reason he can't handle that, either. And if that's the case, of course he would be trying vehemently to pretend everything was okay. Because the alternative meant admitting he was standing, alone, beneath a now-empty sky.

Before

It wasn't always bad, you know, being as in the know as a new-born baby.

"Like a tall glass of water, that man," Megan said, feverishly trying to cool herself down with a homemade hand fan in the likeness of the musician's face. "Literally. A, like, seven-foot-tall glass of water. I hope he plays 'Arsonist's Lullaby.' The set list has seemed more or less the same throughout the tour—from what I can tell from the leaks, anyway—but there's always a few surprise songs and I would die, Birdie, just *die* if I heard him sing 'Arsonist's Lullaby' live. He probably won't do it. Nobody knows that song. I'm gonna keep manifesting, though. I could settle for 'Foreigner's God,' though, oooh . . ."

Megan chattered on, elated to talk whether or not she was heard. Bird didn't have to pretend to understand or nod at appropriate times or give any indication that they even knew she was there. Megan Blackwell, who seemed to have decided Bird was rescued from a deeply abusive Christian cult, had just about demanded they tag along to this concert, citing none of her other friends as having "quite enough religious trauma" to truly appreciate the music. "You might've heard one of his songs on the radio," she'd pressed. "And if you haven't, how nice for you!"

It was refreshing, their cluelessness being regarded fondly, with excitement rather than pity.

Bird had no idea how to correctly pronounce this musician's name, but neither, it seemed, did the diehard fans, which made Bird feel a little less like a loser from a faraway galaxy. And if there were ever a crowd for someone fucked up and fae-adjacent to fit into, it would've been this one. Half the folks in attendance looked like they'd just dragged themselves from the depths of a bog—impressive, given the severity of drought in Southern California, and the endless collar of concrete strangling Los Angeles. Even in their most inoffensive overalls, Bird fit in better than most of the cis dudes in attendance, many of whom were sporting a T-shirt plastered with some variation of *I'm just here for my girlfriend.*

Megan's shimmery green eyeshadow was beginning to smear in the heat. Arriving at a venue several hours early, Bird was to understand, was The Way To Do A Concert if you wanted a good spot. Megan had a whole sack of snacks she was planning to abandon at security, and did that make any sense? No. But Bird was so very content to hand over their autonomy and be completely docile for a night. To be ushered into a human, teenage experience with glee. No one was ever *excited* to dispense common knowledge like an overworked vending machine, filling in cavernous gaps in basic knowledge, but Bird wasn't a charity case this time. They were chosen, happily. For one night, that was enough.

"Doors!" Megan squealed, and the snack sack was forgotten in favor of seizing Bird's bicep in a double-handed vise grip. Bird sucked a breath in through their teeth and tried not to fixate on the pressure against their flesh or the litter bomb they left behind as the line surged forward a few paces. Death would not come for them just because their body was uncomfortable and overstimulated for a few hours, and one of the bored, uniformed people scattered around would keep their trash from killing any sea turtles. Everything was fine, and they were fine, and they were normal enough for this.

"You're gonna love it," Megan was saying, and whether intentionally or not, she was helping Bird through security—plucking things from Bird's many pockets and putting them in a dish, pushing Bird through the metal detector, collecting their items without care for the worker's palpable irritation and guiding them both seamlessly back into the whitewater gush of concert traffic. "You're so book smart and his lyrics are sooo pretty. Too smart for me, sometimes. So you're gonna be obsessed, I fear. Okay, ready? Hold my hand!"

"What?" Bird's voice came out in a croak after hours of silence.

It didn't matter; Megan had grabbed their hand anyway, and was wearing the biggest, most crooked smile her face could hold. "Now run!"

Before Bird could even wonder *why*, Megan plunged them through the venue doors into a welcome blast of air conditioning and dim light. "No running," a venue employee called listlessly as Megan and Bird raced past power-walking fans, and they looked so ridiculous that then Bird was laughing helplessly along with Megan's infectious, maniacal giggles.

"Yes!" Megan screeched when they turned into a cavernous room that stretched a mind-bendingly long expanse before ending in a stage. "Bird, *yes*! *RUN!*"

What had she seen? Who knew. Bird had never been happier

to be clueless. They could've been pursued by a bear and they wouldn't have known to be afraid, not with the excitement resonating through their joined, sweaty hands, fusing their bones into an instrument of pure vibrato. Bird sprinted for all they were worth, ignoring increasingly irate barks of "No *running*!" until they crashed, full-speed, into a chest-high steel barrier.

"FRONT ROW!" Megan screamed. She threw her sweaty arms around Bird's neck and screamed it about a dozen more times. Bird avoided swallowing their tongue by reminding themself that this was how friends expressed delight and shut the mental door between their eardrums and their brain until Megan had repeated herself enough times to quiet a few decibels.

"If you have to pee, no you don't," Megan managed between panting breaths. "I will die before I leave this spot. Holy shit. Holy *shit*."

Bird looked back at the hordes piling in after them, already stacked a few people deep at their backs, and their skin began to feel as if a few thousand larvae were hatching just under its surface. They couldn't do this, actually, and it didn't matter how cheerily they were invited to look through the windows of someone's very normal life—they'd never be anything other than a freakish, humanoid thing dependent on others to function halfway fine.

Clammy palms sandwiched their cheeks and turned their face back toward the stage. "Just. Don't look, okay?" Megan commanded before rummaging through her canvas backpack. It was covered in hot-glued fake moss and Styrofoam mushrooms. She wrestled out a big pair of headphones—a few loose coins and tampons hit the floor in the process, casualties of haste and maximalism—and clapped them over Bird's ears.

Instantly, the growing cacophony was swallowed by calming, cottony pressure, and Bird got a bit of their breath back. For the first time, they felt like they're looking at Megan like *she* was the alien.

"This lady on TikTok who grew up in the Waco cult said she *still* gets really freaked out in crowds," Megan shouted, over-enunciating to a ludicrous degree. "So like, breathe, babe! Don't look backward! And if it gets really bad, security'll haul you over the barrier!"

Bird would never, ever be able to tell this girl that they'd never been around so many humans—certainly not this many this close—and their throat threatened to swell closed with the pressure of holding back the confession. How counter to their instinct, such a secret, when every other scrap of their body was screaming *friend! That was a display of friendship! Bird, we did it! We made a friend!!!* They could never have one of those, not really. Not here.

But for one night, what was within Bird's reach was supposed to be enough, and so for tonight, it would be.

Bird stared straight at the stage for the next hour, breathing slow and deep as pressure grew against their back, eyes tracking people in all black moving wires and instruments in a hypnotic kind of dance. Megan, of course, made fast friends with everyone around them, her muffled voice becoming a comforting kind of white noise after a while, another buffer against the sound of the crowd. When the lights went down, a woman who was certainly *not* the man depicted on Megan's hand fan came onstage, and Bird learned what an opener was, even though Megan couldn't really explain why that was a thing. Again, they weren't the only one in the room kind of confused, and again, it was a relief, and *then . . .*

Then.

Megan's very tall glass of water was onstage, and he was un-hinging his jaw and singing with the voice of something just as otherworldly as Bird. At some point, several songs in, Bird became aware that their mouth hung slack and wide, that they hadn't blinked, that their cheeks were wet and salty. That they'd, at some point, pulled their headphones down to rest on their collarbones, willingly stripping away whatever barrier they could. The crowd was so much more bearable in chorus. Bird was surrounded by thousands of humans, and together they were all, a little bit, otherworldly.

You might've heard some of his songs on the radio, Megan Blackwell had said, *and if not, how nice for you!*

Bird likes to cut the memory there, when they can, like some film editor of old. It's better when they can pretend it ended the way it began. On the nights they can't sleep for how mortified they are by their attempt to play human, that memory of com-munion, a moment hung forever fossilized in amber, is enough to stay the killing knife of their embarrassment.

Chapter 10

Cal

Anger is so much more loving than most people give it credit for.

A person can't get angry if they don't care in the first place. There has to be something worth caring about, something that actually, tangibly matters, or else there isn't any reason to get angry when stuff goes wrong.

Plenty of people have been cruel to Cal, but very rarely have they ever been angry at her.

It's goofy as fuck, the way she watches Hugo and Bird arguing in the rearview mirror, silently suppressing her pathetic jealousy. There is nothing about the two of them that she should realistically be jealous of. They're ridiculous. They're childish. Neither one of them has ever tried thinking a single decision through to its conclusion.

And yet . . .

She wonders if they know how agonizingly obvious it is to the whole rest of the world that they never stopped being in love with each other. They're both trying to hide it, that much is clear. But she suspects they both think they're doing a better job of that than they actually are.

Because Hugo can't do a damn thing without Bird mapping his movements. He inhales, and they exhale. He looks at his hands, and they chart the moles on his knuckles like a road map. There isn't a single moment Bird isn't watching, waiting, poised for flight—though what they're waiting for is a mystery, at least to Cal.

And for all Hugo refuses to look back at them, he isn't any better. Somehow, he's worse. Because he's pointedly not watching, and he's trying so hard to keep his distance, and he's *still* being pulled toward them. He doesn't need his eyes. Even with his back to them all, anytime Bird moves around Cal's RV (doing nothing, so far as Cal can tell, but mess with all her shit and put it where it doesn't belong), he leans as if he's their shadow. Like he's a goddamn compass, and Bird is north. He doesn't have to see them. Gravitationally, magnetically, *whatever*, he's always going to find his way back to them.

It's such bullshit.

Especially because they don't even seem to like each other. Not anymore. What a waste it is, for two people to be so hopelessly wrapped up in each other's orbits, only for it to basically mean nothing because they're both complete assholes. There are so many people out there who spend their whole lives searching for their other half. Most never find them, and either settle for the best they can get or die alone. How selfish and miserable and ridiculous it is that Bird and Hugo were handed their person on a silver highchair tray, able to explore and know and adore their soulmate while shitting in their diapers, and it doesn't actually even matter.

Do they have any idea how many people would kill for what they have?

Cal would kill for someone to want her that way.

Of course, the same person who wanted her would probably end up dead. So Cal will settle for the best she can get and redecorate her RV anytime she gets too up in her feelings about it.

Felix finally exits the bathroom, and Cal watches him in the rearview. He sniffles, jumping a little when he sees her stare, and gives her a sad smile before his attention diverts to Bird.

"You okay?" they ask, all hushed and clandestine, as if they think there's any chance Hugo won't hear them. He's all of five feet away with his nasty little boots grinding into Cal's pillows, his nose in the corner like he's in time-out—Cal *suspects* he can hear them.

"I'm okay. Thanks." Felix squeezes Bird's shoulder before climbing up into the loft over Cal's bed, making himself at home in the nest beside the storage bins. He tugs the heavy blanket over himself until he becomes a burrito.

And Bird keeps watching him, even when it seems like he might've fallen asleep.

So, Hugo isn't the only one Bird watches. It's different with Hugo; that much is undeniable. But Bird cares about both brothers. That's the whole reason they got angry in the first place. They don't want to see the two of them going for each other's throats, because no halfway decent person should want that for the people they love. Whittled down, and their anger and nosiness is just Bird's way of telling the boys they're loved.

Bird has always loved people fiercely. Cal still doesn't understand how they were able to leave the Caravan, how they could make the choice to leave everyone they cared about. It doesn't make any sense to her.

What *does* make sense is the way people reacted when Bird came back. They pulled up that day and climbed out of the car with downcast eyes and people went to their goddamn knees. It was like the messiah had returned.

Yeah, Bird loves people, but people love Bird just as much and probably more. They might be Hugo's extra-special center of gravity or some bullshit, but he's far from the only person who's always watching them, even when he refuses to look at them.

Sometimes, Felix stares at Bird like he's watching some higher power remake the world right in front of him—like the very act of creation sits in the palms of Bird's hands and he's scared and confused and breathless with awe.

Even Eamon started looking at Bird in a way he didn't look at anyone else. Cal has wondered what his deal was since the day he showed up—where he'd come from, what he could do. And he seemed to wonder just as much about everyone around him, always levying suspicious stares that lingered way longer than was comfortable. But the way he looked at Bird was different, like he'd already decided they were innocent. Or maybe like he didn't care if they weren't.

Calling it pretty privilege feels *corny*, and Cal straight up refuses to do that. But what else could it be, really? How is it possible that Bird can just breeze through life, wrapping everyone in their path around their finger, all while remaining clueless to the irrefutable fact that they're making the whole wide world fall in love with them just by being in it? Is that just what it's like for people who look like them? Dead ringers for the classic beauties ancient painters obsessed over, whose half-bared chests and demure expressions are still hung to be gawked over centuries later? Does everyone with a stupid, perfect face and a stupid, perfect body just get to be whatever they want and do whatever they want and—

Cal realizes she's stopped breathing only when Bird meets her eye in the rearview mirror. Her eyes dart away, back to the road, and she sucks in a desperate, rattled breath, her stiff, sore fingers flexing away from the steering wheel cover.

Fuck.

So, okay, whatever, she's not immune to Bird, either. But that's not her fault. She certainly isn't a god, and *she* didn't decide who was going to be beautiful and who was going to be gay.

Besides, her issues with Bird are a lot more complicated than thinking they're a pretty pretty princess—or regent, royal, whatever feels *congruent*, because Cal can't help but file every crumb of information away, all the while cursing herself for doing it.

Because it's about Bird, fine, but it also doesn't actually have anything to do with Bird at all. It's about Cal.

It's about how some people get to walk through the world never knowing what it's like to be unwanted, and other people have only their car to dote on and spend their whole lives on their knees because no one can even be fucked to lend a hand to pull them to their feet.

Cal's knees are blood-soaked by now, but she stopped begging to be forgiven for the sin of her birth a long time ago. These days, she doesn't pray while she's down in the dirt. She just keeps digging the grave. One of these days, she'll figure out if it's hers or not.

Before

The Caravan had authorities called on them plenty of times in Cal's memory. No matter how well they hid, it wasn't like they were locked far away in some secret compound. They were traveling through forests and deserts and mountains and beaches and places where outdoorsy types went to hike away from their human problems, whatever the fuck human problems looked like. And occasionally, someone might catch a glimpse of their camp—always with enough warning to shuffle the most obviously inhuman ones out of sight, the ones never allowed to tread too close to hiking paths anyway. But the *inhumanity* of the Caravan's existence was only one of a list of problems.

Most often, the calls would report one of two things—public indecency or potentially endangering a minor. When it got extra spicy, the complaints might even combine the two. In nearly every single circumstance, the Caravan was able to deal with it quickly and quietly. The Network, after all, was bigger than anyone could possibly wrap their head around. Their kind were hidden in plain sight all over the place, in positions of power and authority, positions where they could make complaints disappear with a signature or a handshake.

Most often, it was fine. This was what they did. They basically had it down to a science. In so many ways, the Caravan felt and *was* completely un-fuck-with-able.

There was the one time, though, when they couldn't make it go away so easily.

Cal was twelve when it happened. Someone on the road in Illinois saw something they shouldn't have, and because of it, a handful of kids from the Caravan ended up in a human group home for *three days* while Basil and Cassandra frantically puppeteered their release. In the end, there would be no investigation, no resolution, just a shuffling of children from the hands of one shadowy group to another, and the Caravan disappearing into anonymity once more. But it would be the first time in Cal's life that, however scary the circumstances, she got to taste the outside world.

It was also the time she thought she was going to murder Bird, because they shared a bedroom for two nights.

"*Stop. Fucking. Crying,*" Cal growled into the dark for the sixth time in the last hour. This time, however, she followed it up with "Or I will come over there and give you something worth crying over."

Trembling in their own twin-sized bed, the glowing lump that was Bird-before-they-were-Bird *hiccupped*. Somehow, that was even more annoying than the sobbing on its own.

"How can you be so mean right now?" they demanded, yanking their blanket away to glower—less than intimidatingly, given the overall dampness of their face—in Cal's direction. "What if we never go home again?"

Where the fuck is home?

Was Cal supposed to be mourning the trailer she lived in by herself, hitched to the back of Basil and Cassandra's RV like a dog in an outhouse? Maybe she was heartless, but she didn't exactly care if she never saw that place again.

And it wasn't like anyone there was missing her, either.

"Then you better start learning how to make friends without just nepo-babying your way through it," Cal suggested.

She wasn't even sure Bird understood what a nepo baby was, but something about her answer kicked off another round of hysteria. They pressed their face into their hands, body trembling so violently they turned the room into a rave of light and shadow.

Cal drug her nails down the sides of her face, clawing at her own skin. She couldn't take this anymore.

Tossing back her blanket, she leaped from the bed and stalked to the pathetic, weeping wonder she'd been left alone with. Without thinking, she clambered into the other bed, kneeling at its edge to grab at her roommate. Her nails dug into Bird's shoulders and she slammed them onto their back, pressing them firmly into the mattress so she could hold herself above them.

"Hey! Enough!"

With the only light in the room coming from the skin under her hands, Cal suddenly had an impeccable view of Bird's shock at being touched at all. Their eyes widened, lips parting—almost immediately, their crying dissipated, turning instead to a quick gasp and then increasingly slow, shallow breathing.

Good. Finally, Cal might be able to get some sleep, now that she could focus on something other than the—

Oh. It hit Cal after Bird, the shock at her having touched

another person. Maybe even *especially* to have touched the one she had.

Bird's skin was warm and soft, yielding and wholly unfamiliar. And as soon as Cal realized she was touching them at all, the terribly sacrilegious desire to touch them even *more* flooded into her. Her hands ached with a desire to slide over Bird's long, bony arms, to memorize every notch of them with her fingertips.

Behind her lips, her teeth throbbed, and it sent a chill of fear like a current over the river of her spine.

Of course, Bird was going to shove her away. They were going to trade in anguish for anger, and yell at her to get off of them *now*. It was only a matter of seconds, probably, and Cal braced herself for it.

But it never landed. Instead, a silent Bird continued to stare up at Cal through the dappled shadows that now carved her face and body. Somehow both too round and too sharp, Cal's features were in flux, beginning to shapeshift away from the softness of youth and into something new, something she was still not sure she wanted. But with this front-row seat in the almost-dark, Cal could watch with confusion and excitement and a sick, heavy pit in her stomach as Bird's eyes hungrily memorized it all.

Their breaths mingled in the illuminated space between them. Delirious, Cal swore she could taste Bird's mouth when they did.

"Thank you," Bird finally whispered. "I couldn't snap myself out of it."

And in some bizarre show of kinship and familiarity, they reached up with one small, still-trembling hand to press their fingers atop the ones Cal was still using to pin them down.

As the girl watched in growing horror, Bird twined their fingers together, clasping Cal's under theirs and giving her hand a squeeze.

Oh.

Oh no.

More speedily than she'd arrived, Cal threw herself from the bed. She stumbled backward, catching herself on the edge of the other mattress, and immediately clambering onto it. As if the thin material of the group home's bedding might protect her from the knowledge that Bird Stieber had just tried to hold her hand.

"Fuck you," Cal snapped. "Just be glad I didn't have to shut you up another way."

The room went silent.

Cal pulled the blanket over her head and curled herself into the smallest ball she could. Inside her head, she made a vow to herself to forget the way Bird's eyes felt on her body, and the way their skin felt under her hands. She would forget *everything* about that moment. She had no other choice.

Chapter 11

Hugo

"Is anyone's fucking phone working?"

It's only after Hugo speaks, the words like sandpaper on his throat, that he realizes he can't remember the last time any of them said anything out loud. They're parked now, scattered about under the wide-open sky. Judging by the settled sprawl of camp chairs and the dirtied dinnerware littered all around their makeshift campsite, they've been here for a while.

How much time has passed since his argument with Felix, and the spat with Bird that followed? How many hours did he spend staring daggers at the corner to keep himself from snapping? Were they on the road all day? They must've been, because they're no longer shepherded by the Rockies' stalwart silhouettes. As it always does this far West, the earth has opened up like a cactus bloom, flattening into endless stretches of desert, the sandstone made scarlet by sunset's dim dusting of pigment. The sheer amount of vermillion is enough to make him dizzy, and the sudden geological shrinkage doesn't make any fucking sense—weren't they just surrounded by mountains?

Maybe he crashed in Cal's bed without realizing he was dozing off and stumbled out here before he was fully awake. Or maybe he didn't, and he's just been glaring at the wall and sleepwalking for like seven hours.

If he thinks about it too hard, he can't remember much of anything about the rest of their day, right up to when they finally stopped for the night and made camp. Somewhere in the maze of his mind, Hugo's thoughts took a wrong turn. He knows this, a self-aware-enough rat to know that if he could only back up and make a better decision at an earlier opportunity, he might still find the promised cheese. And even as he knows that, he can't seem to escape out of the corner he's backed himself into.

Something is wrong. Something is terribly, horribly wrong, and there is nothing he can do to save himself from the trap he can't make himself see.

Everyone else seems as surprised to hear him speak as he is to have spoken. Felix's head snaps up, body jolting as if he'd been asleep with his eyes open. "Hm?"

Cal looks up from the shadow of the RV where she's made a little grotto for herself. Her silhouette blends so seamlessly with the dark around her, Hugo could almost believe she hadn't been there at all until it'd spit her back out. "Working how?"

He opens his mouth to call her an idiot for asking him that, but manages to bite back at the last second, swallowing the unnecessary indignance. He doesn't *want* to be the bad guy, even if everyone knows he is. And with the weight of the morning's confrontations still anchoring the beast in his chest, playing nice feels infinitesimally easier.

"I don't have any service," he elaborates, for all he doesn't feel like he should've had to. Give the boy a round of applause.

"Where *is* my phone?" Bird mumbles in response, the rhetorical directed at themselves or the world at large more than anyone else in their group.

Hugo absolutely does not watch them hunt for their misplaced phone in his periphery as the last frayed edges of sunset struggle and slip below the horizon, the desert beginning to cool and darken almost immediately. He does not blueprint the way they rifle through every pocket of their backpack and then move back into the RV to turn all of Cal's stuff upside down. He definitely doesn't clock how, though he can't hear Bird, he can hear the vehicle's axles shift and groan with their steps. No, Hugo is apathetic and healthily detached and perfectly capable of not noticing Bird at any given moment.

"No bars." Cal shoves her phone back into her boot after giving the screen a cursory once-over, slumping forward with her arms over her knees. When she bites into the sandwich in her hand, tomato juice drizzles down the path of her chin. She swipes it away with the edge of her palm, then traces it with her tongue to mop it up.

He cannot stand her. Which is fine and unremarkable, because no one has ever been able to stand Cal, but it occurs to him sharply in that moment.

Immediately in its wake, he wonders how the hell he's ever supposed to stop being such an asshole if he gets angry anytime someone else has the audacity to be nonchalant and attractive in his range of cognizance.

Oh. *Does* he find Cal attractive?

It's news to him, but sure. That makes sense, in its own unfortunate way. She dresses like she's been under the hood of a car for forty years, and he's not entirely convinced she's ever taken a shower. But beneath her grime and decidedly off-putting attitude, she's plenty pretty.

Somehow, that makes the circumstances of her existence even more sad. Prettiness is entirely wasted on her, for a short list of altogether uncompromising reasons.

"Mine's dead," Felix pipes up, frowning at his blank phone screen. He looks up at Hugo through his golden eyelashes, mouth pinched at the center and tucked down in both corners. "Sorry."

Hugo takes a deep breath before he answers, all too aware that his tongue wants to scream his throat raw at Felix for packing half a dozen stuffed animals but no cell phone charger, and also that Bird has just stepped back out onto the RV's steps. The memory of their accusations, the way they talked about his relationship with his little brother, replays in his head.

As much as he didn't want to hear any of it, there is a part of him that knows it's good he did. He needs to be more careful. No one can know the truth of what happened between Felix and him. No one can know *why* things changed, in exactly the way Bird pointed out.

Even though the idea of his interactions with anyone else being monitored makes Hugo want to *eviscerate* someone—perhaps himself—that reality has always been part of his life. Safe hiding places are nonexistent for anyone who grew up the way he did. Children of the Caravan learned early to keep their secrets buried bone deep beneath their skin, or not to have secrets at all.

And, to be clear, he's never met someone in the Caravan without a minefield of secrets to navigate.

"It's okay," he tells his brother, annoyed that it *is* okay, and also that the lasered branding of Bird and Cal's supervision makes it feel like he's only saying it's okay because he doesn't have a choice. Not being able to give any other answer doesn't actually make his words less true, but it certainly makes them taste that way in his mouth. "Probably wouldn't have service anyway."

He's been all over the country. The two worst places for any cell service? Rural pockets of the Southeast where long stretches of bumpy dirt roads sit tucked between barren fields of once-farmlands, and this flat expanse of desolate, sandy nothingness. The desert is a great place to die, it makes it so easy.

"I can't find my phone," Bird announces.

Hugo still doesn't look at them. Instead, he looks at his hands—and jumps to find he's holding a sandwich, too, matching the one Cal's chewing on. When the hell did that get there? Has he been holding it the entire time? There are no bites taken out of his, just a perfectly put-together tomato and cheese.

Of course they stopped for the night and made dinner. Eating is as important as sleeping. They need to make sure they're doing both of those. Of course. That makes sense.

Where was his head when they were doing all that?

He frowns but takes a bite. When tomato juice trickles down *his* chin, he wipes it away with fury and swipes the mess on his pants instead of lapping it up. He'd look a lot more like a stray dog than whatever strong, hot vibes Cal was giving off.

"Are you sure you brought it with us?" Felix asks Bird, words dripping out slowly like he doesn't like what he's insinuating as much as he knows Bird isn't going to like it. "I don't remember seeing you use it in the RV."

"Dammit," Bird mumbles, and dips back inside.

Hugo rolls his eyes. He ignores the sting of disappointment that he's pretty sure there's no way Bird could see him do it.

"What do you need, anyway?" Cal demands, narrowing her eyes at Hugo. "No one you know's gonna pick up your calls."

He gnashes the bread between his back molars to keep himself from telling Cal she's a cunt. When he swallows, he answers, "I thought it might be worth trying again. Just in case. I'm sure that's hard for you to understand, when you don't have anyone but yourself to worry about."

Goddammit. He tried, he really did.

Felix hops to his feet, holding his hand up like a teacher's pet. "I'll see if I can find a spot."

Hugo tilts his head away from Cal, peeling his attention from the burning distaste in her eyes, to consider his brother's palm. "You sure?"

"Yeah. I'm not really hungry. If I can get service, I'll try Mom and Dad."

"Well . . . Thanks." Hugo sets his phone down in Felix's dainty hand. "Use the flashlight. Watch for snakes."

"I know, I know." Felix smiles, pressing a button on the screen to click the light to life. "It'll be fine."

Barely illuminated by the dim glow of Hugo's phone camera, the younger Beránek makes his way into the darkening desert alone.

"You're really going to let him go off by himself?" Cal's tone oozes with judgment.

Hugo considers scorpions and rattlesnakes and coyotes as he watches the bouncing flicker of light until it disappears behind a red rock face. "He'll be fine."

The beast in his chest growls in warning, scraping slow, sharp claws against the cage of his ribs. It is impossible to say if it fears what might happen to Felix alone out there, or if it fears what Felix might do when no one is watching.

None of the others have any idea what his brother is capable of.

Chapter 12

Felix

You don't need to be afraid of Felix.

Listen—I understand your skepticism. All of these deeply troubled teens have clearly done something terrible, each and every one of them, at various moments in their lives. And clearly, you're being set up to suspect each of them might have been responsible for whatever happened to the rest of the Caravan.

Felix isn't without skeletons in his closet; none of them are. But I can assure you, there's no reason to worry about him. In fact, I wouldn't recommend worrying about what *any* of our chroniclers may be guilty of.

A far better use of your time may be considering what the Caravan has done to back their children into these corners in the first place. And in that vein, what kind of people are they, that someone might have been compelled to make all of them disappear?

For his part, Felix doesn't have any idea what the rest of the Caravan is up to. He couldn't begin to guess where they are or how they got there or if they're trying to reach their unyoked fledglings even now. And for all the guilt he might've felt in the beginning, when he first realized everyone was gone and promptly spiraled into his own shame for secretly wishing this would happen someday, he's feeling a lot better about it now.

As far as he's concerned, there isn't much reason to try and contact the others.

Still, here he is, wandering aimlessly somewhere near Moab, holding up his brother's phone to the maroon backdrop of the barren dust bowl and watching to see if the tiny SOS marker in the upper right corner might turn into a bar or two. It seems unlikely. But what does he know? (Not much.) There's no harm in trying. And maybe if he does this, he can start making his way toward fixing things with Hugo.

For all Felix doesn't care about figuring out what happened to their parents, he wouldn't know what to do with himself if things stayed like this with his brother forever. And everyone's right, even if Hugo will deny it with all the air in his lungs—things between them *are* messed up. They've been messed up since Hugo . . .

Well.

Reader, look, I have to be honest about something. I *am* keeping secrets from you here. It isn't that I think you're untrustworthy, but I've been burned before. I have to keep some things close to the vest. At least until we get to know each other a little better.

So, anyway, things have been messed up between them since Hugo ▍▋▍▍▋▋▍▍.

It wasn't his fault. Felix *knows* that, because he was there. He saw the whole thing happen, and he knows Hugo didn't see any other choice but to do what he did. Seriously, Felix doesn't blame him!

But Hugo blames himself. At least, that's the way it seems. So maybe he's projecting all that guilt onto Felix. Maybe he's imagining Felix hates him as much as he's started to hate himself.

The whole thing sucks. There's a part of Felix that'd like to go back to before it happened, to see if he could intervene and stop it, to see if he could save his brother the burden of shame he's been hauling around. Of course, if he did that, they wouldn't—

He disrupts the flow of his own thoughts by asking, "Who are *you?*"

Felix's head tilts so far to the side that his cheek is practically parallel with the dry, cracked earth beneath his shoes. He isn't sure how far he's wandered, or exactly how much time has lapsed. The only measurement he has to go by are the changes in the world around him.

The rusted copper of sunset has fully drained away to the other side of the world, revealing the veiny underbelly of the desert night sky, mulberry purple and swollen with unshed blood. A million white stars cast the only light besides the flashlight in Felix's hand, like an intricate web of cross-sectioned arteries keeping this place alive. They don't do much to illuminate the vast stone void.

There's no breeze out here to offer a reprieve from the uncanny heat of an October in southern Utah. Instead, the overstuffed air drips in and around itself, coaxing a trail of sweat down the back of Felix's neck. He worries he could drown in air this thick.

When he breathes deep, anxiety making it hard to get his lungs full, he can make out the scent of creosote and agave. The medicinal plants mingled with the faraway choir of coyotes promise that, despite its deceptive impression of an arid wasteland, the desert is teeming with life that does not want to be intruded on.

Felix has no desire to intrude. He never wants to be anywhere he isn't also wanted. Besides, none of those are what grabbed his attention.

The red rock sculptures are so delicately and precisely designed, they couldn't have been stacked together by anything other than the hands of intention. Felix believed that the first time he was driven through Utah, staring out the window of his parents' RV years ago on the trek from one middle-of-nowhere to another, his sticky hands pressed against the glass. He saw them standing like ancient statues and imagined the enormous hands of old gods that must have made them what they were, fashioning the stone when it was still young and wet from the ancient sea that once spanned these lands. The idea something *that* beautiful could just *happen* did not—and still doesn't—make any sense. It had to be a kind of magic.

In this moment, though, it's another kind of magic transfixing him. Because one of the sculptures—huge, at least twenty feet tall, and shaped like an archway over a platform, or the outline of a crystal ball propped on its own enormous dais—*flickers* in his periphery. Certain it must have been a trick of the low light or his own untamable imagination, Felix turns his head to face it straight on, eyes narrowing with misgiving. It won't happen again, surely.

But it does. As Felix watches, a shimmer of glittering blackness, darker than the deepest fathomable shadow and freckled with sparking glimmers, reveals itself within the open circlet of rock. It seems to dance, rippling like a wave from edge to edge. If one weren't looking close enough, they might mistake it for the night sky overhead, an endless darkness dusted in stardust. Perhaps, Felix thinks, whoever's magic this is wanted any passersby to make that very misconstruction.

He walks closer, his hand falling to his side, any thought of illumination evaporating on the spot. The flash from Hugo's cell phone casts a beam behind him, leaving a miraculous illusionary trail of light lingering after the soles of his shoes. He does not think to be mindful of snakes or scorpions or anything else that might lurk in the dark of the desert, so compelled he is by the strange life cradled within the sandstone void.

Is that . . .

No, it couldn't be.

But—no, it is.

Is that shimmering blackness *whispering* to him?

Heart in his throat, Felix creeps nearer, increasingly desperate to make out the subtle sighs of this almost-imperceptible sorcery. And so focused is he on his ominous task, he does not notice when the flashlight aimed behind him catches on a tall, broad figure stalking closer, closer.

WELCOME HOME DARLING NO ONE HERE IS GOING
TO HURT YOU I PROMISE WELCOME HOME DARLING
NO ONE HERE **I**S GOING TO HURT YOU I PROMISE
WELCOME HOME DARLING NO ONE HERE IS GOING
TO HURT YOU I PROMISE WELCOME HOME DARLING
NO ONE HERE IS GOING TO HURT YOU I PROMISE
WELCOME HOME DAR**L**ING NO ONE HERE IS GOING
TO HURT YOU I PROMISE WE**L**COME HOME DAR**L**ING
NO ONE HERE IS GOING TO HURT YOU I PROMISE
WELCOME HOME DARLING NO ONE HERE IS GOING
TO HURT YOU I PROMISE WELCOME HOME DARLING
NO ONE HERE IS GOING TO HURT YOU I PROMISE
WELCOME HOM**E** D**A**RLING NO ONE HERE IS GOING
TO HURT YOU I PROMISE WELCOME HOME DARLING
NO ONE HERE IS GOING TO HURT YOU I PROMISE
WELCOME HOME DARLING NO ONE HERE IS GOING
TO HURT YOU I PROMISE WELCOME HOME DARLING
NO ONE HERE IS GOING TO HURT **YOU** I PROMISE
WELCOME HOME DARLING NO ONE HERE IS GOING
TO HURT YOU I PROMISE WELCOME HOME DARLING
NO ONE HERE IS GOING TO HURT YOU I PROMISE
WELCOME HOME DARLING NO ONE HERE IS GOING
TO HURT YOU **I PROMISE** WELCOME HOME DARLING
NO ONE HERE IS GOING TO HURT YOU I PROMISE
WELCOME HOME DARLING NO ONE HERE IS GOING
TO HURT YOU I PROMISE WELCOME HOME DARLING
NO ONE HERE IS GOING TO HURT YOU I PROMISE
WELCOME HOME DARLING NO ONE HERE IS GOING
TO HURT YOU I PROMISE WELCOME HOME DARLING
NO ONE HERE IS GOING TO HURT YOU I PROMISE

Chapter

Felix

Felix had never been afraid of a new moon before that night.

Maybe he was skeptical of them before. The ways of magic were fluid, after all, and clearly there was no guidebook telling anyone exactly what might happen and when. But for each and every new moon celebration that came before the night everything changed, Felix had faith things would unfold exactly as they were *meant* to, whatever way that may mean.

It wasn't as if he didn't have desires. Of course he wanted for things, and of course they sometimes felt out of reach. He just had a good attitude about it. It wasn't a crime to be optimistic and hopeful.

A far greater cause for concern than his own wishes being left unfulfilled was that *everyone* might get precisely what they asked for. Felix wasn't naive. He'd always known there were those in the Caravan who were capable of a tremendous amount of cruelty. He'd found himself at the sharpened end of someone's whittled-down sense of control on more than one occasion.

But for most of his life, he accepted that as the way things were. He hadn't paid much mind to the bad behavior of the adults in his life. Sure, maybe the best-case scenario would've been for all of them to disappear and leave him to his devices. But as long as the things they put him through were survivable, he was willing to deal with it.

As long as he had the others.

Felix tore his slip of paper free from the communal notebook and folded it in half as many times as the sliver would allow to conceal his chicken-scratch handwriting. With his wish properly prepared, he moved closer to the bonfire, slipping between laughing partiers and celebrating pagans, to toss his hope in the flame.

Watching it catch a spark and turn to ash felt different that night than any of the times before it. Maybe because, this time, he wasn't just hopeful his wish would work. He *needed* it to. Because he couldn't—

Well.

Okay, look, I promise I am working on trusting you, reader. It's just that some secrets can't be shared, even if I want to. And there's a lot riding on this one.

You understand, right?

Anyway, there were *reasons* Felix needed his wish to come true this month. Let's just leave it at that.

It wasn't even anybody's fault things ended up the way they did, where his whole life was upside down and he didn't have any choice but to make desperate last-ditch attempts at fixing things. Felix believed that everyone was trying their best, even when they were upsetting him.

The problem was that everyone's best . . . well . . .

Through no fault of their own, all the people Felix loved

best in the world had been backed into a corner and were just trying to survive. Sometimes survival looked like biting the hands that tried to guide them out.

And even if it made all the sense in the world, it still sucked. It sucked because Felix could see what was about to happen. He didn't think any of the others understood where this was headed, but he did. Anytime now, the rug was going to get ripped out from under them, and they were going to lose *everything*. The stars would be swallowed whole. And Felix, the only one who could so clearly see it coming down the pipeline, had to use his wish to try and stop it.

He just hoped it wasn't too late.

As he backed away from the fire, letting his wish float off to the whims of whoever or whatever was watching it burn, he moved in the direction of the trees. He knew it was late, and maybe he should've gone to bed. But the ball of anxiety in his gut probably wouldn't have let him get much sleep, anyway. And there was always something about the woods that had a way of making Felix feel less untethered from everything around him. Among the trees, he was in no danger of floating away.

Without the moon's face staring back at them, the night sky felt like an empty black mirror looming overhead. It illuminated nothing on the path as he made his way into the thick brambles of the forest.

The air, thick with smoke from the bonfire, threatened to choke him. Or maybe that was just his own anxiety, still refusing to let him breathe, making his lungs feel buzzy and swollen. Maybe he wouldn't be able to breathe again until he knew he'd saved everyone.

He tried, though, struggling to suck in enough air to make

the pounding in his skull go away. For days now, he'd had a headache. If Felix thought about it hard enough, he would have wondered why no one else saw the signs he did, why no one else was as affected as he was by this inescapable *thing* that was coming.

He didn't think about it hard enough, though. There were other things, more pressing in the moment, to grab his attention.

Finally far enough back in the woods that the cloud of smoke wasn't making his panic attack even worse, he sank to a crouch at the base of an old tree. Palms flattened against the bark, he balanced himself on his heels and closed his eyes, willing his heart to stop pounding so loud and frantic.

A whisper of a stray thought tugged at the edge of his mind, but he didn't reach out to touch it. If he had, maybe everything would have gone differently.

If he had just looked a little closer, a little sooner, maybe everything would have been okay.

But he didn't.

And now—

A shadow stalked through the woods toward him.

Felix didn't yet realize it, but his wish *had* come too late.

Chapter 13

Eamon

He is by the truck. He is going to leave. He has just been told he has nothing to fear from the miscreants at this campsite.

"You cannot speak for everyone," Eamon tells Felix.

Felix takes a step toward him. His green eyes are wet. "Yes, I can. Because I love them and I trust them and I have faith that we *all* want everything to be okay. We can figure this out together."

The whispered warnings of the mushrooms become screams in Eamon's mind.

He does not believe these four people will figure anything out together.

"Good luck with that," he tells Felix. And he means it.

Felix is not like the others. He is, although not untainted by the Caravan, at least strong enough to fight back against whatever this place and its people have done to him. Eamon does not know exactly *how* he knows this, but he knows it without question. He would like the boy to succeed.

It is just that he does not wish to be around to witness it.

The truck door rattles as he slams it beside himself, settling into the driver's seat. He and Mister Basil had spent the last couple of weeks fixing up this truck. And while Eamon's unlawful guardian had taught him anything he needed to know about the mechanics of the vehicle, he had not required lessons on driving. Apparently, wherever Eamon came from, whoever or whatever he was in his previous iteration, he had been behind the wheel of a car enough times for the memory of it to remain stored somewhere in his body. Even when his identity became untethered from its vessel, the reflex of putting a key in the ignition and driving away was still rooted at the marrow.

Eamon does not look in the rearview until the campground is long gone behind him and he knows there is no risk of seeing a could-have-become-familiar face watching him leave. Even then, he only glances at the empty dirt path long enough to make sure the rotten heart of the woods did not follow him out.

In some ways, Eamon does not have any idea where he is going. This is because he does not have a destination in mind. If he could go anywhere, do anything, perhaps he would like to see the ocean. For all the things he can and cannot remember, he has either never stood before the sea or else the saltwater memory has since been flushed from his eyes. But he does not know of a beach on either coast that might hollow out a space for him, and he does not know what he would do if he were to show up somewhere and be unable to take care of himself. For all the harm of the Caravan's actions, they have at least kept him fed and warm these last few weeks. He does not know what he will do when he gets where he is going, and he does not know if he will even make it wherever that is.

There is always *so much* Eamon does not know. The weight of his own ignorance is a wound that cannot heal, always throbbing and ceaselessly bloody. He wishes he could put a bandage over it and pretend, at least for a little while. But pretending is the one kind of ignorance he is apparently not afforded.

In any case, there are other ways in which he knows exactly where he is going. This is because he can read road signs. He follows their directions to Interstate 70, and once he's on the interstate, he makes his way toward the unspecified west.

He notices the lack of other cars on the road but does not think much of it. Perhaps the road is often empty this time of day. With the scarlet sun looming too close overhead, Eamon finds it impossible to remember which time that is exactly. He does not think much of this, either.

Eamon makes it to Route 191 before the truck breaks down.

That is concerning.

More than a cause for concern, though, it does not make any *sense*. He and Mister Basil were meticulous in their care of the truck before its maiden voyage with Eamon behind the wheel. Together, they had gone over every inch of its components, detailing every surface under the hood and along the undercarriage. Despite its age, it had been in pristine condition.

It still *is* in pristine condition. Pulled onto the side of the straight expanse of desolate highway, Eamon uses the flashlight from his emergency kit in the truck's glove box to search for the problem. He prods extensively around the engine before slithering beneath the chassis. And though he does not stop to check the time, he is certain he is stopped there for quite a while before finally accepting failure. There is no problem to be uncovered.

The truck has simply given up, quietly and peacefully rolling to a stop as if it had reached its intended destination with no plans to continue any further.

Eamon pinches the bridge of his nose.

Of course, the truck has not *really* just decided to give up. Trucks, as far as he is aware, do not have that capacity for thought. Something must be wrong. And if that problem is neither mechanical nor methodical . . . perhaps it is magical.

The face of Hugo Berának flashes in his mind and Eamon grinds his teeth.

Whatever codification exists around the magics of the Caravan, it has never once been explained in detail in Eamon's presence. In the weeks he lived with them, the bounds of what was and was not possible never once became clear, and no one appeared all that interested in helping Eamon find answers from which to build the framework of his new life. The oversight does not feel unintentional.

As far as he is able to understand it, Mister Basil and Miss Cassandra have only two rules for ordaining a person as a possessor of magic and therefore belonging to their fold. Firstly: This person displays inhuman characteristics or physical features, especially if those features would make it difficult for them to camouflage in human society. (In Eamon's case, his red eyes.) Secondly: If they were not born into the Caravan, they have amnesia regarding their life before.

It is possible the latter is not a requirement, and instead simply the only circumstance in which they have ever found their people. Eamon is unsure if a story exists of one of their kind being found while still holding fast to whatever knowledge of self came *before*. He doubts it, though. So much of Mister Basil and Miss Cassandra's mission revolves around uncovering the truth of their collective origin. If they had ever been given an inkling of an answer, it would have been shared widely.

No, everyone they have found must have been without memory. Or else they lied, the same way he did.

Again, he sees Hugo's face in his mind. Eamon wipes sweat from his brow and slams the hood of the truck shut.

Resigned, he grabs the emergency bag and slings it over one shoulder. The dry hillside curls up behind him like a titanic hand shepherding his path. Still completely without a clue as to the location of his journey's end, he continues down the shoulder of the two-lane highway, treading down toward an endless sunbaked valley. It's difficult to tell how many miles the road stretches before disappearing on the flat horizon, where it's bordered by great red buttes.

Buttes. Another word he hadn't known was rattling around in his skull. He eyes the stark cliffs of the faraway plateaus and thinks of how much he knows about aspens and wonders at how close or how far he is from the mystery of his body's origins.

Because the requirements for belonging to the Caravan are somehow both strict and vague, there are seemingly no commonalities in the magics of its people. At least, not so far as Eamon has been able to deduce. In his time there, he met a psychic and a mind reader and a woman who could fly at least a few feet off the ground—so many people with just as many different types of magics. He had come to learn, however, that some of their magic was ominously indeterminate at best.

Either there were those in the Caravan who have no idea what they are capable of, or they had not wanted to tip their hand and reveal the extent of their power. Both options are troubling.

And both options mean Eamon has no way to know for sure if magic could be the source of his truck's untimely demise. Of one thing, though, he is certain.

If Hugo's magic *could* leave him stranded in the middle of nowhere to meet the inevitability of a slow death, the boy, indelicate in his cruelty, would do exactly that.

The Earth has swallowed the sun.

Eamon has no idea how long he has been walking, but it cannot have been *so* long. He is not even tired yet, his body having fallen into a thoughtless kind of rhythm, the automatic forward motion continuing him along the unwavering side of his lonely highway. His progress is halted only when he realizes there is no longer a sun in the sky.

As soon as the thought occurs to him, however, he turns to stare at the horizon and the Earth spits the sun back into orbit. It reminds him of a guilty child opening their mouth and letting cookies fall to the counter, fingers still speckled with stolen chocolate crumbs.

What was his life before this one, that he is even able to summon such an image?

More pressingly, what is he actually seeing ahead of him?

Because that most certainly did not happen. The sun was not spat out of anywhere. It has been beside him this entire time. He just wasn't looking at it.

Eamon pulls his water bottle from his bag and takes a long, slow sip. The desert is beginning to get to him. He needs to be more mindful of his hydration.

"Everything okay?"

The voice—feminine in the frothiest of ways, pitched high and spun out into the suggestion of a bleat—pricks the back of Eamon's ear. He jumps, backing away from the edge of the road when he realizes a car has pulled up next to him without making a sound.

Driving the sedan is the most beautiful girl he has any memory of seeing. Her green eyes take up half her face, perfectly round, a mosaic of shades, framed with long golden lashes like stalks of wheat. Her features are impossibly dainty, as delicate and perky as a hummingbird, her soft brown skin speckled in a thousand tiny auburn freckles. Her hair falls all the way to her seat in a collection of swirling ribbons the color of dawn.

Eamon is not a romantic, but this girl is poetry embodied.

Her car is disgusting, though. It is filled near to bursting with piles of trash, the floorboards a mountainous collage of empty soda cans, lipstick-painted coffee cups, and fast-food wrappers. The garbage across the backseat has a thick layer of visibly dirty clothes rendering the rearview mirror pointless. This is notably less poetic, and it helps to ground him in the face of her storybook charm.

"Sure," he answers, and turns away from the window, intending to continue on his way.

The car crawls slowly alongside him.

"Well, that was convincing," the girl chuckles, though he suspects she does not mean it. "Where are you headed? I can give you a lift."

He knows where he is going, he thinks, in the way that he can tell he is moving toward something, even if he cannot actually picture what or where that something might be. The problem is that he does not know how to convey that information to someone who does not live inside of his head. In his limited experience, any attempt results in ludicrously inconvenient translation errors.

So instead, he says, "I do not take rides from strangers."

Not anymore, anyway.

"Oh, come on." The girl laughs, and Eamon knows it is *at* him, not with him, though he is not sure what he did that was so funny. "Do I look like a threat?"

He glances at her again, his steps slowing and then halting. She eases onto the brake, idling next to him, the encroaching dark swallowing her headlights.

Those long cornsilk lashes flutter.

"Threats rarely look the part," he finally settles on.

She smiles, seemingly bemused but ultimately unbothered by his refusal. "If you say so. I hope you get where you're going."

"Yeah. Thanks."

So does he.

The darkness is unknowable until a light emerges, the night having slipped in and smothered everything so slowly Eamon was helpless to notice it. Only when a beacon ahead, a luminescent orange glow, appears on the other side of the winding cliffside, does he realize he has been stranded in an endless pitch for he cannot say how long. Maybe since the girl drove off. He is not sure how long ago that must have been now.

It would be best, he believes, to steer away from the light. The Caravan cannot be trusted, but neither can anyone else. Not until Eamon solves the mystery of his own existence, anyway. And he is aware of these things, yet still finds himself creeping closer, as if he might catch a glimpse of the source. He has not experienced a particular need for closeness to another living thing in his so-far-short new life, but the idea of laying eyes on people again makes his pulse quicken.

Part of him—a not insignificant part—regrets not getting into that girl's car. At least people who cannot be trusted are still people.

How lonely has he been and for how long? Is this one more happening he was unaware of until a solution presented itself?

And what sort of mind game is that, anyway? A medicinal denial toward the horror of one's own existence. A safety latch of ignorance that ensures survival but cannot prevent the aftermath when everything inside comes tumbling free.

When he hears voices, he wants to cry. Eamon cannot remember ever crying. So he is not sure how he knows the lump in his throat and the burning in his nose mean tears are trying to make themselves uninvited guests on the house of his face. And still, he does know.

He cannot let them see him. He is not as easily distinguishable for his *wrongness* as others in the Caravan—perhaps, in the low light, he could even play his eyes off as a trick of humanity's inclination toward fantasy—but there is still no guarantee of safety, especially not when he is one and they are several. Rather than continuing toward the orange light like some firefly forced to walk the porchlit hallway to its own execution,

Eamon ducks, at the last moment, behind a person-sized rock. His hiding spot is just close enough that he can still tilt his head around the corner to try and get a glimpse of—

Is that Bird?

As Eamon watches, the waif of a hybrid stalks up the RV stairs to let themself inside. A few feet away, gathered around the campfire, are Cal, Felix, and Hugo himself.

Eamon's stomach threatens to meet his tongue.

There is no question about it now. It must have been magic after all. He was sabotaged on the road, only for the enchantment to lead him here, to the exact same people he meant to leave behind. It is too wide a world and too vast a desert for this entire farce to have been anything other than trickery.

His eyes flick across Hugo's face. The boy's soft skin and sharp bones give the impression of a paper lantern when contoured in firelight. His antlers make him seem like some ancient god, displeased at having been woken.

What has he done now? Moreover, what awful thing will Eamon have to do *this time* in order to make things right?

Predictably, Hugo is arguing with Cal about anything and nothing. Their bickering is finally interrupted when Felix, hovering on the edge of the conversation with his teeth gnawing at the inside of his cheek, has had enough. He flings his hand into the air.

"I'll see if I can find a spot."

"You sure?"

"Yeah. I'm not really hungry. If I can get service, I'll try Mom and Dad."

"Well . . . Thanks. Use the flashlight. Watch for snakes."

"I know, I know. It'll be fine."

Light in hand, Felix turns from the camp and begins to

pick his way into the desert. Such a weak pinprick of electricity seems unfit to equip a defenseless boy under a sky so boundless. Eamon hesitates for only a moment, tucked behind the rock. When the moment passes, he slips like a shadow and follows.

All Eamon intends is to wait until they are far enough away from the others that there is no chance of being overheard. Unfortunately, he is set on fire before he gets the chance.

Before

It was purely human, the sky under which they danced—atmosphere shielded by steel, stars captured and overwritten by robotic pulsing lights. Bird raised their hands toward it, pale fingers flexing, painted new colors every few heartbeats, and laughed as their phalanges buzzed with sound unnaturally magnified so as to make one's skeleton sing. Such beauty in such an inorganic state of being. They felt as if, at any moment, they might be detached from their muscles and teeth and float, incorporeal, above the surge of their crowd.

Their eyes fluttered shut, and Bird feasted on the way their eyelids became a thundercloud, lit in flashes, capillaries thrown into shadow like pitch bolts of lightning. Sensation was funny in this state of rapture. It was almost an echo on their periphery, easily ignorable. Bird's body moved in current with those around them, all their blood and bones made seagrass, anemone, ripples and flows weaving a great and singular body that heaved in ecstasy. They were vaguely aware of Megan Blackwell at their side, and oh, they'd come to enjoy this together, hadn't they? Even as the thought pecked at their consciousness, Bird couldn't bring themself to care. Petty interpersonal politics had no place here. There was no point in fixating on their body's neighbor. Not when they were so much bigger than their own flesh, for a time, woven watertight by song and pulsing light.

Not when they'd found a pocket of humanity where, at last, they could belong.

A girl behind them broke from the choral refrain, her solo suddenly staccato and dissonant and plain grating against Bird's bliss. They clung to the music. The music clung back. But the girl was shrieking now, screaming, her solo crescendoing into cacophonous harmony as others joined. The movement of the sea was becoming disrupted and discordant.

Bird was aware, abruptly, that they were not actually an underwater creature. That their lungs screamed for air.

"Birdie, holy *shit*!" Megan Blackwell screamed with glee, or perhaps fear. And when Bird opened their eyes, some part of them—the part that had been convinced they could ever really pass as human—died a quick and painless death.

For when they opened their eyes, hands still stretched toward an artificial sky, Bird saw their skin was incandescent, glowing, lit from within for all to see.

Chapter 14

Bird

When a thing is *known* and cannot yet be named, it sits like a lead weight in the belly, demanding to be acknowledged, threatening to claw its way up the intestines and into the throat, the mouth, across the tongue. Things felt but unseen have a way of running their phantom talons along the skin, leaving gooseflesh and a thousand paper-thin slivers in their wake. These things can be ignored by the mind, but the body always knows. The body keeps watch where the mind closes its curtains. The body raises the alarm the mind tries to suppress.

Bird does not have a healthy relationship with their body. It has never done a damn thing they've asked it to, and, in fairness, they've never been very good at being its caretaker. In this way, they've both disappointed the other. After years and years of trying and failing to find their footing in the temple of their own bones, years and years of wishing they would stumble into monstrosity or else ascend fully into humanity so they could stop living life in the half-light, years and years of picking at the skin in the mirror and wondering how much it would take to rip the mask of their face off entirely, Bird learned to pretend their body didn't exist. They became cerebral, some sentient mood floating in the void, and nothing more.

Tonight, as Bird rummages through their and Calliope's things in the RV, hunting for their misplaced cell phone, their body tries to send a warning. It floats from their belly to their nose like a smoke signal, making their eyes burn at the too-closeness of open flame.

But it has been so many years since they've talked to their body. Whatever it's trying to warn them about, they no longer speak the same language. Whatever this thing is in the room with them, skittering in their periphery, moving closer with every jerky marionette movement, they can't make out the shape. And perhaps they won't until it's too late.

Oh.

Bird looks up from their suitcase, head jerking and twisting toward the shadow that's tucked up beneath the RV's pull-out kitchenette table.

Was there something moving closer? They could've sworn . . .

But no. Now, in the burnt yellow of the overhead bulb, flickering and pulsing with a quiet electric hum from the crappy generator, shadows bounce without intention, simple tricks of the light instead of the prowling ghouls of an overactive imagination. It is anticlimactically mundane, actually, this lack of a thing where a thing could've been, the *unhauntedness* of Cal's van that, even briefly, promised ghosts.

That's what Bird's mind latches on to—the mundanity, which is so very safe and comfortable and understood, like one of the many science textbooks they absorbed so thoroughly it might as well have been osmosis. Bird's mind is content now. But Bird's body is still desperately trying to send a message.

And Bird's body won't calm down at the lack of a thing lurking beneath the table. The tense muscles of their shoulders don't relax, their spine doesn't loosen, their breath doesn't come any easier. When fear overstuffs itself into their mouth so they can't scream, it tastes like raw meat, squishy and wet and oozing blood down their throat until they might choke on it, until it's all they can taste or think or remember.

Something is *wrong*. Bird doesn't know how they know—they can't even be sure they know they know—but their every tendon and vessel and muscle fiber and skin cell and *follicle of hair* is screaming out in the same strange chorus. They don't need to understand their body's words to intuit the meaning behind them.

Run.

Forgetting entirely whatever inconsequential task led them inside, they sprint to the RV door, flinging it open to rejoin the others. Hugo jumps, startled by the slamming of metal against metal, and Calliope shoots them a dirty look from her side-eye. It isn't that Bird pretends not to notice either reaction. It's only that they have more important things to notice, like the fact that someone is missing, and the fact that they already knew that, somehow, before laying eyes on his absence.

"Where is Felix?" they demand, eyes drifting from the ring encircling the campfire to brush against the desert horizon.

"He's looking for service—what's your issue?" Calliope's single raised eyebrow is as sharp as a hot iron slotting between Bird's ribs.

It doesn't help they don't *know* what their issue is. Instead of attempting an answer that would only butcher their tongue, their eyes find Hugo's from across the flame.

Please, they think. *Please, please, please, just find him.*

For a moment, they wonder if it's a lost cause. Hugo can't hear their signals any more clearly than they can hear their body's. He's long since severed whatever cable once existed between them.

But as soon as Bird's had the thought, Hugo rises to his feet. "Felix!"

Bird ambles after him, feet slipping across the rippled surface of the amber sand, unsteady beneath their legs—already too thin and knobby, now suffering from the added burden of anxious shaking like molted feathers in an unforgiving winter wind. Their voice follows Hugo's deep, rough-hewn bellow, an imperfect and eerie echo. "Felix!"

A shadow flits maybe ten feet to their right, ducking behind a rock face. Bird whips in its direction, eyes narrowing in a futile attempt to make out a single detail in the near-nothing light of the starry night sky. Accepting defeat, they suck in a deep breath and lift their hand in the direction of the specter gone to ground.

And finally given permission, their skin erupts in a bright white glow, illuminating the desert all around them.

In time, the Caravan would come to realize that Bird's power could be easily hidden. They were their father's child, too, after all, and it was just as possible for them to tuck themself into the folds of the human world as it was to grow up alongside beasts and miracle workers.

When they would eventually choose that human world, it would be the ultimate betrayal. No one would forgive them for it, not really, not even beneath the layers of gratitude expressed on their return.

But all of that would come much later. On the night Bird was born, however, Holly's only child took their first breath with skin that shone like moonlight. A glowworm, a firefly. A lantern in the dark. Their own Polaris.

Our Star, the Caravan whispered, *will lead us home.*

"Eamon?"

Crouching behind the red rock, Eamon, now cast in Bird's light, tilts his head up to meet their eyes. His own crimson tidepools glint with something bleak—some fury Bird is afraid to touch, or even look at too closely.

"What are you doing here?" they demand, chest creaking painfully with breaths too fast and heavy for their bones. "How did you find us?"

Up ahead, at the outskirts of Bird's illuminated circle, another figure turns to face them. Half shadowed, the sharp planes of Felix's face contrast with the softness of his downy ears and pillowy curls and plush mouth. "What's—*Eamon?*"

It doesn't look good. Bird *recognizes* this doesn't look good, and they reach blindly for some benefit of the doubt. Why is Eamon here? Why is he sneaking around in the dark? Why was he following after Felix? What does any of this have to do with the warning signs their body has been trying to throw at them?

If it were up to them, they might've had a conversation about it. As it turns out, it isn't up to them. After all, they're just the eerie echo in this situation.

"What is it going to take for you to learn to stay out of our fucking business?" Hugo demands, though he doesn't pretend to want an answer. His question is immediately made rhetorical by the unfurling of his fist. Fire blooms from his palm in an air-warping display. With perfect, effortless aim, his mouth a grim slash of long-awaited satisfaction, Hugo hurls the cannon inferno directly at Eamon's stooped body.

"Hugo!"

Bird can't be sure if it was their voice or Felix's screaming, but it doesn't really matter. Shocked out of concentration, the light in their skin goes dim, like Hugo's delight in violence has sucked it right out of them. Now they have only the firelight engulfing Eamon's chest to keep the dark at bay.

The hypnotic boy *yowls*, an animal sound unlike any Bird has heard from him before, and slams his palms against his chest in a frantic attempt to put the fire out.

"Stop this!" Bird demands, addressing Hugo even as they can't tear their eyes away from Eamon.

"No." Hugo's voice is steady. His hands rest still at his side; he is not consumed by blind rage, lashing out because he's become convinced he has no choice. He knows he has the magic to put it out, but he's enjoying the show. Hugo has wanted this moment for a long time—maybe even longer than he's known Eamon at all.

"*Huey*," Felix pleads in a voice that could not be *less* steady if it were following a script for collapse. "Don't make me do this again."

Do what? Bird wonders. *Again?*

There's no opportunity to ask the question or get an answer. Calliope's heavy boots announce her appearance at the fringed edges of firelight. Had she been following them this whole time? Had she been watching from beneath the darkened desert house lights, entertained by the conflict playing out across the illuminated sandstone proscenium? Bird had stopped noticing her the moment they'd flung themself after Hugo.

Calliope doesn't dawdle. Somehow, perhaps by proxy of a lifetime of knowing and hating Hugo, she'd thought to come prepared. She's already unscrewing the lid of her sticker-plastered Nalgene as she storms to Eamon's side. Calliope's boot meets flame. She kicks Eamon onto his back and upturns the bottle over his chest. Water meets fire and smothers its fury into smoke, dousing the horrible sight out of existence. As quick as it began, it's over. All that's left is a memory that makes their throat burn.

With all of them plunged into sudden dark, it's hard to say whether Eamon coughs or sobs.

Chapter 15

Hugo

His fire is snuffed out and his lungs become a vacuum chamber, the air siphoned from Hugo's body as if the mechanics of oxygen and inferno have undergone some paradoxical reversal. Deflated, he struggles to drag in a breath, suddenly hypercognizant of what he's just done. Were he a better person, his anger might've been extinguished alongside the flame, the awareness of his own actions forcing him to grapple with the weight of their severity.

He is not a better person, nor will he ever have the chance to become one. Even when everything else is taken away, Hugo stands there with his rage in his hands and nowhere to set it down.

"Why would you do that?" he demands of Cal, taking a step closer to the silhouetted suggestion of her, difficult to make out in detail through the dark.

"You were hoping we'd stand here and watch him die?" She snarls her response, and Hugo watches her shadow lean in rather than back away.

He knows the risk of proximity to Cal, and still can't seem to stop himself. Only when he can make out the furious whites of her eyes in the low, low light does he finally stop advancing. "For all we know, that *thing* is dead already."

"For fuck's sake, Hugo," Bird whispers at his back, and he cuts the thread that reaches, on reflex, to surrender.

"I did not do *anything* to you," Eamon growls. There's a shuffling from behind Cal, and the almost-cremated apparition masquerading as a real boy manages to push himself to his feet. There's a sulfuric reek of burned hair about him, cut by a scent uncomfortably close to pork in a cast-iron pan. His outline stumbles to Cal's side. "I did not hurt *anyone*. That is *always* you."

Hugo knows that's neither entirely true nor untrue. Per usual, the truth exists somewhere between the things people are and aren't willing to look directly at. Well, most people— not him, though. He sees everything. It's part of the reason they all hate him.

The other part, he knows, is because he isn't very pleasant to be around. But that's not the point right now.

"Why were you stalking my brother?" he demands, throwing out an arm to gesture in Felix's direction. The other Beránek makes a soft, strangled noise like a whimper that second-guesses itself and tries to curl back into his throat.

This is the truth: Felix is a prey animal, and Eamon is a predator, and if Hugo has to turn himself into a hunter in order to protect his family, is he really the bad guy? Is violence really so violent when it's the only option left?

"I was not stalking anyone," Eamon argues.

Cal, loyal to nothing but her own foul reclusion, turns to him with her arms crossed. "You were absolutely stalking him.

You were creeping around the rocks so you wouldn't be seen. Just because I didn't want to watch you get barbecued to death doesn't mean I can't recognize there's something fucked up about you."

"How did you find us?" Bird questions. The feel of their voice sits like the weighty palm of a handler on the back of Hugo's neck, as if they're seconds away from scruffing him with their teeth. It drops something heavy deep in his belly and makes him want to self-immolate. "Have you been following us this entire time?"

"No." Eamon shakes his head. "The truck broke down. I was walking along the highway when I saw the RV lights."

"That's really *fucking* convenient," Hugo snaps. Embers, accidental this time, spark at the click of his front teeth, the taste of smoke flooding over his tongue. He huffs it out like the hellhound he is.

"No," Eamon says again. "In fact, it was actually incredibly suspicious. The truck was in perfect mechanical condition. Someone *wanted* it to fail and made sure it did."

Hugo's heart floors it, suddenly thundering in his eardrums. "What are you accusing me of?"

"Interesting," Eamon sneers. "The accusation had not yet come. But now that you *mention it*—"

"Who is this helping?" Bird sighs, disappointment like a thick, clear lacquer over their every intonation. Hugo feels a little bit like a school child. He wants to dig his fingers into the sticky coating and peel it off, if only to examine the imperfections underneath. "I don't understand this desire to villainize each other. Someone is *hunting* us. We're being played with. Don't you see that?"

Whatever vicious retort he might've otherwise let loose

backs away from the tip of his tongue and tucks itself behind his molars. By no fault of their own, Bird doesn't understand what's going on here, but there's no way to get them to see it without telling them *everything*. And Hugo can hardly stomach looking at Bird already. Facing them in the aftermath of his confession would be unendurable.

Felix shuffles closer to the group, Hugo's phone clutched to his chest. "You think someone's hunting us?"

"They might be on to something, for once," Cal agrees. "First the disappearance of the others. Now Eamon's truck breaking down? All of us finding each other here, in the middle of nowhere? It's like we're being . . ."

"Herded," Eamon answers when Cal's voice drifts off. "Like cattle."

"Why? Where?" Felix asks.

"And who," Cal adds. To Bird, she asks, "What enemies does the Caravan have?"

When Bird is too quiet for too long, Hugo is the one to answer. "The group at Port Haven is the closest thing to enemies the Caravan has."

"Port Haven," Eamon echoes, something acerbic altering the font of his words. "The place you are leading us to."

"I'm not leading anyone anywhere," Bird stumbles over their words. "I just thought—I don't know where anyone else—"

"Why did you come back when you did?" Cal demands. "The timing—it's interesting, isn't it?"

"You cannot be serious."

"Why not?" Hugo asks, twisting his body toward them. "It wouldn't be the first time you'd been accused of being a traitor."

He doesn't need to be able to see Bird's eyes to feel the way they slice into his throat.

After a beat too long, they reply, with a barely contained tremor, "One of us betrayed the other, Hugo. We both know it wasn't me."

Is it betrayal, really, to know your atoms are meant to exist alongside someone else's, even if that existence is nothing but suffering? Because Hugo might be an asshole for that, but as far as he's concerned, shattering their quantum entanglement to run off and play human is a sin far worse.

"Okay, great, just—everyone shut the fuck up." Cal groans, pressing the heels of her palms into her eyes. "We're not getting anywhere like this. And I'm not standing around with my head up my ass arguing with all of you morons for the rest of the night."

"We need to stay together." Felix takes a deep breath. "I know you all have your issues to work through. But if there is someone out there who wants us hurt, we're safer together. Even if it's *one of us*—we need to keep an eye on each other."

"It does not appear we would be allowed to separate, regardless," Eamon hisses, a cryptic reminder. Hugo doesn't ask him to recount his time away because he doesn't care to acknowledge Eamon's existence any more than is necessary, and it would probably be a string of lies anyway. That doesn't mean he appreciates the blind spot.

"I think this is a bad call." Hugo shakes his head but doesn't linger to argue. He suspects no one intends to listen to him, anyway.

Felix's next words drift over his shoulder, following him back toward the RV.

"Not every problem demands we scorch the earth, Huey."

Not every problem. But this one?

Hugo sees what no one else will look at. He knows how this *thing* with Eamon is going to end. And the sooner they let him see it through, the less it's going to hurt.

Before

"Knock, knock, Penguin."

Bird bit back their acerbic tongue and leveled a flat look at Opportunity. The betta fish shimmied in his cup, his pouty mouth bumping up against the plastic. Bird, elbow deep in smelly aquarium water and struggling with a gravel vacuum, had little sympathy for his temporary plight.

"What," they called flatly over the curated cadence of *All Things Considered*. Their dad undoubtedly thought it was weird that they listened to NPR on the daily, but Bird thought it was weird that they had walked into high school not knowing what the three branches of the federal government were. When presented with the monumental task of memorizing the ever-changing labyrinth of pop music or gaining enough geopolitical awareness to understand current events, Bird really only had enough bandwidth for one and couldn't justify picking the fun option.

They'd tried it for one night, anyway, and look how that had ended.

They heard their dad let himself in. They knew his workflow

had just been interrupted by an unexcused absence call. It was the third day in a row, and each morning his knock had come like clockwork when he'd been reminded of their existence.

"Hiya, Bluebird. How's it going?" he asked, and again, Bird directed their irritation into Opportunity's smooth-brained, unblinking stare.

"Peachy," they said. "What's up?"

Unable to stomach a conversation where he was not being visually appreciated, their dad stepped past them and sat awkwardly on the very edge of their bed. Bird drilled their eyes into the filth floating up from Opportunity's aquarium gravel, but they couldn't erase him from their periphery. He was all bones, this forty-year-old bachelor, like a gangly boy who got put through a taffy stretcher and slapped with a Roth IRA. He looked like every other white man in tech, and plenty of those guys had kids, but somehow nothing about Dylan Reed looked like a father.

He leaned back, simultaneously crossing his arms and legs with a loaded sigh. "Well. I'm worried about you, kiddo," he said. "You've been locked in here since Saturday night. And I don't wanna trample any boundaries or anything, but I'm starting to get pretty concerned something bad happened at that concert."

Bird had known it was only a matter of time until their truancy stacked up enough to warrant this talk, and it still managed to take them by enough surprise to sink their stomach like a stone. "Why would you think that," they said to the draining fish tank.

"Well, Pigeon . . . you came home a bit of a zombie and seem to have developed a spot of agoraphobia."

"Don't use real disorders to hyperbolize. It's ableist."

Their dad let out a long sigh through his long nose. Everything about him was stretched out. Bird thought about it every time they looked at their own hands. Holly was short and well-rounded, a mosaic of pleasing curves she displayed with (perhaps too much) pride. Bird had spent their childhood wondering if their body would soften to mimic hers, all while this stranger's noodly DNA was laughing in their veins.

"Thanks," their dad said, a little pained. "Do you want to talk about it?"

Yes, desperately, so much so that their teeth ached in their skull. Bird gripped the edge of the fishtank to keep their words stacked behind their tongue. Dylan didn't know about the Caravan. Dylan *couldn't* know. As far as he was concerned, Holly had just been some mesmerizing hippie he'd encountered with a little too much enthusiasm while on a summer backpacking trip in undergrad. And Bird? They were just the accidental free-range organic grass-fed result. Weird, sure, but that was par for the course when it came to vanlife kids, wasn't it?

Dylan could never know his kid wasn't human. Bird had known that when they'd decided to leave, and had deluded themself into thinking that choice was realistic and sustainable. And here they were, three years in, alone, without anyone but a punchy betta fish with whom they can share a damn thing of substance.

"No," they got out through their clenched teeth, the sound almost a snarl.

"I've scheduled you for a telemed intake with a therapist," their dad said, immediately, like he had been waiting for the faintest hint of pushback so he could plop that bomb right in their lap. "They're really cool, Chickadee. They've a cool haircut, some piercings, they specialize in anxiety and depression with queer teens . . ." He gave Bird the most tight-lipped, awkward double thumbs-up. "Their name is Pebble, which I thought was really original."

Bird had made it this far without looking up from Opportunity's tank, but their hands had begun to shake. They slapped the gravel vacuum into the rocks and wheeled to face him. With his Patagonia puffer and wool snapback and general vibe, their dad looked completely out of place in their room. Until three years ago, it had been his home office. Now he worked from the sunroom, which was a far cry from a real workspace, and Bird thought about it multiple times a day. He was all clean, moisture-wicking fabric and flat-packed furniture, and they were a ball of moss that had decided to set upon his simple life and grow like mold. Their bed frame was a stack of pallets, by *choice*.

You could take the freak out of the Caravan, but the Caravan would never truly let the freak forget where it first rooted.

"Cancel it," Bird demanded. "I have no use for a therapist."

"Respectfully, kiddo, I super disagree."

"That's nice. I won't be going. Save yourself the no-show fee and cancel it now."

He gave that long nasal sigh again, and Bird had to turn away to avoid screaming. He didn't know them. They were just a stranger taking up his second bedroom. Any reaction they could've given would've seemed ludicrously outsized. He didn't know they'd spent every night since that wretched concert plagued by nightmares. How could they possibly explain the vivid, strobe-painted scenes of them being hoisted and splayed out over the crowd, drawn and quartered, roasted, eaten, all the while somehow alive and bawling as they shone like the North Star? Had they even tried, he'd have been forcing them into involuntary inpatient instead of therapy with some nonbinary martyr with a noun for a name.

"I gotta pull rank here," their dad said once he was finished with the longest sigh in the world. "You're doing this intake appointment. I'm sorry. It's what's best for you, Finch—"

"Oh my god just call me my fucking *name*, Dylan." Bird went back to cleaning the fish tank, too forceful, too loud, but the alternative was throwing something through a window, and that version of themself scared them.

Their dad made a sound like a wounded animal and oh, they wanted to sprout the wings of their namesake and take off over the Pacific until exhaustion claimed them and they fell, Icarian, into the brackish void.

"Okay," he said, attempting to recover. "Can do. Anyway. You're struggling, Bird, and it's my job to make sure you reach adulthood with your best foot forward."

"Your job."

"Yes. As your parent."

"You're a roommate who bankrolls my life."

From the corner of their eye, they watched their dad recoil. Bird felt bad, beneath the stormy sea of angst. They didn't mean to be ungrateful. They were pragmatic, realistic, and so damn tired of keeping their inhumanity bound and gagged while desperately trying to shine a spotlight on their barest hints of normalcy.

But they were tired. God, were they tired. Tired of being asked if they were an alien, asked which religious cult they were from, stared at, gawked at, shared loaded, knowing looks about. Even if their father found a therapist who handled ex–cult members, he'd never find one Bird could actually confide in.

And that was the whole keystone to the agony of this false little life, wasn't it? They would never be able to trust anyone, let their guard down fully, experience the vast and varied patchwork of life's fullest potential. Their knowledge gap would never hit zero, no matter how much *Morning Edition* played over their alarm clock radio. No admissions board would deem them worthy when they couldn't name all the parts of a cell.

And they'd spend every second of their long, lonely, human-adjacent life concentrating on keeping themself dimmed. Always alone, never seen, never off their guard.

Never human, no matter how normal they looked with their light off.

"I am your dad," Dylan said, "and I love you."

Silent, teeth muzzling the frenzied scream that begs to tear itself from their sternum, Bird seized the nearest item and hurled it at him in one great sweep. Opportunity's tank and all its many accessories hit their dad in a tumble of plastic and glass and wet, fabricated rock, bottles of ammonia neutralizer and water conditioner spilling on the original hardwood floor, a mix of paper detritus from Bird's desk fluttering down like the feathers of a bird snatched midair by a hawk. This house was not theirs, and no house ever would be, and if Bird could have made a single wish on a star, it would've been to stop existing.

Their dad did not shout, did not react at all. He simply sat, wide-eyed and frozen, confused and upset and waiting for a larger explosion that never came. It took a long time for Bird's heart to stop pounding, deafening, in their ears. By the time they could hear again—by the time they noticed the plastic cup, fallen, now lidless and empty—Opportunity's fins were limp and still, no longer flapping in desperate search for water, on the toe of their dad's sneaker.

Two strangers, they were, staring silently into the unknowable depths of one another.

Chapter 16

Cal

The next day, Alanis Morissette and Johnny Cash try to kill them all.

There's no Bluetooth in the RV and the radio stations in this windy mountain stretch of the middle of fucking nowhere are more staticky sermons than music. There's a CD player, though, and Cal has an old shoebox full of discs shoved under the bed, a charming collection of secondhand finds she's picked up for a dollar each at different hole-in-the-wall thrift stores across the country. It should be simple enough to pick one out and put it on so none of them have to listen to each other breathing or—god forbid—try and fill the silence with conversation.

None of these bitches make anything simple, though.

"Babes in Toyland, *Fontanelle*," Cal instructs, glancing in the rearview mirror to watch Bird fish out the box.

Bird digs through the different cases before plucking out the one they're looking for. Their nose crinkles, studying the cover. "Hm."

Cal rolls her eyes, grip tightening around the steering wheel. "It's the best one in there. Sorry I don't have any Taylor Swift."

To their credit and Cal's deepening irritation, Bird takes neither the bait nor the request. They keep rifling through the CDs until they pull a different jewel case free. "I know this one. What about this one?"

Hugo yanks it from their hand. "*Jagged Little Pill?* Sounds cringey."

"Then it should be right up your alley," Bird quips, snatching it back from him.

"Babes. In. Toyland." Cal realizes no one is listening to her, and as long as she's driving—and therefore unable to throttle them without abandoning the steering wheel—they're simply not going to. *Cool.*

Hugo yanks the box right from Bird's arms, doing his own rifling. After a moment of incredulous one-sided staring, Bird takes the high road and *Jagged Little Pill* up to the front of the RV, where they stand at Cal's side, bracing themself on the dashboard. Their arms almost touch when Bird presses the button to switch on the CD player. Every muscle in Cal's body gets coated in invisible wet cement.

"It's a good album," they assure her.

"It's my fucking album—I know it's good." She's going to drive them all off a cliff.

"Wait." Hugo tosses the box down and stomps up to them, shoving his own CD selection in front of the player. "I found one."

"Good for you." Bird rolls their eyes. "We weren't looking anymore."

They try to swat his hand away, but Hugo waves the CD in their face instead. The movement is way too fucking close to Cal, as far as she's concerned. She shifts a little to the left, craning her neck, increasingly uncomfortable but trying to focus on the road.

"Johnny Cash?" Hugo asks. "*The Man Comes Around?* Come *on.* Everybody likes Johnny Cash."

"I already picked something." Bird pops open *Jagged Little Pill* and slides the disc into the slot. The board lights up a nostalgic analog green, the player booting up. "We can listen to that one next."

"Or," Cal growls through her teeth. "We could listen to Babes in Toyland, since that's what I asked for and it's my goddamn van."

Everyone ignores her.

"This one's a book!" Felix offers from behind them, having started sifting through the CDs himself. *"The Subtle Art of Not Giving a Fuck."*

Everyone ignores him, too.

Cal glances at Eamon in the rearview, wondering when he's going to pipe in with his own brilliant suggestion. He barely looks like he's paying attention to the conversation, though. Sitting at the back in a too-tight Dolly Parton T-shirt (Cal's least favorite of the four she owns), he stares out the window with a ramrod straight spine, features expressionless and eyes a thousand miles away.

Whatever. Dude probably doesn't know what a CD is anyway.

Hugo slams the eject button as soon as the first note of track one starts to play. He swipes Alanis Morissette from the player and jams Johnny Cash in its place.

"You're acting like a child," Bird informs him, pressing

the eject button again before the speakers have even realized which CD they're supposed to be playing.

"I *am* a child," he reminds them smugly. "At least I'm not acting like a spoiled brat."

Bird grinds their teeth and reaches up to grab their CD back from him. Hugo casually raises his arm until the disc dangles effortlessly out of their reach on his pointer finger. The two of them tussle and lurch at Cal's side.

She knows it's gonna be bad before it is, but there's no time to holler with any effectiveness. For a moment, Hugo's arm covers up Cal's field of vision. When she ducks her head to look around him, there's a hairpin bend approaching, curving sharply around the mountainside with nothing but a guardrail between the RV and the drop-off. She yanks the wheel, sending them careening too quickly at a weird angle, kicking up red dust all around the wheels. For one sickening moment, she feels the driver's-side tires go featherlight, but then the road straightens, and she slams them back onto solid pavement.

Cal managed to keep herself upright by holding on to the steering wheel, but everyone else went sliding. Hugo and Bird are collapsed in a tangle of limbs against the passenger door.

"Why don't the two of you just lock yourselves in the bathroom and screw each other already?" Cal refuses to look directly at them but can see them twisting and jumping apart in her periphery. "Maybe then you'd both be a little more bearable to be around."

"Fuck you," Hugo mumbles, pushing away from the door and stomping back to his place at the kitchenette table.

"No, fuck *Bird*," Cal corrects with a snap of her teeth.

"Fuck both of you." Bird gathers up the jettisoned discs,

putting Johnny back in his case and sliding Alanis into the slot once again.

This time, when the green board lights up, it reads "ERROR" and then switches over to AM radio. An audioscape of static fills the RV.

"Great." Cal shakes her head, slapping the sound system off entirely. At least the mountains that almost killed them have spared them from the fervent exclamations of a very excitable Mormon sermon. "You dumbasses broke the CD player. Thank you *so much*."

Bird's eyebrows tighten in the center of their face. "Well— why don't you have an aux cord or something?"

"You cannot *seriously* be insinuating that this is my fault." The road is straight for one blessed moment, and Cal twists her head to glare directly at Bird. "What do you want, an apology that the accommodations here aren't up to your standards?"

"You don't know anything about my standards," Bird mumbles, crouching down to study the CD player at eye level, not meeting Cal's glare. "This idea you have of me—that person only exists in your head."

"I know the whole Caravan would turn itself inside out to make sure you never heard the word no, and it still wasn't good enough for you." Cal shakes her head back to the road, disgust and rage and some kind of quiet, simmering, maybe unfair envy and something worse that she can't even think about all bubbling up just beneath her skin. "Why did you even come back? You don't exactly try to hide how much you hate everyone."

"I don't *hate* everyone." Bird sighs, dragging their delicate, long-fingered hands over their face. "I just didn't want to be here again."

"Then *why* did you come *back?*"

"It's complicated."

"I'm sure my tiny little brain can manage to keep up. No one is as stupid as you think—"

"Oh, for fuck's sake." Bird rips their hands from their face, surging back up to their full height. "I came back because I didn't have anywhere else to go! Is that what you want to hear? That I failed? That I tried to be human and I sucked at it? That no one there wanted me? Does that make you feel better?"

Uncomfortable silence is the only thing playing in the RV now.

Cal knows she should feel bad about pressing—clearly, this isn't something Bird wanted to air out in front of everyone— but all she can really summon is curiosity. There are a dozen questions she wants to answer, and she knows Bird won't have a lick of interest in responding to a single one.

Luckily, Cal isn't the only one who's curious.

After a long moment, Felix ambles toward the front and sinks down to sit on the carpet next to their feet. "What about your dad? I thought he was happy you were moving in."

"He was." Bird wipes the back of their hand under their eyes, sniffing, and drops into the perpetually empty passenger seat. "And things were good, for a while. But . . . we were strangers, really. We didn't actually know anything about each other. And he . . ."

They suck in a deep breath through their nose and shrug. "I guess he wasn't actually a very good person. Just like my mom warned me."

Cal can't help but notice that they don't sound entirely convinced about that.

"What did he do to you?" Felix asks softly, his tone clearly preparing a soft place for trauma to land. He reaches for Bird's hand.

They squeeze his fingers. "No, he didn't—he didn't do anything. God, no, I . . ."

For a moment, their voice trails away. And then finally, softly, they admit, "It was my fault it didn't work out."

They don't elaborate.

"You're eighteen now," Cal reminds them. "You had other options. Right?"

"Did I?" Bird laughs without humor. "Let's see . . . I applied to a bunch of colleges that didn't want me, and a bunch of jobs that didn't want me, and I asked my friends for a place to crash and it turned out they didn't want me, either."

"Yikes." Hugo's being an asshole, trying to press Bird's buttons with his levity, but Cal sees right through it. He's not *actually* a monster. His eyes are distant, clouded by fog, and she knows he's imagining what the last few months must've felt like for the person he's so obviously still in love with.

Bird rolls their eyes in response, and they look to Cal. "I know *you* think that *I* think I'm some kind of chosen one or something—but it turns out I'm not very good at anything, actually. Least of all being human."

Cal's knuckles are white on the steering wheel. Never in her life has she stared harder at a road. She doesn't want to meet the burning stare Bird's leveling at her cheek.

"I came back because I didn't have a choice not to. I'm not some evil mastermind who wants to ruin everyone's life—" Their voice hitches, and Cal can swear she feels holes burning into her face from the heat of their unblinking, unrelenting stare. "I'm actually just pretty fucking pathetic."

"You were really brave," Felix assures them, dragging their attention from Cal's face.

Only when Bird's eyes leave her does she feel like she can breathe again.

Felix continues, "And I'm really glad you remembered you can always come home."

Bird makes a sound that might be a sob or a laugh. Cal knows Felix means to be reassuring, the same way she knows his words cut down to the marrow.

In the rearview mirror again, Cal meets Eamon's eyes. He's watching the entire exchange, silent but intense, not missing a thing. When he stares back at her, some silent understanding passes between them.

The two of them can always come *back*. But they can never go home.

Chapter 17

Eamon

Just across the border into Idaho, a few days after leaving their abandoned camp, Cal announces that the RV's gas light is on. Neither Hugo nor Felix has been able to get cell service since they lost it in the desert, and Bird still has not found their vanished phone. Following road signs and quietly begging the RV to keep going just a few more miles, Cal navigates them to the first gas station she can find.

The aforementioned station is a tiny A-frame building with a metal carport off the front and a single analog pump with one flickering light bulb hanging over it like a spotlight. No one moves for a long moment, all of them staring through the windows at the grim reality of their only hope.

"Are we certain this place is even operational?" Eamon asks, eyes floating from the rusted-over pump to the front door of the building itself. He cannot detect any life within.

"We better fucking hope so," Cal answers, pulling the RV

the rest of the way forward before bringing it to a stop. "If anyone wants to use a bathroom that's not in the middle of my bedroom, now's as good a time as any."

Eamon . . . adamantly disagrees with that statement. Now is not as good a time as *any*. In fact, he can think of many times that would be infinitely better for going to the bathroom. Times that include, to give one example, properly lit buildings.

"You know," Bird says. "When I'm out by myself, I always look for some bourgeois coffee shop with plants in the window when I need to pee. They almost always have an all-gender bathroom. And I realize I can use the women's restroom, no one's going to harass *me* in there, but it's nice. It's a little more comfortable—it's affirming, I guess."

"Why exactly are you telling us about your piss habits?" Hugo asks.

"Because this"—and here Bird waves their hand demonstratively at the gas station—"is whatever the opposite of that is. This is where you use the bathroom when you are actively hoping to get hate crimed."

"Give me a break." Cal rolls her eyes. "I think you're inventing boogeymen, your highness."

Eamon thinks he agrees with both of them and knows he does not care enough to be part of this conversation. He stops listening, pulling his wallet from his back pocket and stepping over to the pump. When he was taken in by Mister Basil and Miss Cassandra, they gave him a card connected to their bank account and told him to use it in case of emergencies.

They never spoke explicitly about what an emergency

might look like, and Eamon obviously does not remember ever living through one, but he is willing to assume this constitutes.

With the card poised between his thumb and forefinger, he considers the pump for a long moment. Ah. Interesting. Okay. Finally, he interrupts the back-and-forth the others are doing.

"I believe this is cash only."

Cal stops in the middle of whatever nasty thing she was saying to Bird, turning to look at him. "Of *course* it is."

"At the very least, I suspect it must be paid inside."

"I'll go!" Felix offers with a too-bright smile, bounding to his feet. He had been slumped on the RV steps, head in his hands while he despondently watched the other three try to verbally eradicate one another. "And I'll check out the bathrooms. Maybe they aren't that bad."

"You can't go in there." Hugo is looking at Felix like he's lost his mind.

"Sure I can. It'll be fine."

"You have ears," Eamon reminds him, in case he has forgotten.

Felix grins and pulls something from his back pocket. He unfolds a thick piece of beige fabric and tugs a beanie over his head before doing a little pose. His ears are squished down underneath it, the lumps blending in with the piles of his curly hair. "Not anymore!"

"Be careful," Hugo snaps. "Don't try and make any more *friends*."

Felix rolls his eyes but offers his brother a smile before heading inside, the bell over the door jingling in welcome when he does.

Hugo stares after him long after the door closes. Eamon stares at Hugo.

Eventually, the older Beránek brother notices he is being watched.

"What?" he snaps, the blades of his eyes narrowing against the sharpeners of his cheekbones. "Why the fuck are you looking at me?"

"Why do you have such little trust in him?"

"Not this shit again." Hugo snakes a hand through the hair between his antlers, fisting a clump of it and tugging. "I'm gonna need everyone to stop psychoanalyzing my relationship with my brother."

"You love him, but you have no respect for him. What kind of love is that?"

"You know who I have no respect for?" Hugo asks, mockery dripping from his tone. He tilts his head, hand curling around the back of his neck while he does. It cracks under his palm, vertebrae popping in a line.

Eamon shrugs. "I do not care if you respect me. But I think the way you feel about him is unkind."

"A feeling can't be unkind," Bird suggests, leaning against the side of the RV and crossing their arms over their chest. "Feelings are just feelings. They're neutral. What's kind or isn't is all in the way you treat people."

Eamon does not agree with that, but he does not have the language to explain why.

When he does not answer, Cal bites out, "Don't be naive. Of course feelings can be cruel. *Nothing* is neutral."

"*Everything* is neutral," Hugo argues.

"If everything were neutral, then nothing would be neutral," Bird scoffs.

These people make Eamon want to drive broken glass through his temple. Head pounding—and so, so far removed from the original point he was trying to make—he presses a hand to his face to massage the throbbing veins in his forehead.

He pretends he is unable to hear them, and it works as well as he could expect it to. Only when Hugo says his name is he called forward again, summoned by the still-unfamiliar sound of it leaving the boy's lips. He is unsure he will ever enjoy hearing that name, bestowed by a woman he grows more suspicious of by the day, but it is a special kind of torment when it comes from Hugo.

"What the hell would Eamon know about loving someone, anyway? Who has he ever loved?" His mouth curls to show off his teeth. Eamon watches them, stark white and black shadow mixing in the light of the single gas station bulb. "Who's ever loved him?"

Eamon considers that and answers honestly, "By the looks of it, I have been as loved in the last few weeks as you have been in your entire life."

Sharing his thoughts was, he muses in retrospect, another unkindness. And to it, Hugo does not respond well.

Eamon watches from between his fingers, hand still pressed over his face, as Hugo straightens to his full height. The air, still in the moments just before, begins to pick up its hem, shaking itself out at their ankles. A breeze wafts up against Hugo's body, making his clothes dance. Sparks flicker to life around the hazy outline of him, embers beginning to crackle in the smolder of his frame.

"Hugo," Bird warns, their tone gone low. "*Not* here. You wanna blow us all up?"

The honest answer to that question, Eamon suspects, is not one Bird would like to hear.

His head continues to pound. It may be that exhaustion is catching up to him. He has not gotten a decent night's sleep since before the new moon ceremony. The others certainly do not abate the symptoms of enervation, instead exacerbating them with their . . . everything.

Hugo does not bother to answer Bird's question, nor give any indication he heard them at all. He instead raises his hand and flicks his fingers toward Eamon, sending a spray of sparks flying at his face. There is no real way for Eamon to defend himself, and he knows this. Well beyond the end of his rope, he moves his hand from his face and holds it in front of himself like a small, ineffectual shield. If he is lucky, maybe only his palm will be burned this time.

But the burn never comes. Eamon frowns, tilting his head and looking down at his hand—no, not at his hand, not exactly, but at *a* hand.

From his skin, a shadow has leapt free. Not *his* shadow, not really, but a perfect doppelgänger. Five black fingers stretch beyond his own and cup Hugo's pyrokinetic magic in their own dark palm.

Eamon has never felt the pulse of his own magic. For weeks, he has been waiting to see what he might be able to do, desperate to understand the life he was dropped into without ceremony. Has the time come? Is this shadow his gift?

"Holy shit," Cal whispers from somewhere beside him, and he cannot say he disagrees.

The shadow continues to emerge. It pushes forward further

and further, first a hand extending past his own, then an arm, until finally a dark torso breaks free of his chest, carried by a pair of tenebrous legs. Still cupping the small open flame, the shadow walks across the dimly lit gas station parking lot until it is face to face with Hugo himself. The boy is as frozen as the rest of them, stunned into inaction.

Slowly, the shadow reaches out to press its fingertips against Hugo's mouth. In doing so, it returns the fire from where it came, the sparks scattering over his tongue and sliding down his throat, briefly illuminating his neck golden and blue and streaked with red. Eating his own fire does not seem to faze Hugo. He swallows, his lips tightening around the tips of the shadow's fingers.

Carefully, almost as if to be gentle, the shadow curls its palm over Hugo's jaw.

"What the hell are you doing?" Hugo finally asks, the question directed at Eamon.

Eamon cannot bring himself to answer; he can only watch in fascination with the rest of them. *I am doing nothing*, he wants to say, but he's not sure if that's true.

The shadow's other hand rises to mirror its twin, now cupping both sides of Hugo's face.

"Hey, let me—" Hugo's words are interrupted by the broken sound of a gasp, the shadowy hands slipping from his jaw to his throat and tightening until his air supply is cut off entirely.

"Let him go!" Bird finishes for the boy who can no longer speak for himself.

Eamon does not move. The shadow's grip on Hugo's neck only continues to tighten.

"Eamon!" Cal shouts. "That's enough!"

Is it?

Hugo's legs go out from underneath him. Even as he falls to his knees, the shadow crouches with him, staying level with his eyes the whole time, its hands never moving from their stations. Hugo claws at its arms, trying desperately to peel it off of him, but he is not strong enough. His cheeks begin to turn the faintest shade of indigo.

Cal grabs Eamon by the back of the neck and jerks him away, as if breaking his concentration might get the shadow to stop. It does nothing. Hugo is still going to die.

Bird slams their hands against the creature's back, illuminating their palms, as if enough light might simply snuff out the dark. It does nothing. Hugo is still going to die.

His eyes begin to roll back into his head, the whites overtaking everything else. His lips part. Eamon's mouth opens in response, and he does not understand why. All he can hear is his own heart beating, but he could swear he feels the slowing of Hugo's beneath his hands.

Another light appears. Glowing golden like the dawn, it shimmers into existence from nothing and begins taking shape just beside Hugo and the monstrous shadow. When a stag appears, formed by the glow, it leans its head forward and slams its antlers into the shadow's side, ripping open a seam at its rib cage.

The black figure is thrown away from Hugo and sucked back beneath the surface of Eamon's skin. As Hugo falls to his hands on the pavement, struggling to catch his breath, the stag glides into nonexistence as quickly and seamlessly as it appeared. In its wake, Felix steps forward from the shadowy gas station doorway.

A flood of questions assaults Eamon's mind, none of them with answers that he can reach for. But a single clear thought stands out among the chaos of the rest.

It would have been better if Hugo *had* died. Because whether it is true or not, that is what everyone is going to believe he was trying to do anyway.

Chapter 18

Felix

Okay, not *everyone* thinks Eamon was trying to kill Hugo. At least, specifically, Felix doesn't think that.

"I had no control of it," Eamon insists for the dozenth time. He's sitting on a tree stump a few yards away from the RV, hands balanced on his thighs. "Nothing that happened was intentional—it just happened."

"I know that," Felix reassures him for the dozen and oneth time.

"*I* don't know that," Cal argues. She's perched on the tow hitch of the RV in a crouch, arms crossed over her knees, narrowed eyes watching Eamon like she's waiting for the boogeyman to appear. "And I think it's pretty fucked up that you're pretending you do."

Felix sighs. He understands her anger comes from a place of fear. And he can't fault her for that—it's a tool that's likely served her well. There's a lot of stuff out there they all need to be afraid of. Plus, he can't be mad at her for being cautious on his brother's behalf.

Felix wouldn't do anything to hurt his brother—not ever. And if there was any part of him that actually thought Eamon was a threat to Hugo, that he'd had any control over what happened back there, this would be an entirely different story.

"Besides," she continues, teeth grinding like saw blades against each other. "It doesn't make it better if he didn't have control. When your magic can hurt people, you don't have a choice but to have control."

"Are we still talking about Eamon?" Bird is sitting on the other side of the RV's back end, knees curled to their chest, ass in the gravel of the parking lot, watching the road in front of them. Felix can't see them from where he's standing with Eamon, but he knows they're watching Hugo. Their voice is quiet enough that he *could* pretend he didn't hear them. And maybe he should. "Or are you projecting?"

If Cal's glares were as lethal as her fangs, Bird would be dead by now.

Felix sighs and tugs a hand through his hair. "He didn't know that was even an option. Now he does. And he'll figure it out. He will. You just gotta give him some time."

Neither Cal nor Bird looks convinced. Even Eamon looks like he's struggling to believe what Felix is saying about him.

"Look, all of us are still figuring out how much we can actually do with our magic, and we were all *basically* born in the Caravan." Cal wasn't, he knows, but she was still in diapers when they found her, so that distinction hardly feels important. "He's *brand new*. How was he supposed to know how to rein it in? He didn't even know he could do that until it was happening!"

"I'm sorry, all of us are what?" Cal asks, raising an eyebrow.

"I've known the limitations of my own magic since I was old enough to understand what magic was," Bird says in a flat monotone. "I think you might be the only one who's still figuring this out, Felix. Like what the hell was that thing with the deer, anyway?"

"Well, that's just . . . me." Felix waves a hand over his body, which . . . does *not* look anything like the stag they all saw. So, his gesture probably loses some of its credibility.

In fairness, the others have never really understood Felix's magic as well as they think they understand their own. Hugo has his fire, and Bird has their light, and Cal has her kiss. All of those are fairly straightforward and easy to understand, even if they only know what they know and they don't know anything about what they don't. On the other hand, Felix has his faith. In the simplest terms, he makes things where they weren't before.

It was a cool party trick when they were younger. He could pluck flowers from behind someone's ear or pull a rabbit out of a hat, a tiny magician without any trapdoors or smoke and mirrors. Just Felix and his heart and him standing in front of the world, saying, *This is going to work because it has to.*

He still thinks it's a cool party trick. He's just figured out a bunch of new ways to use it.

"I guess it's sort of like . . . astral projection?" That sounds right. "I believed I could save Hugo without hurting Eamon, and so I could. And I did."

From down the road, Hugo says something. He's too far away for Felix to understand it.

"What'd he say?" he asks Bird, frowning.

They sigh. "He says you've done it before."

"Yeah." Felix smiles. "See? Huey knows what I'm talking about. And I *believe* that Eamon is telling the truth, so—"

"So he is?" Cal asks, visibly skeptical.

Felix does not let her doubt bring him down. He knows how bad things can get if he starts to let doubt creep in. If faith is his magic, then cynicism is his Achilles' heel. It turns everything upside down.

"Yes," he answers. "So he is."

"That is just so . . ." Cal's voice trails off and Felix watches her struggle to find the right word.

"Delusional." Hugo steps out from around the back corner of the RV. His throat is smeared blue with Eamon's finger-painted bruises, his eyes red from the popped blood vessels. "You are fucking delusional, Felix, and you are going to get us all killed just because you want to live in a world where nothing bad ever happens. How far do things have to go before you can admit that he shouldn't *be here*?"

Felix's chest hurts. Still, he says, "There's nothing wrong with believing we can still be happy, despite everything that's happened."

Hugo glares at him with those borrowed red eyes.

"Besides, no one's going to die." Felix's smile is weak but honest. "I can keep us all safe. We're going to figure everything out and we're going to do it together. Just trust me."

Okay, pause. Hello again, reader. I imagine you might be having some thoughts right now.

Let me see if I can guess what you could be thinking.

I absolutely do not trust Felix, what the hell does this little twink know that I don't?!

Or maybe

Are all of these people just the worst *people in the whole wide world? Seriously, why is there not a single likable character in the bunch? Who am I supposed to be rooting for?*

Or even

Is it just me, or was the thing with Hugo and the shadow kind of gay?

And, honestly, any of those thoughts would be fair. If you're thinking any of that, it means you're probably on the right track and you're seeing this story for what it is. Because of course Felix knows things you don't. And of course all these people are terrible. (And yes, the sexual tension is way too much, but we don't have time for all of them to work that out.)

Did you think you were reading a story about good but deeply damaged people surviving against all odds and finding hope for the future in each other?

Because there are plenty of books telling that story, but this isn't one of them.

This is a book about haunted houses, except the houses are bodies and the hauntings are the lies children tell and are told. This is a book about how dangerous it can be to dream when you grow up sleeping with something under your bed. This is not a book about an exorcism, because these houses cannot be saved by anything short of burning to the ground.

Hugo knows that already. That is why he says, "Whatever. Let's just get going."

Because he believes that, soon enough, none of this is going to matter anyway.

And Felix believes that, too, even if he and his brother would disagree on what the end is going to look like. As far as Felix is concerned, everything is going to be okay, because they'll make it okay. And if it isn't, they'll remake the ending themselves. Together.

So, he smiles at Eamon and tilts his head toward the RV. "You heard him. Let's get going."

Before

No one found Eamon. In his own way, he found them. He wasn't there and then he was, as if he'd materialized from morning fog or been delivered to them by the trees themselves.

It was early. The Caravan was beginning to rise for the day, bodies shuffling out of tents and campers, fires just being built to brew first cups of coffee. Someone on their way to the porta-potty noticed him, standing upright but as still and rigid as a corpse, at the edge of their encampment. For a moment, they felt a jolt of fear—was this a human come to spy on them?

But then they caught sight of his red eyes. No, not a human. They breathed a sigh of relief and stepped a little closer.

"Hey, are you okay?"

Eamon didn't answer. He didn't even turn to look at them as if he'd heard them.

They took another step, a new kind of worry bubbling up in their gut. "Hey, kid. Who are your parents? I can run and grab someone for you."

It was odd that they didn't recognize him. The Caravan wasn't tiny, but it wasn't so large that its members struggled to know each other all by name. How was it possible that a teenage boy lived among them and no one had any recollection of him?

Still, they chalked it up to the nature of things around here. Magic got in the way of logic sometimes, and vice versa. Besides, their numbers were always changing, fluctuating in one direction or another. They must've missed something.

"What's your name?" they called out, stopping a few feet away from him.

At this, finally, he seemed to recognize he was being spoken to. He turned his head and met their stare. But when he opened his mouth to speak, it was not language that slipped free. Instead, the sound was an awful gurgle, a rasping, rattling, desperate cry for help.

It didn't take long for a crowd to gather. Someone went to fetch Basil and Cassandra, banging on the door of their RV to wake them. Others helped the boy to a seat by the biggest fire, where they wrapped a blanket around his shoulders and offered him food and water.

When the elders finally joined them, the boy had no answers to their questions. He did not know who he was, or where he had come from, or how he had found them. He felt he had a name, the same way he felt he had a family, but he could not recall either.

Cassandra stroked his back through the thick blanket. "You must have some kinda guardian angel, ending up here of all places. That's what we do—this whole community exists just so we can find people like you."

He said nothing, face blank, but she thought he heard her.

"What do you think of the name Eamon?" she asked, still

petting him. "It means protection. And I think that's what you've got, some kind of protection."

From the other side of the fire, a pair of green eyes met Eamon's—now Eamon in truth. He couldn't be sure how he knew, but he knew he'd seen those eyes before. And unbidden, fear and rage in equal measure threatened to consume him. Detached from reason, an echo of something awful pushed at the back of his skull. It begged him to remember.

And Hugo continued to stare, wordlessly praying that he wouldn't.

Chapter 19

Hugo

Hugo has lived his whole rotten life in cramped quarters with the demons who begot him. The shape of his youth was determined by hiding spots, his childhood whittled by the scrutiny of a knife. By comparison, sharing Cal's studio apartment on wheels with four other bodies should've been easy. And it might've been easy if those bodies had belonged to entirely different people.

When their RV pulls into a campground for the night, Hugo announces he'll be the one to leave cash in the drop box. That way, at least, he can get a few minutes alone. Three sets of eyes follow him until he disappears around a curve in the path: the first, a brand; the next, a target; the last, a cage. Only Cal doesn't bother to stare after him. If he had to guess, she's too busy Birdwatching.

The park is blessedly quiet. Most of the other spaces are empty—it's off-season for outdoorsy types, after all, closer to Halloween than Labor Day, and even the ones with other tents and campers have turned in for the night. Boise National

Forest is still and cold, and as Hugo tugs his corduroy jacket tighter over his torso, the only sounds to be heard are his own footsteps, the stubborn buzzing of the last mosquitoes of the year, and the distant calls of a great horned owl.

Hugo loves being in the woods. It's easy to disappear here, to slip between the trees and become something else entirely, at least for a little while. The trees may as well have raised him. It doesn't matter that these specific trees in this specific park aren't familiar. He knows how deep the roots go. He knows the way trees talk to each other, across hundreds and thousands of miles.

There's something comforting in knowing these trees knew who he was before he ever showed up here. That they've heard stories for the last eighteen years about him and every good and awful thing he's ever done. That their cousins have seen him at his best and worst and passed him along in whispers buried under the soil. Not to judge him—what good would such a judgment do for *trees*—but only to recognize him.

Here, Hugo is seen and known and nothing else. Here, he is only exactly what he is, and it means only what it means, and he will never be asked to hide or defend anything.

The drop box is at the end of the road, right next to the bathrooms, whose showers will only offer up a dribble of hot water for a few extra quarters, and the bulletin board with flyers advertising everything from how to throw a birthday party at a national park to kids who've been missing for years. Hugo's eyes linger on the latter, scanning over names. It's a grim collage, the photos picked and provided by loving parents whose fear flavors the air like ozone before a storm. Awkward school portraits, tongue-out bathroom selfies, frantic attempts to sum up their precious, half-grown babies in a single snapshot. One flyer in particular holds his attention, terribly familiar.

On it, an unsmiling teenager who disappeared on a camping trip just like this one, the head in the picture made heavy by a massive pair of headphones and a too-intense stare that sears Hugo through the paper. That stare, hazel-eyed and serious, presses in from all directions, itching at every exposed inch of him.

The others can't see this face. Not in this context. It would be traumatizing, at best. Hugo reaches out and tears the paper from the corkboard wall, balling it in his fist and tossing it into the trash can beside the drop box. Wayward souls never get found anyway.

He yanks down an envelope and one of the cheap plastic pens and scribbles Cal's license plate number, their site number, and the day's date. From his wallet, he crams in a twenty, then shoves the envelope in the box.

When he turns to head back, the peaceful break from his begrudging companions already ruined, there's a deer standing directly behind him.

Hugo's heart thunders as he hurriedly backs up, spine colliding with the edge of the drop box until metal digs into his lower back and pain shoots down his legs. No. No, there *isn't* a deer standing behind him. Because whatever that thing is, it isn't a deer. And Hugo, of all people, would be qualified to recognize the distinction.

It's wearing a deer's body. That also isn't an entirely accurate explanation, but Hugo isn't sure how else to describe it. His eyes take the thing in, but it's as if they can't focus on the details. There is the suggestion of a deer, sure, but it's wrong. Its limbs are too long, too thin, its eyes too big—too many? Its gnarled antlers are twisted, warped, curled in on themselves as if to make a nest or a crown.

And it's talking.

Except it isn't, not really, it's not like its mouth is moving. This isn't Bambi. But it's staring at him and he's staring back at it and Hugo swears, he *swears* he can hear it. He can hear it whispering, or maybe he can hear something else whispering, maybe something else is crawling up right behind him and he won't notice because he's too busy staring at the fucking *thing* pretending to be a deer.

Its too many eyes glimmer with a shiny blackness, an endless ink spill, a void that threatens to drag him down and drown him. And for a moment, Hugo thinks about drowning, thinks about leaning in closer and being consumed by this thing, this not-a-deer.

The whispers grow louder, just a little. Just enough that he can make out what they're trying to say.

GOD FORGIVE ME **YOU** KNOW I LOVE YOU THE ONLY
WAY I KNOW HOW GOD FORGIVE ME YOU KNOW I
LOVE YOU THE ONLY WAY I KNOW HOW GOD FOR-
GIVE ME YOU KNO**W** I **L**OVE YOU THE ONLY WAY I
KNOW HOW GOD FORGIVE ME YOU KNOW I LOVE YOU
THE ONLY WAY I KNOW HOW GOD FORGIVE ME YOU
KNOW I LOVE YOU THE ONLY WAY I K**N**OW HOW GOD
FORGIV**E** ME YOU KNOW I LO**V**E YOU TH**E** ONLY WAY I
KNOW HOW GOD FO**R**GIVE ME YOU KNOW I LOVE YOU
THE ONLY WAY I KNOW HOW GOD FORGIVE ME YOU
KNOW I LOVE YOU THE ONLY WAY I KNOW HOW GOD
FORGIVE ME YOU KNOW I LOVE YOU THE ONLY WAY I
KNOW HOW **GO**D FORGIVE ME YOU KNOW I LOVE YOU
THE ONLY WAY I KNOW **H**OW G**O**D FORGIVE **M**E YOU
KNOW I LOV**E** YOU THE ONLY WAY I KNOW HOW GOD
FORGIVE ME YOU KNOW I LOVE YOU THE ONLY WAY I
KNOW HOW GOD FORGIVE ME YOU KNOW I LOVE YOU
THE ONLY W**A**Y I KNOW HOW **G**OD FORGIVE ME YOU
KNOW I LOVE YOU THE ONLY W**A**Y I KNOW HOW GOD
FORG**I**VE ME YOU K**N**OW I LOVE YOU THE ONLY WAY I
KNOW HOW GOD FORGIVE ME YOU KNOW I LOVE YOU
THE ONLY WAY I KNOW HOW GOD FORGIVE ME YOU
KNOW I LOVE YOU THE ONLY WAY I KNOW HOW GOD
FORGIVE ME YOU KNOW I LOVE YOU THE ONLY WAY I
KNOW HOW GOD FORGIVE ME FORGIVE ME FORGIVE
ME FORGIVE ME FORGIVE ME FORGIVE ME FORGIVE
ME FORGIVE ME FORGIVE ME FORGIVE ME FORGIVE
ME FORGIVE ME FORGIVE ME FORGIVE ME FORGIVE
ME FORGIVE ME FORGIVE ME FORGIVE ME FORGIVE
ME FORGIVE ME FORGIVE ME FORGIVE ME

Hugo shoves away from the drop box and swerves around the creature's body, stumbling backward down the path. He refuses to take his eyes off of it, and it turns its head to watch him go.

"You can't hide your real face from me. I know who you are," he manages to warn. "I know what you've done, and I already know how this is gonna end."

The not-deer tosses its bramble-crowned head and stomps at the ground, the muscles under its fur quivering with the anticipation of a charge.

Hugo, for all his insight, turns tail and runs.

Before

Even when drowning—and he'd been drowning for a year, now, the most torturous of baited deaths for a boy woven by licks of fire—Hugo found it difficult to hate the Catskills in autumn. Soggy summer air turned crisp as the apples found aplenty, and daylight painted the hills in fiery swathes that rolled, flame oceanic. Nestled at the base of unfathomably old mountains, ground down by relentless time, Hugo felt he was nothing.

This was not a bad thing. It was peaceful, here, to be small.

Nights this time of year were pleasantly cool, just enough so as to flavor a campfire with appreciation. So when he saw Felix alone in the dark, curled up inside his oversized sweater, long ears draped down his narrow shoulders with the skyward tilt of his face, Hugo gathered wood. His little brother didn't look away from the stars as Hugo cleared a patch of dirt and positioned his timber, nor when Hugo closed one eye and snapped fire from his fingers to the dry wood with perfect precision. His fires never required kindling. Hugo made for a damn good firestarter, even—and maybe especially—when there wasn't a drop of kerosene involved.

Felix was still bound to the cosmos when Hugo returned to the fire with provisions, eyes shimmering with pinpricks mirroring the expanse above. Sometimes Hugo swore he'd light the whole world on fire just to see the flames dance in Felix's ever-wide eyes. He tossed the canvas bag on the ground beside his brother.

"What have the stars got to say that's so goddamn interesting?"

Felix blinked out of his reverie, surprised to see Hugo there. "It's always something, Huey. Don't you think you'll have endless stories at that age?"

It was tremendously earnest, that question. Sometimes Hugo didn't know if Felix was naive or just really bad at delivering jokes. He skirted the discomfort of the unknowing by tugging the bag into his lap, unearthing a pack of jumbo marshmallows, a box of graham crackers, and two dark chocolate bars.

Felix's eyes were full of stars, and he wasn't even looking up. Hugo ripped the marshmallow bag open with his teeth and, wordlessly, shoved two on a stick. He handed it to his little brother, who shimmied with glee before extending the marshmallows, just so, over the flame, steadily turning his stick like a spit.

Hugo jammed his own marshmallows onto a stick and held it with his knees while fishing out a pilfered, lukewarm can of Pabst. Felix's lips plumped and pouted with disapproval but quirked to the side when carbonation cracked into the peaceful dark of the night.

"Can I . . ." He bit his lip. "Can I try it?"

"Don't be ridiculous." Hugo threw back a mouthful, boggy wheat bitter on his tongue, and forced himself to swallow it down. He retrieved the stick from between his knees and jammed his marshmallow directly into a dancing lick of fire. It immediately ignited. "Drinking's bad for you."

Felix, still turning his slowly, perfectly toasting marshmallow, gave him a once-over and must've decided to find him funny, because he threw back his head and laughed. The sound twinkled through the air, stars for audiophiles. Hugo would've committed war crimes for that laugh. He pulled his blackened, flaming marshmallows, blew them out, and feasted upon their charred exoskeletons before shoving their white, half-melted innards back into the inferno.

Were Bird here, they'd've said something about the marshmallows' fate feeling very in line with *The Divine Comedy*.

Were Bird here, Hugo wouldn't've been gagging on secret beers.

"Show me your favorite constellation," Felix said, stars on the brain, and pulled his perfectly toasted marshmallows from the heat.

Hugo ripped a chocolate bar open, portioned out graham crackers, and made a bed for Felix's pillowy treat to land. "Well, that right there is Orion's belt."

Felix giggled, licking strings of sugary goo from the edges of his s'more. "What about the rest of him?"

"What about it? It's probably in the same vicinity."

Stars had never been a subject of his study. He'd had his star—snuffed, now—and he still had his star catcher, and if he kept thinking like this he was going to punch something.

Felix took the moody onset of silence and relieved Hugo of the pressure to converse, pointing to a scatter of stars near the horizon. "Look there. Do you see the bear?"

"Course," Hugo lied, for he, of course, saw a scatter of stars.

"Ursa Major. The Great Bear. That's my favorite, because it has an accompanying constellation, and—oh, is that cheating, Huey? To name two when I asked for a single favorite?"

"I think you make the rules of your own game and you can do whatever you want."

Felix beamed. "Well, then. The legend is muddy and there's a smattering of variations, but! All conclude that the nymph Callisto, who hunted alongside Artemis, was seduced by Zeus—"

"Weren't they supposed to all be virgins?" Hugo popped the burnt remains of marshmallow into his mouth and washed it down with beer.

"Well, yes, and that's why it was such a big deal when it was revealed she was pregnant. Someone turned Callisto into a bear—Zeus, or Artemis, or even Hera—and her son was raised a bear hunter."

"Brutal. Though, why exactly was she punished with bear-hood?"

"Oh, because myths are often unkind to women, I think. Anyway, one way or another, many years passed, and then Callisto, still a bear, saw her grown son for the first time. In her delight, she ran for him. He, of course, just saw a bear charging, and went to strike in self-defense. But before he could kill her, Zeus saved them both and turned them into stars. So there"—and Felix pointed into the field of pinpricks—"the Little Bear plays forever alongside the Great Bear."

Hugo nodded slowly, then sat up and pointed. "Hey, I know that one! That's the Big Dipper."

Felix threw back his head and laughed into the heavens until tears glittered at the corners of his eyes. "Huey! The Big Dipper is *part* of the Great Bear!"

Hugo scowled, some flavor of embarrassment burning in his cheeks, misplaced—Felix would forever be the last person to make him feel any kind of embarrassed. "And how exactly does it make sense to subdivide constellations, huh?"

"Because people are funny little creatures, that's how. And look." Felix pointed again, to the same smatter.

This time, though, Hugo's gaze followed his brother's gesture to the single star he'd know anywhere in the sky.

"Polaris," Felix said softly. "The North Star. It's the tail of Ursa Minor, Huey, see? The Little Bear was separated from the Great Bear, but returned and hung, forever, in the sky."

He turned and looked, full of meaning but completely lacking in tact, at Hugo, who could not divorce his stare from Polaris even as its shine unglued him and began to pull his muscles away from his bones like slow-cooked meat.

"Bird will come back," Felix said slowly, the corners of his lips sticky and dark. "I don't know when, but I believe they will. And once Bird is back, Huey, you have nothing to worry about. They will never leave."

Hugo decided he hated the stars and shotgunned his first beer.

Chapter 🔲

Cal

From the safe distance of her RV, Cal watched the new moon celebrations through a dusty windowpane, a mug of cinnamon tea in one hand and a pocketknife in the other. With the practiced tip of her thumb, she opened and closed the blade methodically, the repetition soothing and familiar.

Up. Down. Up. Down.

Each swish of metal on metal offered its own small comfort. Cal would take that wherever she could find it, in whatever ways big or small.

Outside, someone screamed with a fanatic joy that made her fist clench tighter around the knife's handle. Immediately after, she felt like she'd committed some sin, loosening her grip before tossing it away from her altogether. Guilt was even more familiar, and nearly as comforting.

After all, what sort of person was driven to anger by the happiness of others? What did it say about the bleak reality of her own damnation that she resented everyone around her for things that were no one's burden but her own? Her soul was a grim and long-expired thing, shriveled up and rotting at her core.

At least, that was the way she imagined it. Likewise, it was the way she assumed everyone else must have seen her. It wasn't like she'd ever been particularly successful at hiding her feelings, as much as it would've made things easier on her and all the others. Instead, she wore her fucked-up heart like a banner in the bags beneath her eyes, a masquerade of allegiance to her own emotions.

Her bitterness and her anger, anyway. She'd *never* been good at putting those in her pocket and letting them go unnoticed. They refused to be denied. Other emotions, of course, were easier to box away. And of those, there were a select sacred few she set aside, only taking them out to examine when she was alone.

This new moon's festivities were on an entirely new level of debaucherous glee. Cal's eyes traveled the raucous crowd, half-naked (sometimes entirely naked) adult bodies twisting and vibrating next to the open fire, embers sparking and dancing like lightning bugs in the air, the endlessness of a black sky interrupted only by the occasional star. All of it lacked interest to her. She was looking for something in particular—*someone* in particular.

If she'd worn her anger like an emblem all her life, any trace of Cal's fondness had been tucked like a pebble into her shoe, unnoticeable to anyone but her, and eventually fading away into a minor discomfort she'd more or less forgotten about. This specific pebble had been lodged in her shoe for as far back as Cal had memories to call on. But after three years of distance where it seemed that the rock might've fallen out on its own, its sudden return was even more annoying than it'd been when it first got stuck in there.

She really hated how much she didn't hate Bird fucking Stieber.

Of course it didn't take long for her to find them in the crowd. Bird's skin might go dim when they wanted it to, but there was still an incandescent blush that followed them everywhere they went. Maybe everyone couldn't see it but everyone could feel it, pulled in like moths to bulbs, even if they didn't understand why. If Cal wanted to find Bird, all she had to do was look toward the light.

They were standing at the outskirts of the celebration, wild curls like a mane framing their face. Cal's hungry eyes devoured the lines of their body, every inch of them drawn as tight as the cable cord of a crossbow. Tension turned the softness of their features into stone etchings. Cal studied the wall of their shoulders and the way it met the unflinching paths of their arms, ending in two curled fists.

Cal remembered Bird as a small child—they'd been wistful and clever, too old for their age, but happy, for the most part. It was only when they got older that they got sad. Older and sadder and sadder and older until finally they said goodbye to the Caravan. Cal remembered that day, sketched in her head in permanent ink.

She'd been perched in the back window of Holly's van, having crawled in when no one was looking, when Bird left the bathroom, eyes red-rimmed and bloodshot, ten conspicuous pinpricks on the sides of their face.

"You're seriously doing this?" she demanded.

Bird yelped, jumping and twisting toward her voice, eyes

widening before narrowing. "What the hell are you doing in here?"

"You're actually leaving?" Cal jerked her thumb at the suitcase on the floor. "Today?"

"Yeah—that's been the plan." Bird sniffed, grabbing their shoes and sitting down on the edge of the kitchenette table to start yanking them on.

"Yeah, but . . ." It sounded bad, maybe, but, "I don't think anyone actually thought you were going to go through with it."

"Well, maybe everyone should have spent more time getting to know me a little better before I left." Bird yanked on the laces of their boots, sniffing again. "Why do you care, anyway? I'm sure you're going to throw a party as soon as I'm gone."

Maybe you should've spent more time getting to know me *a little better before you left,* Cal thought. She didn't say that, though. It wasn't fair, and, even if it was, it wasn't a hand she intended to show.

"Already put in a cake order," she said instead, flashing fangs in a cruel grin.

Bird paused, briefly, in tugging on their other shoe, to look up and glare at her. There might have been more heat behind it if it weren't obvious they'd just been having a meltdown in the toilet.

She opened her mouth to land another blow, only to be cut off by banging on the camper door. A second later came Hugo Beránek's voice in a vicious howl. "Open the door! You can't actually be going through with this!"

Cal watched Bird's face. Bird watched the door, cheeks going pale.

"I'll leave you to deal with all that." She swung her legs back out the window, poised to slide to the ground. At the last second, she paused and glanced over her shoulder. "Hey—I sincerely hope I never see you again."

That was the last thing she'd ever planned to say to Bird. She didn't think they ever realized it was meant to be a kindness.

In her own RV, Cal watched anger tighten the screws at the corners of Bird's jaw. They'd been sad when they'd left for California, but the anger hadn't come until later. Not until they'd shown up again.

Cal wanted to know what happened out there. She didn't think she'd ever get the courage to ask.

Maybe courage was the wrong word for it. Maybe it was more like stupidity, all things considered.

The lanterns of Bird's eyes lit a pathway through the crowd, searching for someone else the same way Cal had searched for them. She didn't need to know who Bird wanted to see to *know* who Bird wanted to see. It made her hate them all the more. *Why?* Why would someone give their heart away to a boy who only knew how to eat it?

Cal recognized the hypocrisy in the question. Although, in fairness, she'd never expected anyone to give her anything.

She noticed when Bird's expression shifted, their eyes finally landing on someone and pausing. Cal followed their gaze, expecting to find Hugo on the other end of the stare. Instead, it was Eamon. The dark-haired, red-eyed boy watched Bird with his usual intensity, like if he looked for long enough he could see everything about a person unfold right in front of him.

Cal's eyes flicked back and forth between Bird and Eamon,

watching each other as a literal fire danced between them. Finally, she had enough. She grabbed the window curtain and threw it closed.

She had never known anyone who wasn't a little bit in love with Bird Stieber.

Hugo Beránek was an animal wearing a people suit, but at least he was housebroken.

Eamon, though? *Really?*

Sometimes, the reality of her endless isolation was harder to swallow than others. That night, she choked.

Chapter 20

Eamon

"Why are you staring at me?" Hugo deadpans the question without looking up from his dinner, a grilled cheese cooked over the campfire, toasted until the crust is blackened but a warm meal nonetheless. "Why are you *always* staring at me?"

Although he does not direct the question at any specific person, Eamon has no doubt he is the one being addressed. He knows this, because he has known for several minutes now that he needs to stop staring at Hugo, and has been entirely incapable of forcing himself to.

He realizes this is a problem, in the sense that it makes other people uncomfortable when he looks at them for too long. He does not entirely understand *why* it makes them uncomfortable, and he is not altogether certain if that makes it a him problem or an everyone else problem. His inclination is to believe this makes it an everyone else problem, since he is decidedly unbothered about where his eyes do or do not rest.

Still. The length he has spent staring at Hugo is . . . excessive, he knows, and he did intend to stop himself. It was only that he could not.

This has been a constant occurrence for some time, the way he follows Hugo, in one way or another, wherever the boy goes. It is not that Eamon even wants to be looking at him, ever, it is that he cannot seem to *not* be.

It is just that, the morning Eamon was blinked into existence from wherever he came from, the only memory he had was of Hugo's face. And no matter how vile a memory it was, some part of him feels pathetically like an imprinted duckling.

Perhaps if he had let his shadow kill Hugo, he would no longer feel such a loathsome connection.

As if reading his mind—though he knows she is not and cannot—Cal fills the silence that follows Hugo's questions with "Maybe he's thinking about finishing the job."

The job, in this case, being strangling the boy to death.

Which, he supposes, is not wrong. He *was* just thinking about that.

That was not why he had been staring at Hugo for too-long, stretched-thin moments, though. Eamon had been unable to look away from him since he had returned from paying the overnight fee. There was something . . . unsettled in the shape of him. As if he had seen something on his walk that shook out the webbing of his nerves and tugged it a little closer to the surface of his skin.

He had left one way, and he had come back another. That was all. And Eamon, who had been looking at him for weeks, just happened to notice.

Being openly discussed by the others seems to do the trick, however, because he is finally able to tear his eyes away to look at Cal, instead. "I do not have to stare at him to think about killing him."

Felix groans. It is enough to make Eamon feel a smidge of admonishment. He knows how much Felix had to do to keep him here. He is not trying to cause problems for him or anyone else by saying the things that come out of his mouth. He just also does not always understand why the things that come out of his mouth bother them all so much.

Deciding he will change the subject, for Felix's sake and no one else's, Eamon's eyes glide from Cal to Bird. They are stuffing their own sandwich in their mouth when his gaze lands on them, a thick glob of cheddar pooling over their bottom lip.

It is difficult to say with certainty, given the campfire between them, but he could swear their cheeks redden. Around their mouthful of food, they ask, "What?"

"You said you applied to several colleges that rejected you."

He continues to stare, and Bird continues to stare, and no one says anything for a long stretch. Finally, they swallow and ask, "Are you just . . . reminding me? I'm sorry, did I look like I was enjoying myself too much?"

"Oh. No." He is not good at having conversations or being around other people. That is what he has decided. "I was curious . . . what were you intending to go to school for? I was not with the Caravan for long before all of this happened. But I struggle to think of a career path you might have been prepared for by your time with them."

At least not one that required a degree from a university in order to pursue. He supposed Bird could have had a lucrative career as a phone hotline psychic or a social media–based salesperson.

Not for the first time, Eamon finds himself entertaining a thought and then wondering how he was led there. What even is a phone hotline psychic? Who are social media–based salespeople? How does he know them and when did he forget them and why did he not forget them entirely?

Bird frowns but attempts to cover up their expression by sucking more oozed cheese from the tip of their thumb. When it pops free from between their front teeth, they say, "Well, that was kinda the whole problem. I wasn't prepared for anything."

"Why apply for college at all, then?"

They narrow their eyes. Still, they set their sandwich down on its disposable paper plate, balanced in wobbly precarity on the ledge of their knee. They are sitting crisscross in a fold-out chair, and they adjust a little as if getting comfortable for whatever this conversation is going to become. "Because that's just . . . What I was supposed to do? I don't know. It was the next step in humaning. I'd managed to fake it all the way through high school. I thought I could do the same in college."

"But you failed," Hugo reminds them.

Eamon's eyes twitch toward him, only briefly. He has to force them to pull away and move back to Bird, like prying magnets apart.

It is just that . . . Hugo is constantly cruel with no end goal. He is violent for violence's sake. But there is something new in his voice . . . something new tucked behind his throat . . . This particular cruelty comes with the barest suggestion of desperation—if anyone were watching him less closely than Eamon, they might not notice it at all.

For his part, Eamon wonders what it would take to pull Hugo apart and hunt down whatever new mechanism has slipped inside. He questions if he would remove it like cleaning away a bacterium or stitch it into the lining of his skin so Hugo could claw and claw at his own body, but he would never recognize the shape of himself again.

Anyway. Eamon looks back at Bird. *They* are looking at Hugo. He wonders what they see when they look at him. It is obvious enough that Bird doesn't see the same boy he does. He wonders which of their Hugos is closer to the real one.

"What did you apply for?" he reiterates.

Bird continues to stare at Hugo until their shoulders droop with silent resignation. At that point, they look back to Eamon. "I— It's stupid."

Without more information, Eamon does not have any ability to convince them otherwise. It is entirely possible that whatever Bird hoped to accomplish in the human world was stupid. He considers that for a moment. Something that Felix said about him brushes at the back of his mind. He reaches in and grabs it with his fist, pulling it to the forefront.

"I am *brand new*. I do not even know enough to know a thing is stupid."

"For fuck's sake, this has got to be the most embarrassing meeting of the minds that's ever happened," Hugo grumbles, rubbing his hands over his face.

"Why don't you shut the fuck up for once?" Cal snaps.

Eamon keeps his eyes on Bird's.

Slowly, they admit, "Aerospace engineering."

"Whoa," Felix breathes. "That's *so* cool, Birdie. I didn't know you knew anything about space."

"Yeah, well, I failed, remember?" They roll their eyes, leaning back in their chair. They pick at the crust of their sandwich. "But . . . yeah, I thought it would've been cool, if it had worked out."

"Aerospace engineering," Eamon repeats. "Astronauts?"

"Sort of."

"You wanted to go to Mars and shit?" Cal clarifies. He does not think her tone is intended to be harsh—he does think that is just the way her voice sounds.

"Well, I wanted to go to Houston." Bird chuckles. Eamon does not know why it sounds self-deprecating, but it makes him sad for them just the same. "I had this whole idea that maybe someday I'd work at the Johnson Space Center. I don't know. I've always had a weird soft spot for Texas."

"Yeehaw," Felix agrees.

As if they cannot help themself, Bird looks back to Hugo. And, unable to keep up with the effort of holding magnets apart, Eamon takes that as permission to give in and let himself look back to Hugo, too.

Hugo is not there. Which is to say that physically, Hugo is there and he is fine, but his eyes have gone vacant, the shell of his body still and hollow. Eamon wonders which deep pocket of his own mind he wandered off to hide in. Eamon wonders what it would take to crawl in there and smoke him out.

This Hugo is a lot less interesting to look at. This Hugo is a lie and it does not even have the decency to be a convincing one. Eamon turns his attention back to Bird. "Why were you rejected?"

"Geez." Their eyes shoot back to him. "*Why* are you asking?"

"To hear the answer." He does not understand that question. "Why else?"

"I—" Their eyes narrow in on him. He has seen suspicion levied so many times that it is no longer anything novel. He still does not understand what he did to warrant the skepti-

cism the rest of the world seems to have in him. Just because
he is fairly certain he is a soulless eidolon who is not supposed
to exist at all does not mean he has done anything *wrong*.

"I bet I can guess what happened." Eamon glances at Cal
in time to watch her flip her chair around to straddle it, facing
Bird. She balances her forearms against the backrest, tilting
forward until her chin hovers just above her wrist. "All those
schools you applied to realized you were *also* brand new."

Back to Bird. They swallow. Then shrug. "Basically."

"What does that mean?" Felix asks. "You're not brand new."

"No, but I might as well have been." Bird sniffs. They look
at their knuckles. They meet Eamon's eyes, then quickly look
away. "I didn't—it's actually insane how much our parents
didn't teach us, you know? About anything. Everything. Do
you know the reason we don't float off into the sky or fall off
the side of the planet when it spins is because of something
called gravity? It's a whole thing with, like, the moon, and
you're supposed to learn about it when you're, I don't know,
five years old or something."

Cal nods, stoic and knowing and angry in each and every one of her pores. Felix cocks his head, appearing genuinely confused—and perhaps a little distrustful—at the idea
of some invisible force tethering him to the Earth. If Hugo
has any reaction at all, it is entombed beneath his practiced
catatonia.

As for Eamon, he did not know he knew what gravity was
until Bird said it. Once it is mentioned, though, he realizes he
has, of course, always known what gravity is. It was only that
someone misplaced it somewhere, and it got lost behind one
of the revolving locked doors in his own mind.

"The Caravan does not educate their children." It is not a

question, but Eamon supposes it is not *not* a question. He is not certain he can make the statement definitively—but if he had to guess, he would feel good about his odds of making the right call.

Still, Cal responds as if it *were* a question needing an answer. "Oh no, they educate them. They don't teach them about the moon's gravitation pull or anything, but they teach them all about how the moon can grant magic fucking wishes."

"Them?" Eamon raises one eyebrow. "You do not consider yourself a child of the Caravan?"

Cal's mouth opens. Then closes. Opens. Closes. Then, very slowly and with such care, she explains, "There's a difference between being a child *of* something and a child *in* something, and I was never a child *of* anyone's."

And once again, he could not say how he knows he knows what she means, but he knows with certainty that he does. He considers that, and everything else, for a moment. Perhaps the others consider things, too. The campsite goes quiet but for Felix's and Cal's occasional chewing.

When he has finished his considering, Eamon asks, "Do they never intend for their children to leave?"

"Most of us don't have that option." The fleshy puppet fashioned in Hugo's image seems to come alive, shaking off despondency and latching instead to this newest turn in the conversation. His green eyes, more moss than sage tonight, slice right into the contours of Eamon's face.

If Eamon did not know better, he might believe *he* were the puppet, and Hugo the wood-carver whose sharp gaze alone was enough to bring him to life. He does know better, of course. If Hugo could sculpt Eamon any way he wanted, it would be into a corpse, not a real boy.

"And those that do?"

"It's not like it's forbidden," Bird begins, and already Eamon can hear the slow crawl of unfounded justifications in her teeth, trying to make themselves seem sturdier than they actually are. "I mean, I left, right? No one made me stay. People *leave*. That's how the whole Network exists."

"The Network," Eamon echoes.

"That's how the Caravan finds people," Cal explains. "There's a bunch of people like us, scattered all over the place, who *have* been able to go out and build lives in the human world. And whenever they find someone new, they get in touch."

"Someone new."

"Magic powers. No memories. You're familiar with the concept."

"Brand new," he repeats in understanding. "And . . . they say they have no idea where these *new* people come from? We just appear—no memories, magic powers, somehow always in reach of someone who can contact the Caravan on our behalf?"

Cal blinks.

"Or," Eamon amends, "in my case, we are already in walking distance."

"What are you suggesting?" Hugo asks. There is startlingly little heat in his tone. Somehow, this is the one conversation where he maybe does not want to immediately set Eamon on fire. Thrilling and curious.

"I am not suggesting anything. I am asking questions." Eamon shrugs. "And my question is . . . the Caravan travels from place to place, picking up people they claim to have found, with no memory of where they came from or who they were before, promising to teach them control and offering them a safe haven from the threat of . . . what, exactly? Humans?

Has there ever actually been an instance where a human outed one of these people and caused real harm?"

"Um . . ." Bird frowns. "Well . . . I don't think so. But it's obvious what would happen, right? If people knew what we are, what we can do?"

"What would happen?" Eamon does not believe it is obvious.

"Well, they would . . ." Bird's voice trails off.

Felix offers, "They would kill us. Or—or put us in cages. They would treat us like animals."

"Why do you assume that?"

"Why are you *defending them*?" Bird demands. "You're acting like you're one of them, but you aren't—you aren't human. You're one of us. *You're* a member of the Caravan, too, whether you like it or not. None of us can outrun what we are."

Okay. This has now gone slightly awry. Eamon clears his throat and takes a deep breath, careful to cultivate his response. "I am not trying to defend anyone. I am just asking questions because they are the questions I have. It is confusing to me, the way the Caravan serendipitously finds the people who need them and then makes it nearly impossible for those same people to ever leave again. Even in your case, Bird. You could have had a human life if you wanted. But they sabotaged you before you ever tried."

They bounce their leg, not realizing how bad the jitters have gotten until their plate tumbles from their lap and their sandwich lands in the dirt. Bird curses under their breath, leaning forward to gather up their ruined meal.

As if by itself, the waning fire flares with new verve, but Hugo is already, automatically, reaching for the sandwich fixings. Eamon wonders how much he must hate himself for this ingrained tenderness.

"When you lay it all out like that," Cal says slowly, resting her cheek against the back of her hand, eyes glossy and far away. "It all clicks into place, huh? We're so fucked."

"We were *born* fucked," Hugo mumbles.

"*You* were born fucked, antler boy," Cal bites back, head snapping up to stare across the fire at him. Eamon can see the glistening tips of her canine teeth where her venom begins to pool. "You have always been theirs. I don't know anything about how they got their hands on me."

"Maybe that's a good thing." Felix's whisper is so low that it nearly disappears beneath the crackling embers of the low, quiet campfire. Eamon can only be certain he heard him speak because the others all look to him at the same time. "Some of us wish we didn't know anything about the way we came into the world, Cal. Maybe the truth would just make you feel worse."

Hugo tosses Bird's new grilled cheese onto the skillet. It sizzles in the near-unbearable hush.

Eamon understands what Felix is saying in that he understands the individual words and the way they string together. He does not understand what the hidden message is behind them. He does not understand why it is enough to end the conversation for good, Cal and Bird and Hugo all admonished into silence by whatever Felix did not have to explicitly say.

He does not understand what secrets this Caravan is hiding. But he certainly intends to find out.

Before

"What are you doing?"

Fuck.

Their mother's voice shattered the repetitive, if frenetic, rhythm Bird had fallen into, their hands stilling before they could shove another wadded-up piece of clothing into their suitcase. Their shoulders tensed, tensed, jerking up around their ears. Immediately, they felt as if they might lose the contents of their stomach.

Bird couldn't make themself turn to face her. They were not actually very brave at all. They were only pretending to be and hoping that eventually, maybe, it would feel true.

"I told you, Mom. I'm leaving."

Holly's breath hitched on a whimper, and Bird winced in response. Guilt burned its way down their throat. Though they hadn't moved at all, they could swear they must've kicked their mother right in her belly.

"I—I told *you*, I won't drive you to the airport. I'm not going to let you do this!" She was already crying, already wounded.

What kind of monster would Bird be, to leave their own mother to bleed out in this camper all alone?

Something brushed against the back of their mind. A dark warning, increasingly louder, more and more familiar by the day. What kind of monster would they become if they stayed?

"I'm sorry," they whispered, shoving balled-up fabric into their luggage, resolved but trembling just the same. "But I already have my ticket. And Dad said he would send a car to get me. It'll be here soon. Please, Mom, I don't want this to be the last—"

"You cannot do this!" Their mother's nails dug into their arm, yanking Bird away from their task. Forced to face her, they stared into Holly's wide eyes gone impossibly wider, two frantic hunter's moons like spotlights on the dust motes between them. "Please. Please, honey, if you have to go, if you're sure this is really what you want, just wait a few days. Okay, just—"

"No. Mom, no, I'm not—" Bird shook their head. This, too, they'd been over with their mother. Again and again. Would it never end? Could the only resolution between them ever be a cord-cutting ceremony? "I'm not staying for the new moon."

They *knew* it meant something special to their mother, this idea of having one last lunar celebration together as a family. But they couldn't figure out *why* it meant as much as it did. The Caravan celebrated the moon every two weeks. It wasn't as if they hadn't just been here, beneath the full moon together, not that long ago.

Even if Bird believed everything their mom did about the moon and its magic and whatever influence it had over their lives, they didn't understand her desperation for this one particular night. You couldn't do a thing every single month of the year and still think it was that special, right? For most people, mundanity would've set in a long time ago, the way it had for Bird themself.

Holly was apparently *not* most people, though that was not news to her only child. Tears leaked from those giant eyes, and her lips wobbled with the kind of plaintive helplessness that had kept Bird tethered to this place for basically as long as they'd lived here.

"But . . . new beginnings," Holly whispered. "We haven't been given the opportunity to . . . to celebrate you . . . your new becoming . . ."

The invisible hand of some spectral guardian, some ancient and primal ward at the gates of pain, brushed its knuckles down Bird's spine. They swallowed past the gravel in their throat. "I appreciate the idea, Mom, but I don't need a celebration."

"Of course you do!" Holly's shriek straddled the line between unhinged confusion and a black pit of rage, and Bird took a step back without truly making the decision to do so. "You are becoming an entirely new being! You are being exalted into a new purpose! That moment must be marked! It must be memorialized!"

The bend of Bird's knees tucked against their threadbare mattress. Was this display really meant to convince them to stay?

Tread carefully, they told themself in silence, alone in the safety of their thoughts—the only place in the Caravan that could ever be truly safe. (Though just because a thing *could be*, didn't mean it always *was*.)

"I think . . . if you really want to make me feel celebrated, the best way to do that is to listen to what I want." It should not have been the job of a fifteen-year-old to talk down their mother from a cliff's edge she concocted in her own frazzled mind. But there were many things in Bird's life that were not as they should have been. "And this is what I want. Besides, you can always still throw a wish in the fire for me, even if I'm not here."

Holly had never been a particularly agile woman, nor someone with any vested interest in fitness or athleticism. But she moved then with such speed and vicious precision that she might as well have been an Olympic medalist—or an animal.

Suddenly, in less than a breath, she was practically nose to nose with Bird. Her hands clutched either side of her child's face, nails digging into Bird's cheeks and temples. Her wild eyes seemed more fiery than wet, in that moment, her pupils blown wide, wide, wide until each eye was its own abyss.

"YOU WILL NOT ABANDON YOUR PEOPLE! WE WILL GRANT YOU WHAT YOU DESERVE, YOU UN-GRATEFUL BRAT!"

Silence.

Stillness.

In the aftermath of their mother's rage, Bird dared not move or breathe or think. In the rock, paper, scissors roulette of fight, flight, or freeze, Bird always wound up carved from ice.

Slowly, after a time that might've been seconds or minutes, Holly's hands began to lower. She let them fall to her sides, shoulders eventually slumping, the anger draining out of her or at least finding a good hiding spot.

"I'm . . . I'm sorry, honey." She sniffed, stepping back, swiping at the poisoned apples of her cheekbones with shaking fingers. "I'm just so sad to see you go. I'm sorry, I didn't mean to scare you."

The words came as if Bird had memorized them, their tongue operating on some autopilot they hadn't consciously flipped a switch for. "It's okay. I'm sure this is really hard for you."

"Yes . . . yes, I knew you would understand . . ."

Holly continued to back up, moving toward the door, hands still shaking. Those wild eyes, bled of their fury, glazed over entirely. Wherever their mother was, she was not really in the camper with them.

"I need . . . I need to speak with your grandparents. Yes. They will know what to do. Yes."

Without a goodbye, she turned and left, the metal door clanging closed behind her, only catching the latch on its third attempt.

Bird stood still until they could feel their own pulse again. And then, slowly, they made their way to the tiny RV bathroom to examine the wounds their mother had left them with.

Chapter 21

Bird

Dangling over the bathroom door on the left is a sign with a fishing pole on it. On the right, a fish. With barely three disjointed and restless hours of sleep on their scorecard, squinting hard against the punishing beams of the early morning sun, Bird stares between the two for what feels like a long, long time.

So . . . which one looks more like their genitals?

Obviously, this is not the true heart of the predicament. Its heart, Bird decides as they try in vain to rub the headache from their temples, probably lies somewhere with cis men who've been reassured they're funny enough times that it now poses a problem for everyone else.

They know, though they almost would rather be ignorant, what the signs are trying to indicate. And they know which one they're supposed to choose, based on other people's ideas about them. If it were only an issue of the signs being offensive and ridiculous, that would've been one thing.

It isn't only that issue, though. There's also the fact that

Bird is neither a fishing pole nor a fish, not in reality or in this grotesque little euphemism.

They are not a girl, though they have survived—or are perhaps still surviving—girlhood. They are not a boy, though they still wish boyhood had been gifted to them, even a taste, even just once. The concepts of woman and man are as distant and impenetrable as the stars themselves, though Bird has remarkably low interest in exploring those particular corners of the galaxy.

From a nebulous childhood, they evolved and are still evolving, and whatever lies beyond remains unanswerable for now. As evolution is prone to do, they will become whatever they need to become, whatever that looks like, in however long it takes for their becoming.

Though they know there are those who would argue with their assessment, those who have always believed they comprehended them in a way they could never quite grasp themself, Bird's sabbatical into human society held very little influence over their discernment of their gender. On the contrary, it was only their understanding of human language, of words old and new and all invented to describe experiences Bird once believed were entirely unique to their own life, that evolved at all. They do not feel they see themself more clearly after living in California for three years, at least not insofar as their gender is a concern. They only feel they have words now to put to the way they've always felt—words that would have been denied to them for a lifetime, had they never stepped outside the Caravan's perimeter of control.

Perhaps that line of thinking is too dangerous to entertain. Because if Bird allows themself to think about *that*, it may stoke the same feelings that'd shaken out the night before while they'd listened to Eamon talk about his skepticism of the Caravan's lore.

What an inexplicably discomfiting thing, to be told something so familiar is likely not the thing they thought it was. What an even *more* upsetting thing, to realize in the quiet cavern of their chest that they'd maybe always known it was not the thing they were pretending to believe it was.

With a sigh, Bird sets aside their moral code and enters the goddamn fish bathroom, placing a mental sticky note to write someone at the National Park Service a *very* nasty email when all of this is over.

The interior of the women's bathroom is more or less what they would've expected, having spent their life in and out of a thousand campgrounds exactly like this one. The linoleum of the floor was probably once white, or maybe a pastel mint, but has long since gone the way of smeared taupe and globs of unfortunate greenish yellow. The lights over the ceramic sinks buzz, a warning chorus that they might blow out at any moment. Not that their absence would be cause for much concern; they hardly provide any light to begin with.

Each of the toilet stalls is open, though Bird would not consider each of them to be in a usable state. Those aren't why they're here, though. There's a half bath in the RV—what there *isn't* is a shower. The promise of warm water—even if it cost extra—was the only thing to convince them to finally unfurl from their hiding spot in the smallest, darkest corner of the RV's kitchenette. There's only one shower stall in the bathroom, and someone else is already inside. Bird can hear them humming under the gentle spray of the tap.

Fine. They can wait. They consider setting their towel down on one sink, but decide that may negate the whole point of taking a shower at all, what with the thick layer of slimy brown grime on the edge of the ceramic. Instead, they curl their arms around their belly, tucking the towel into their torso. From their tightened fingers, their bag of toiletries hangs limp. Left with nothing else to do, they study themself in the dirty mirror over the dirtier sink.

Looking into the dimmed mien of their own reflection, one thought stands alone, the singular frontline soldier in the war zone of their psyche: Sometimes, familiarity is so much more jarring than the macabre could ever hope to be.

The last few days have turned the fabric of Bird's life inside out. Ever since the disappearance, they've been walking around like their organs are on the outside—like every tender stretch of them is laid vulnerable, bloody and exposed to the elements, and there's nothing they can do about it.

And the thing in this moment that really makes Bird want to cry, the silly, inconsequential thing that makes them feel as if they're about to go falling over the edge, is the sight of themself in the bathroom mirror in a too-big sleep shirt and a pair of cheap flip-flops, their curls gone frizzy and extra big from the humidity trapped in the bathroom with them. Because there is something so *ordinary* about that sight. Because they have seen this version of themself looking back from the mirror hundreds, maybe thousands, of mornings before.

There is something maybe reassuring and maybe cruel that, even when the worst thing happens, there is still everything else happening at the same time. Life goes on, right up until it doesn't. And for everyone else, it goes on even after.

"What are you doing?"

Bird jumps, looking over their shoulder at the sound of the brash voice iced with a thick layer of judgment. They hadn't even noticed when the shower turned off, too busy staring at themself. If they had, they might've realized Calliope was the one in the bathroom with them, before she stepped out in her towel and caught them having a whole *moment*.

Honestly, Bird isn't sure what they must've looked like from the outside. There doesn't seem to be an answer that allows for anything short of dismissal or over-the-top sincerity. They frantically cast about for one, though. While they do, their eyes snake—absentmindedly—over the water droplets on Calliope's shoulders, the white cotton of her itchy looking towel pressed tight to her cleavage, the water droplets on her knees.

When Bird realizes they're wearing identical pairs of cheap flip-flops to protect their feet from the nasty bathroom floor, they can't help but quirk a half smile.

"Huh. I didn't peg you for someone with a foot fetish, Stieber."

Calliope carries her black toiletries bag to another sink and tugs out a wide hairbrush. Bird stands there with their cheeks turning red, even more incapable of forming a response than they'd been seconds earlier. Finally, too embarrassed to do anything else, they stomp into the stall Calliope just abandoned.

Some ten minutes later or so, scrubbed raw, their own towel wrapped around their chest, Bird emerges. They're delighted to discover Calliope is still there—they've been thinking about their response the entire time they were in the shower.

"You've never pegged me at all!"

Calliope blinks. She's halfway through pulling a pair of

camo joggers up her legs, and she freezes with them around her knees. While Bird was behind the shower door, she'd brushed and dried her hair, and put on a clean bra and underwear. The all-black sports bra and boy shorts could almost be workout clothes. Bird could almost pretend they were at the gym.

"Um." Calliope drags her pants over her thighs. Movements gone liquid and slow, she carefully ties the drawstrings at her waist. "What?"

"I mean—" Ten minutes thinking about that in the shower and it only just now occurs to Bird that it's a double entendre. "I *just* mean, you have never really understood anything about me."

"Are you . . . are you agreeing that you have a foot fetish, or . . ."

"That is not the point! Wait—I mean, no!" Bird presses their hand to their face. This conversation is not going the way they'd imagined it would when they were practicing their lines in the shower. It's actually very unkind of Calliope not to do exactly the things Bird had scripted for her in their head.

Cal doesn't bother with her shirt. Instead, she crosses her arms over her chest and leans back against the sink, raising an eyebrow. And she *smirks*.

"You are such an ass." Bird doesn't know why they're trying here. They aren't even entirely sure *what* they're trying.

"And?"

"And . . ." They throw their hands up, tilting their head away. Maybe all of this would be easier if they weren't looking at Calliope. "You obviously hate me and I think it's really easy for you to see me as the bad guy because you already hate me and you always have. It's called confirmation bias."

There. That's the thing they're trying.

For a moment, the only sounds are the buzzing lights and

the steady *drip, drip, drip* from the shower head, and both of them sound a thousand times louder than they could possibly be when no one is talking. The dripping water, in particular, is going to make Bird's skin crawl.

Calliope comes to their rescue by finally responding. "I don't hate you."

"Well—" That just isn't true. Bird shivers, clutching their towel a little tighter. "What do you mean? Yes, you do."

"That? That I hate." Calliope rolls her eyes.

"What?"

"This belief that everyone's everything revolves around you. Do you realize you have an incredibly inflated sense of self-importance?"

Bird . . . laughs. It takes a second for Calliope's words to sink in and then, well, they can't help it. It's ridiculous enough to be comical, intentionally or not. "Is that a joke?"

"I don't get what's funny about it." Calliope shrugs. "I haven't *always hated you*. But I have spent our whole lives watching you get handed everything and everyone you've ever wanted."

"I have never gotten a single thing I wanted."

The two of them stare each other down, both tensed like they're anticipating blows about to land, and—at least for Bird's part—unsure of how to move forward. They have never looked at someone and felt the sensation of staring in a fun-house mirror until this conversation with Calliope. How . . . *inexplicably discomfiting*. How very familiar and how very not.

"Everyone in the Caravan adores you."

"Everyone in the Caravan thinks I'm going to take over for my grandparents someday. It's sycophantism, just preemptively."

"Does that matter? Love is love."

"You sound like a bumper sticker." Bird winces. "Sorry. My instinct here is to be a bitch to you."

Calliope rolls her eyes but waves it off.

"Um . . . besides, it's not that simple. Love isn't love, or—whatever." Bird sucks in a breath. "'Cause most of them don't actually love me. They love what they think I can do for them. People in the Caravan just . . . they all love some version of me they made up in their heads."

"Except for me," Calliope reminds them.

"Right. 'Cause you hate your version."

"Yeah." Her eyes bounce off Bird's face, landing on her own nails. She studies them and shrugs. "Except no. Like I said—I don't hate you."

Bird's still trying to make that make sense, but they can't seem to get from point A to point B. It feels like knowing the answer to a math problem, like having a cheat code that shows them exactly where they're supposed to end up, without actually knowing how to solve it or being able to show their work. "Then why do you act like . . . *that?*"

"Maybe *my* instinct is to be a bitch to *you,*" Calliope suggests. She still doesn't look up from considering her own hands.

"Oh."

"Maybe I thought *somebody* should be." She snickers, finally glancing back at Bird's face. "I was trying to keep you humble."

Bird's throat becomes the barrel of a gun, words like bullets loading themselves behind their tongue, every stand-your-ground law giving them permission to open fire because Calliope shot first. Except the safety slots back into place when

Bird's tongue presses tightly to the roof of their mouth, probing the space between their front teeth.

Because Calliope is making a joke. It takes Bird a second to notice it. Calliope is trying to be funny, not cruel—she's *teasing* them.

Huh.

"Yeah, well, I should've just let you read my diary, then," Bird finally answers. "'Cause I was doing enough of that for the both of us."

"Damn." Calliope clicks her tongue. "Now I get it. You think I hate you as much as you hate yourself. Now who's projecting?"

And she's still trying to be playful, still trying to tease them, or at least Bird is pretty sure she is. But the question still makes them full-body flinch, fist tightening again in their towel, thighs rubbing together as they shift uncomfortably beneath Calliope's stare.

Yeah. Their instinct really is to be a bitch to her.

"I'm sorry for saying that." They can't look at her when they apologize, so they stare at a glob of *something* on the floor instead. "It was too far. I knew it was and I said it anyway."

In their periphery, they watch Calliope shrug it off. "Maybe. It was also fair."

"No, it wasn't."

"Sure it was. I killed someone. That's a thing I did."

Bird's eyes snap back to Calliope's face at her blasé mention of that night. "You were a baby. A literal *baby*. Someone died—I don't know if that's the same thing as you killing her."

Calliope's tongue rolls across her teeth. Bird is helpless but to follow the trail of that pink muscle, watching it map the sharpened points of her ivory fangs. "I was a baby, and it'd be fucked up to be mad at a *baby* for biting someone in the middle of a tantrum. That doesn't make me *not* a murderer, Bird. You know that, and I know that, and everyone else in the Caravan knows that, and they definitely never let me forget it."

A canyon sits between them, a chasm of loneliness Bird has never noticed before. Has it always been there? Have the two of them spent their whole lives yelling from across this uncrossable divide?

And if they have, how could they have ever been expected to hear each other clearly?

"Maybe I wasn't actually even angry that everyone was in love with you." Calliope chuckles, dry and flat and sad. She sucks in a deep breath and all the air in the dirty public bathroom disappears. "Maybe I was just pissed off because you were allowed to love all of them back."

The words are so palpably heavy, Bird can't help but hope she feels a little lighter now that she's said them out loud.

"You deserve to be loved, too, you know." They don't even know they know that until they've said it. But it's so obvious now, having tasted the words for themself.

"Yeah." Calliope doesn't actually agree. She slides one tooth over her lower lip. "By someone with a death wish."

Bird stares at her mouth and Calliope stares at the fluttering pulse point in Bird's neck and both of them breathe with considerable concentrated intention.

The ravine that divides them feels a little smaller. And in turn, Calliope feels that much closer. From this new distance, Bird can almost smell her. Something shakes loose beneath the floorboards of Bird's rib cage. A thing that is known but not yet known. Familiar and not. Buried potential, long forgotten, that might've been a seed.

From outside the bathroom, Felix's voice interrupts whatever is not happening.

"Um . . . Cal? Bird?"

Bird's rib cage feels like the shaking branches of a tree when their breath punches free of their chest.

Calliope doesn't look away from them when she calls out, "Yeah?"

"Um . . . sorry to interrupt. It's just, uh, Hugo and Eamon are trying to kill each other again."

Chapter 22

Felix

His first mistake was not paying enough attention to Hugo.

Well—no, maybe that wasn't it. Maybe his first mistake was making it his job to pay so much attention to Hugo in the first place. Felix was the little brother. He was supposed to be the one who was being looked after.

And, to Hugo's credit, Felix is pretty sure that's what his brother thinks he's doing. Hugo has always believed he was looking out for Felix and not the other way around. And, for the most part, Felix has let him think that.

But Felix doesn't need a babysitter. He never has. People think he's too soft, but that's just because he's not afraid of being soft the way the rest of them are. It's a cliché, but he thinks it's probably a sign he's braver than the others, his willingness to be vulnerable.

Hugo is not brave, but that's okay. He doesn't have to be. Felix can be brave for both of them.

Hugo doesn't let himself be soft. Hugo would rather die than make himself vulnerable. And *that* is why Felix is always having to keep an eye on him. Someone has to make sure he doesn't get himself Big Hurt in his efforts to avoid all the small hurts one right after the other.

So, yes, maybe that was Felix's first mistake—making himself his brother's keeper. Maybe, if he hadn't done that, if he hadn't done everything in his power to protect Hugo from the reality of his own pain, if he'd just let him face the hurt head-on for once, Hugo would have learned to live with it. Maybe all of this could have been avoided.

Or maybe it would have ruined him and all of this could have been avoided because Felix would have buried his big brother a long time ago. And that was an even less acceptable outcome than the current one. So, *maybe* it was his first mistake. But he *definitely* couldn't bring himself to actually regret it.

Today's mistake was not paying enough attention to Hugo. Sometimes, Felix got a little lost inside his own head. One minute, he'd been tidying up the campsite from the night before, trying his best to be helpful to get them all on the road as quickly as possible, and the next he was in the woods. He might as well have blinked and transported himself to the base of a Ponderosa pine, sitting in the dirt with his legs tucked underneath him. And he could've actually done that, though he hadn't. It's just that keeping track of time lately is getting harder and harder, the thread of it all falling away from him. Sometimes the days and nights aren't sure who's who. Felix doesn't know what to do about that.

It was when he started to hear the yelling that he knew he'd screwed up. He'd run back to the RV to find Eamon and Hugo going at it again, fire and shadow and spittle flying as accusations were thrown into the space between them. Something about a car engine, something about a lie. That was when Felix went to see if he could recruit backup.

Now he sprints back in the direction of their campsite, Cal following after him and yanking on her sweatshirt as she goes.

Hugo glances up when he hears them approaching and points a finger in her direction. "Why don't you try explaining to *her* what you were doing? I'm sure she'd love an explanation about why you were messing with her fucking house."

"What?" Cal skids to a stop, head snapping from Hugo's direction to Eamon's. "What are you doing up there?"

Ugh. Felix's head is aching, overfull and stretched thin, like a balloon about to pop.

Eamon is perched like a gargoyle on the hood of the RV. He narrows his eyes at the question, giving a small shake of his head. No. To what, Felix isn't sure. "I was attempting to avoid being set ablaze *again*."

"That's not what I'm talking about." Hugo throws his hands up. "He was tampering with the engine! I caught him under the hood myself!"

"I was *examining* the engine." When he speaks, Eamon's words are pushed through clenched teeth. "I was not tampering with anything."

"Yeah, right," Hugo says at the same moment Cal asks, "Why?"

"Because someone already left me stranded and I am not interested in that happening again. I was just giving everything a once-over before we got on the road again. It was that simple."

"Bullshit," Hugo growls. "Drop the Good Samaritan act. Nobody is buying it."

Cal sighs. "I believe him."

Felix exhales in relief that makes his limbs feel a little warmer than they did a second ago. But Hugo stares at Cal as if he's thinking about her DNA under his fingernails.

"Why?" he finally demands when he gathers himself enough to speak at all.

"Because he's not actually doing it out of the goodness of his heart or whatever you think he's claiming. He's stuck in the RV, the same as the rest of us. And if he wanted us all to be trapped in the woods together, he wouldn't have taken off the morning everyone else disappeared."

"He—maybe he—you don't—" Hugo's face gets redder and redder as he struggles to come up with something, *anything* he can pin on Eamon.

Felix understands why. He does. He knows that it would be easier, that it would feel better, if Hugo could convince himself Eamon was a bad person. After what happened between them . . . Felix knows Eamon being the villain here is a much better story than the one that's actually being told. At least as far as Hugo's heart is concerned.

He wishes he could make it easier on him. But he can't make Eamon the bad guy just to assuage Hugo's guilt. That's an unfair game he won't play along with; that's one hurt he can't protect his brother from.

"Just let it go." Cal answers whatever it is that Hugo can't make himself say. "I'm not in the mood for this today."

"You have got to be fucking kidding me." Hugo shakes his head and turns away from them, staring into the woods as if thinking of disappearing himself. "You're all getting sucked into this. He's convinced all of you he isn't what he is."

"What am I?" Eamon asks.

There isn't any anger behind the question, and it doesn't

sound particularly mocking, and both of those things would confuse Felix if he hadn't already accepted that Eamon is just . . . Eamon. He's genuine. He's asking because he wants to know.

Hugo doesn't answer. So, Eamon asks again, "What am I, Hugo? You seem to know more about me than I know about myself. So *tell me*."

"I don't know what you are," Hugo snaps, turning back around. "But you aren't one of us. Cal might let you haunt her RV, but as soon as we get to Port Haven, you better stay the fuck away from me, and Felix, and Bird."

"What about me?"

The air shifts to make room for Bird's presence when they step into the circle of the campsite, hair still wet and their dirty clothes bundled against their chest. Hugo won't look at them. Felix watches his brother, hoping, hoping, but he knows some things are too late to hope for, even for a boy whose whole world has been stitched together from make-believe and resolution.

It's Eamon who finally answers them. "He was telling me to stay away from you."

"Why?" Bird's nose scrunches up, their eyes darting back and forth between the two.

"Because he believes I am dangerous, or at least wants you to. Because he is in love with you and our interacting makes him uncomfortable." Again, Eamon's words come without malice. The blow isn't even meant to be a blow. Felix wonders if that makes it hurt less or more when it lands and then thinks he already knows the answer.

"Oh." Bird is polite enough to have no other response to that, though Felix is sure there are a thousand things they could say.

Hugo stares at Eamon like he's thinking of roasting him over a fire; stares at him like he's already making a meal of his face.

Felix's chest aches for him and his anger and his pain that clouds everything else.

Because he knows the truth of Hugo's heart, and he knows his pain makes it difficult for him to recognize who he is beneath it. He knows how frantically he does not want to be backed into a corner and forced to play the cannibal in order to survive, just like Felix knows he would do exactly that if he convinced himself he was *already* in a corner.

He knows his brother never really wanted to be the one holding the butcher's knife and leading the lamb to slaughter.

Never, ever again.

Before

"Everything is going to be okay, darling," Daphne Beránek promised, gripping her two-year-old against her chest. "There's no reason to be afraid, Hugo. You are a brilliant boy, you know. That's why you get to do this."

She held her toddler's hand inside her own, helping him to guide the knife as long as his own forearm, as it began to carve the fawn's head from her neck. Her husband, Nevin, held the animal to the ground with one palm on her face, the other on her belly.

Charlotte screamed in desperate bleating gasps until she didn't anymore.

Hugo continued to wail long after she'd gone quiet. But he stopped trying to wrench his hand away when his wrist turned purple with the mottled reminders of his mother's resolve.

And all the while, Felix watched, silent, from his crib in the corner.

Before

The morning after the new moon, Nevin knelt with the fire at his back, looking up at his eldest son. He balanced a plate in one hand and brushed his knuckles down Hugo's cheek with the other.

"You haven't had anything to eat all day, bud."

Hugo said nothing. The little boy stared at the fire until it found a home in the hollows of his eyes.

"Here," Nevin whispered, pressing roasted meat past his child's lips, setting it between his teeth. "You earned this."

Something in Hugo's brain decided it had enough. It broke away from him, tucking itself into a grave somewhere in his body. Someday, a garden of rage would overgrow that burial ground and he would never quite understand why. But all of that would come later.

That morning, he chewed and swallowed and, blessedly, began to forget.

And baby Felix, cradled in Daphne's arms a few feet away, nursed from his mother's breast while she licked his sister from her fingers.

Chapter 23

Hugo

The others load up the last dregs of the RV and Hugo stays behind and sits near the embers of an extinguished fire, knowing that if he dares to enter that space with them too soon, he's going to do something *someone* will regret.

Bird stays with him. He wishes they wouldn't—he wants to scream and tell them to go away, to leave him alone, to not talk about whatever did or did not just happen here. But any of that would require acknowledging them at all, and that feels impossible. Instead, he sits and he stares at his hands. And when he cannot handle staring at his hands for a moment longer, he stares at the trees.

The trees will not hurt him, and he will not hurt them. When all becomes too much, Hugo goes to the woods. The trees' love is unconditional and, more importantly, uncomplicated.

Too long has passed by the time Bird finally speaks. Long enough that Hugo could almost have forgotten they were there at all, if it were possible for him *not* to feel Bird's presence anytime they were in the same fucking zip code.

"We don't have to talk about it," they say, which is a hell of a way to begin talking about a thing. "But—"

"But nothing. There's nothing for us to talk about."

There is so much they *could* talk about. There are lifetimes of words gone unspoken between them, and there is a very stupid part of Hugo that would like to lay them all out in the open for Bird's consumption. Let them know it all, let them see him for exactly what he is, and let them decide accordingly. If he would trust anyone with the ugly thing inside his body, it would be them.

And, he knows, that would be a mistake. This is why he cannot talk about this. Because something in him wants to trust Bird, and that stupid something might actually win if he lets up on its leash. And then?

Bad. Just bad.

Bird says nothing for a long enough moment that Hugo is naive enough to hope they might drop the conversation as advised. *Hope* is such a cancerous thing.

When they inevitably do speak again, they say, "You have to know I never stopped loving you."

God fucking dammit.

No, no, no.

He presses the heels of his palms to his face. He needs to forget.

Before

"Open the door! You can't actually be going through with this!"

Hugo pounded on the door of Holly's place so hard he thought it might just give way beneath his fist. He wished it would. Maybe that would make them afraid enough to understand why this was a bad idea—and it was a *bad* idea.

He called their name, not knowing it didn't feel like their name even then, and slammed his fist again. Again. Again.

Finally, it flung open. He almost ate shit, stumbling into the camper and catching himself with one hand on the nearest wall.

Golden eyes, bright and wet and furious, were only inches away from his own.

"What do you want, Hugo? I don't have much time."

"That's—that—you can't be serious." The coldness in the words, the detachment. Who the hell was this person? What had they done with *his* person? "You don't have much time? You aren't going! You can't actually go!"

"I've already done this with my mother." They take a deep breath and check their phone screen. "I'm sorry—I can't do this with you, too. Not again. We already had this conversation, and I told you how I felt."

"And I told you how *I* felt!" He pressed his hands to his chest. What upside-down version of reality was this? Where had they gotten trapped, in what vivid hallucination or nightmare, that the only person in the entire world who made him feel safe was leaving? Was leaving and didn't seem to care? "You can't do this to me!"

He threw his hands up and they flinched and he pretended not to notice.

"I'm not doing anything to you." They shook their head. "I'm doing this for me. It's about me. I told you—I can't keep doing this. My mom, my grandparents . . . they just keep getting weirder, and worse, and I'm . . . I'm dying here, Hugo. I feel like I'm going to die here."

"We're both going to die here! We're supposed to age and rot and die here together!" His voice cracked, throat threatening to come apart around the splintered edges of a sob. Whenever and however death eventually found them, it was always supposed to find them together. Because they were meant to *live* together first. "Look at me. You know I can't go with you."

"I—" A tear had the audacity to slip from their eye, leaving a glittering trail of starlight in its wake. "You're supposed to love me enough to let me go."

They might as well have slapped him, and all Hugo could see was red. For a moment, he was nothing but a carnivore, and they were nothing but a warm body with a wounded leg. He screamed, howling his rage in their face until it burnt the edges of his mouth and scattered sparks across the apples of their cheekbones. They yelped, scrambling away from him, swiping at their skin to brush the embers away.

Hugo stumbled backward, struggling to catch his breath. He stared at them, wild-eyed and hungry and knowing he needed to get as far away as he could.

"You . . . you were supposed to love me enough to stay." He shook his head, hands lingering on the edges of the door-way, like his body was still trying to grab on to the moment while the rest of him wanted so badly to get away. "Sometimes things get hard and it's scary, and yeah, maybe we both die, but when you love someone, you don't leave them to die *alone*. I would have never left you alone."

Their lower lip trembled, their hand pressed to their cheek. "I loved you enough that I would have forgiven you, if you had to."

Hugo howled and howled and slammed his fist through the window on Holly's door on his way out. Shards of broken glass erupted in the air and imbedded themselves in his hand. They reminded him of this moment long after the car came and his heart was carved away.

Chapter 24

Hugo

He pulls his hands away from his face and looks at the tiny white scars on his knuckles. He remembers the feeling of sitting alone and picking glass out of his skin for hours, knowing he was never going to get every sliver, some masochistic piece of him feeling grateful at the prospect.

"I know," he says, and he can't look at them. If he looks at them, this might all be over, and he needs it to not be over. "And you know what you know. And there's still nothing for either of us to say."

"You—how can you *say that*?" Their voice trembles. He can feel the air move as they shift closer to him. His own bones tighten their hinges in response. "There is so much for us to say. Don't you wonder if we were supposed to end up here? Maybe all of this is a second chance at something."

"Shut up." He winces, eyes sliding closed. "You need to stop, before this gets ugly."

"How do you imagine this getting any uglier? Three years

ago, you loved me so much you wanted us to die together, and now you can't even look at me."

"If I look at you for too long, Bird, we're not just going to die together—I'm going to find a way to kill you."

And just like that, the conversation evaporates. The tension brewing between them, the back-and-forth pressure that's been making his jaw hurt since Bird showed up again, all seems to just . . . ease up. He said the thing out loud, and no one died on the spot. He said the thing out loud, and he felt a little more like he could breathe.

Slowly, Hugo does manage to drag his eyes to Bird's face. They wince when he does, and he doesn't pretend not to notice. It's okay. He'll go back to looking away in a second.

"I love you," he admits, for the last time. "And I hate you for leaving me. And I can't be near you, because I don't *want* to want to hurt you."

"What . . ." Bird shakes their head. "I don't understand. You love me, but you hate me, and you . . ."

"If you even understood the things I want to do to you, you would be terrified. If I ever did half of them, we would never recover." He swallows. "I am not a good person, Bird. And I cannot love you in a way that you could survive. And so I can't look at you, and we can't talk about it, and there is no second chance, because I am fighting like *hell* not to let myself love you to the point of ruin."

Their breathing hitches. They lean away from him. It makes him want to claw his throat open, and it makes him breathe a sigh of relief. Finally, he looks away from them again.

"You could be a good person," they say, after a beat. "It isn't your fault, you know. They did this to you—the Caravan, Hugo, your parents and Basil and Cassandra—they trapped you in a thousand barbed-wire snares, trying to convince you you'd snared yourself willingly, that you wanted it. They did this shit to all of us."

"I know. And I know it doesn't change anything." He traces one scarred knuckle with the thumb on his other hand. "I am what I am."

"But you don't have to be. You don't have to accept the inheritance of their violence. You could change. If anyone could burn away the marks they left and start over, it would be you." Bird's voice trips over itself. "You could *learn* how to love me."

"Maybe. And I could still do every awful, unforgivable thing before I finally did. And by then, it'd be too late."

They shift again. He knows they're pulling their knees to their chest, resting their chin there. He knows it without having to look in their direction.

"This isn't fair."

"No—but it *is* what we are."

The door to Cal's RV pops open and Felix sticks his head out. At the sight of them—whatever they look like—he flushes, obviously embarrassed to be interrupting.

"Um, sorry. Was just letting you know we're ready to head out. Cal is threatening to drive off without you both, so."

Hugo nods and stands up. "No need. We're all finished here."

Finally.

Chapter ⚏

Hugo

When it all became too much, Hugo fled to the woods. This was nothing new.

The party was too much that night. The mothers were too frantic in their festivities, the elders too coiled and coy—or perhaps it was just him, a raw nerve, screaming and exposed. His eyes kept finding Bird, no matter how many times he tried to force them away. When they weren't on Bird, they were on Eamon.

He couldn't deal with either of those. And so he ran.

He ran from his problems and he tried to hide. He ran from his problems, and he tried to hide, and he thought about how he wished all of it could just disappear. All of them. If everyone else could just vanish overnight, maybe, *maybe*, the world would finally be safe for him to live in. Maybe every minute wouldn't still feel like he was eating barbed wire.

He thought about that, and he hid with the trees, and he almost didn't notice when the whispering started.

Almost. But Hugo saw things other people didn't. He saw

things coming that other people didn't want to look straight at. He always had.

When the whispering started in the woods, interrupting Hugo's fantasies of the entire Caravan disappearing, he moved toward it.

Chapter 25

Eamon

"We could get to Port Haven by tonight if we drove straight through," Cal suggests, one boot propped up on the dash of her RV while she studies the map spread over the steering wheel. "Or there's a beach *right* here with hookups. We could get a full night's sleep and still get there by early afternoon tomorrow."

Eamon glances out the window, as if he might be rewarded with a glimpse of this beach she is talking about. Naturally, there is nothing. They are sitting in a gas station parking lot, after all. Why did he think he might see the ocean behind the Chevron?

"Let's stop," Bird suggests. They're sitting up in the queen-sized bed, lounging against the pillows. Felix is asleep next to them, curled up with his head in their lap. Their fingers pull gently through the threads of his hair, knuckles rubbing the base of his oversized ears every time they go back for a new bunch. "We don't want to show up sleep deprived and delirious and not even be able to explain what's going on."

"Do you feel you can adequately explain what is going on if you manage to secure eight hours of sleep?" Eamon asks.

They roll their eyes at him, and he frowns. It was a genuine question.

"Anyone else give a shit one way or another?" Cal asks, eyes bouncing from one person to the next.

Eamon shakes his head.

Hugo, sitting at the kitchen table and staring into an empty coffee mug like he is looking for a message in the left-over grinds, does not respond at all.

"Great. Guess we're stopping." Cal folds the map back up and snaps her fingers at Eamon. "Shadow boy. Go put gas in the tank before we head to the shore."

Shadow boy is not a nickname he enjoys. Still, at least it makes it clear who she is addressing. Sometimes, the name Eamon hits his ear the wrong way. He is not entirely sure he will ever get used to it being his own. Whoever he is, he leans forward, pulling his back from the pantry door, and heads outside alone.

The sun is still up and only just beginning its descent, and the thrill of pleasure he experiences at such a perceived rarity is . . . peculiar. He knows the sun sets earlier in the cold months—though he does not know where he learned that or how long he has known it—but it seems as if the sun has been hiding for *so much* of their trip. Somehow, no matter how long the days stretch, the nights go on for even longer, plunging them into infinite darkness illuminated only by the occasional flickering pit-stop light bulb.

He removes his wallet from his back pocket, steps over to the pump, and—

Hm.

Well.

Odd.

Okay.

Tucking his wallet back into his pants, he turns right around and heads back to the RV. Cal looks up when he enters, raising her eyebrows.

"There is no card reader here."

Just like the other place, which would only let them pay in cash.

"That's . . . not possible." Cal scoffs, making her chair spin around by shoving off with her boot, then flying to her feet. She stomps down the steps beside him, mumbling something under her breath about having to do everything herself.

"Are you certain you know what a card reader looks like?" Hugo asks, perhaps deciding that sparring with Eamon holds more interest than the sludge at the bottom of his cup. "Would you like me to draw you a picture of one?"

"No." Eamon frowns. Why would he possibly want that? "If you believe I am missing it, you could simply go and locate it yourself."

Hugo grinds his teeth. Eamon wonders what it is he is imagining crushing between his molars. Unbidden, his pulse quickens.

"He's not missing it," Cal announces, storming back onto the RV and throwing herself into the captain's chair. "There's just no fucking card reader. Not at all."

"That's weird," Bird offers.

Cal does not say anything. She does give them a very *strong* look, clearly meant to communicate something Eamon does not understand, before grabbing her phone from the cup holder. "I wonder if there's some kind of national . . . I don't know. Something. What if we're in some weird state of emergency and we haven't heard anything? Dammit. I still don't have service—how the fuck do I not have service? We're like an hour outside of Portland. Does anyone else have service?"

Eamon does not even have a phone. Hugo shakes his head no.

"I . . . huh." Bird frowns, their hand stilling in Felix's hair. "I don't think I've seen my phone since the first day we were on the road. Weird. I forgot to keep looking for it."

Eamon has noticed the attachment other people seem to feel toward their phones. Forgetting theirs existed does not seem like something that would have just happened to Bird organically. Nor do the issues across the western half of the country with card readers and cell service. And Eamon wonders in what ways it is connected to a convoy of people being erased in the span of a few hours, and in what ways it has nothing to do with that at all.

"I will go inside and talk to the attendant." He turns toward the door. "Maybe they know something we do not. And maybe they will let me pay inside."

This is not a terrible plan, but it does *immediately* go terribly off-course.

Most everywhere they have stopped along this drive has been some quiet hole-in-the-wall, with peeling paint and dirt on every surface. This place is different. Inside, the gas station is the cleanest, brightest place Eamon has seen in . . . well, he cannot actually remember. The stark white fluorescents overhead are a sharp contrast to the soft glow of golden hour outside, and they make all the plastic wrappers on the shelves look brighter and more buyable. A bell chimes—sounding happy, somehow—overhead as the door swings closed behind him.

On the speakers, music plays, too quiet to be distinguishable but music nonetheless.

Eamon is not focused on any of that, though. He notes it all, but none of it is what seizes his attention. He is staring at the attendant behind the counter.

"Hi, welcome in," she says without looking up from a thick book in her hand.

"Hi."

How is this happening and what does it mean and is he just going crazy? That would, perhaps, make more sense. Eamon does not know what his life was like before his life was this. Maybe he has *always* been crazy. Maybe none of this is real. Somehow, he thinks that would be easier to explain than this—which he does not think he can explain at all.

He moves to the counter and places his hands on its cool surface. "Do you remember me?"

The attendant, in her little blue collared shirt, name tag written in swirly, glittery Sharpie, forces her eyes slowly to his face. There is a moment of confusion, followed by a toothy grin. "Oh my god, hi. What are *you* doing here?"

"I was wondering the same about you."

The girl behind the counter at the gas station in Oregon is the same girl who pulled over and asked him if he needed a ride on the highway in Utah. He is certain of this. Her face is not one he would have easily forgotten—her too-big green eyes, her thousand freckles, her delicately upturned nose and the softly rounded apples of her cheeks. Her thick blond hair, long enough that it hangs past her waist if left down, has been pulled into a massive bundle at the back of her head.

She laughs, looking around at the gas station behind him. "I work here."

He narrows his eyes and wonders if that is how he sounds when he answers people's questions sometimes. "Then why were you in Utah?"

"Well, why were you?" She smirks, laying her book spine-up on the counter, leaving it open to the page she is on. "I was on the way home from visiting family. *Why* are you so suspicious?"

Maybe that *is* the way he sounds when people ask him questions. The realization knocks him off edge, if only a little. Maybe he is crazy and maybe everything has gone turned upside down and maybe sometimes there are strange coincidences that do not mean anything more than they mean and trying to create a monster where only shadows exist does not do anything to help anyone.

"I am sorry." He sighs. "It has been a long few days. I was just surprised to see you again."

"Well . . ." She balances her chin in her hand, eyes twinkling. "I think it's a happy surprise. I was hoping you found your way home okay."

He does not tell her that he does not know where home is or if one even exists. He is learning to keep some thoughts to himself. Instead, he asks, "Do you know if there is something going on with the cellular service in this area?"

She frowns, cocking her head. "Ah, not that I know of. You need to make a phone call? We have a landline."

Eamon does not know anyone's phone number. He shakes his head. "Thank you, though. I need to get gas. Is there a reason there are no card readers at the pumps?"

"Oh, *that*." She rolls her eyes, sitting up a little straighter. "Owner yanked 'em all out a few months ago. Apparently, people were using prepaid cards with, like, a dollar left on them to fill up their tanks. It was a whole thing, totally drove him nuts. Like—I'm so sure *this* is better for business. Who's going to come inside to pay?"

"Me." He pulls his wallet out and tugs free the emergency credit card, sliding it across the counter to her. "I need one hundred dollars on pump four."

She grins, taking the card and turning to her cash register. "You got it."

As easy as that. Within seconds, he has his card back, and a receipt, and all of the suspicion from the last few minutes feels strange and faraway. As if he cannot entirely remember why he was so suspicious at all. Perhaps, sometimes, a thing is just exactly what it appears to be. Perhaps he spends too much of his time looking for explanations that are not needed and maybe not even there to begin with.

"Till next time." She smiles, balancing her chin in her hand.

"Next time?"

"Sure." She shrugs. "I figure maybe we're supposed to be in each other's stories, you know? Some people just are."

He considers that. He does not know why it makes his heart feel strange and lofty. It feels as if he is suddenly meant to be sprinting—but should he be running toward something, or away?

"Next time," he agrees. The bell dings again on his way out.

Chapter 26

Cal

For the only time in her life, Cal can't seem to take her eyes off a boy.

Parked right along the shoreline, she finishes getting the RV connected to the hookups at the campsite while Felix gets a fire going in the pit. When she finishes, she has every intention of offering to take over for him—until she notices Eamon, standing a few yards away, his profile facing her as he stares out at the ocean. And something in his face takes her so off guard that her words freeze before they have a chance to leave her mouth.

The salt air tickles her cheeks and makes her shaggy hair dance against her face. The smell of seaweed and sand and the whole wide ocean engulfs her, making her toes curl. She rocks back on her heels. And still, she can't look away from Eamon.

He stands directly at the spot where the gentle waves of low tide meet the rocky shore. His shoes are getting wet, though he doesn't seem to notice. His red eyes are latched on to the sunset dipping behind the sea, the way the orange-and-pink light reflects off the surface of the water. His lips are parted like he's in shock, or . . . awe.

"Do you see him?" she asks, voice soft—she doesn't actually want him to hear her.

Meandering around the campsite collecting well-worn sea glass and pebbles, Bird pauses. They and Felix both look to Cal, and then Eamon.

"Hm." Bird stands straighter, tilting their head. They stroke one rock between the pad of their thumb and the knuckle of their middle finger. "Is he okay?"

"I . . ." Cal struggles against the tightening of her throat. "I don't think he's ever seen the ocean before."

"Oh." Felix breathes the word like a sigh, or a prayer, or both.

The three of them stand there and watch him watch the water until the sun sets fully and the night crawls in around their shoulders. Only then does Eamon turn to face them, the campfire casting shadows on his face when he does.

Cal thinks he might blush when he sees them staring. But it's hard to tell.

"Where is Hugo?" is the first and only thing he asks.

"Oh, uh." Cal hadn't actually realized Hugo wasn't outside with them. She was too busy enjoying the blessed quiet of his absence.

"He's still inside," Felix answers, rubbing his palms together in front of the flames. "He's . . ."

"Pouting?" Cal asks.

Felix gives her a *look*. "He's just having a hard day."

What Cal would like to say is that Hugo's entire life has been one hard day after another, each of them stacked on top of each other until they made some kind of fucked-up Jenga tower of trauma. Maybe not a Jenga tower. That implied some instability. Hugo's trauma is perfectly cemented, like brick—and he walks around using it to hit everyone else over the head.

She *doesn't* say that, because she's on this new kick where she tries not to be a total shithead every waking minute. So far, it's lasted about twelve hours and she is proud of herself.

Bird drops onto the piece of driftwood Felix is using as a bench, settling in next to him. Eamon joins them on the other side, on a smaller piece of his own. After a moment, Cal sinks into a crouch, forearms stretched across her knees so she can turn her palms to the fire.

For a while, no one says anything, but it isn't quiet. The waves echo off the cliffs as they beat against the shore, the jutting stone hills looming all around them like sleeping guardians at their posts. Actual birds cry out in the distance. From somewhere too far offshore to see, a pod of something is swimming together, occasionally breaking past the surface of the water to let out a song.

When Cal does speak, she addresses Eamon. "I've been thinking about what you said. About the Caravan not telling us the truth about where we come from."

Everyone, not just Eamon, turns to look at her.

He nods but says nothing. She wonders if there is a silent understanding between them or if she is projecting—again—her feelings onto a guy who may as well have been a blank canvas as of a week ago.

"I've been thinking about the possibility that we aren't found but made."

"What do you mean?" Felix demands, eyebrows knotting.

Cal sighs and shrugs. "He's right—it's weirdly coincidental how the Caravan just happens to always find us, how we've never heard stories of people like us existing that the Caravan *didn't* know about. And that none of us have any memory of what life was like before?"

"Sometimes coincidences are just that." Eamon sounds uncertain he believes his own words.

"And sometimes they're patterns," Bird answers, eyes on Cal. They nod. "I've been thinking about it, too. I've always known my mom and the others were capable of lying. I don't think there's anything they wouldn't do if they convinced themselves it was somehow sacred."

"How . . . how would they be *making* us?" Felix asks, expression nauseated.

"No—*us*. Not you." Cal shakes her head.

Bird agrees. "People like you and I were born into the Caravan. If Calliope's right, I think people like you and me are . . . the next step in whatever they're doing."

Special children with special gifts. Some more special than others.

Felix's cheeks pale. Cal wonders if they're thinking about the same very special child. She doesn't ask.

"But *how*? And . . . and from *what*?"

"Like where did we come from?" Cal shrugs. "I don't know. But if we're right, they definitely don't want us to know. If we're right, it's on purpose that nobody can remember anything."

"I remember some things."

Eamon says it with such casualness, she could've believed he was commenting on the weather if she hadn't heard the actual words. Cal stares at him, blinking. Felix's eyes widen and widen and widen.

It's Bird who asks, "Excuse me? What do you mean you remember some things? No one ever remembers anything."

"So I have been told." Eamon's eyes flick toward the RV. "There is not much to go off of; it is mostly flashes and feelings. But I was someone else, once. Of that, I am certain."

"Human, you mean." Cal doesn't mean for the words to come out biting, but they do anyway. She isn't angry at him. She's angry at people who aren't here and can't answer for what they did—if they did what she suspects, what a quiet, vicious part of her has maybe suspected for a while. "We used to be human."

Eamon doesn't disagree, but he doesn't really acknowledge her at all. Cal follows his gaze to the RV window.

Hugo stands on the other side, eyes locked with Eamon's. Cal knows he can't hear them through the closed glass, but she'd almost think he could, with the expression on his face.

Felix sighs and stands up. "I don't know—that's a lot. How can you know for sure?"

Bird tips their head up and looks to the sky. Their golden eyes, twin suns, map the constellations overhead. "Maybe we can't. Some things are unknowable. If I had to guess, I think there's more we'll never begin to understand than there is that we can ever figure out."

"I need to check on him," Felix mumbles, inclining his head toward the glowering boy in the window. He slips away, and as he opens the door to the RV, the window curtain falls closed over Hugo's face.

"I believe I need to take a walk." Eamon stands, disappearing into the darkness almost as quickly as he does.

In the blink of an eye, Cal and Bird are suddenly alone in front of the fire. The heaviness of the conversation hangs over them like a weighted blanket. There is the threat of suffocation, but somehow it feels like a small comfort.

Breathing as deep as she can, feeling a little like she can't get her lungs all the way filled, Cal shifts from her crouched position to join Bird on the driftwood bench. Not because they're alone now. Just because suddenly there's an open seat.

Bird prods the fire with a metal poker. "So."

"So," Cal agrees. "What do you think?"

"About?" Bird raises their eyebrows, tilting their chin in Cal's direction. She waves her hands around vaguely, and Bird nods. "I think . . . it makes my skin crawl to think about being the Caravan's best beloved pet project that they've been *breeding toward* for some secret, stupid reason that probably has something to do with the phases of the fucking moon."

Yeah, that sounds about right. Cal grimaces at the word "breeding." Not that it isn't the right word. Just . . . yikes. Gross.

"And it makes me think about . . ." Bird's voice trails off. They tilt their head toward the RV. "You know?"

"Yeah. I was thinking about her, too. The way they talk about what they did to her—like they're fucking gleeful."

"Like, what if . . . Ugh. I don't know." They set the poker down to rub their hands over their face. "How is it possible that our childhoods could have been even more fucked up than we realized?"

Cal nods, picking up Bird's discarded poker. They press the spokes into the red hunks of wood at the bottom of the pit, watching the black marks that appear as it rapidly cools at the metal's touch.

"What about you?" Bird leans in and curls their arms around their shins, resting their cheek against their knees. "You might've been human once."

"Not just human. A baby. A human baby that someone . . ." She doesn't actually know how she could've gone from one to the other. Cal's jaw clenches, her hand tightening around the handle of the stick. "Yeah. Skin—crawling."

"You would've had a family." Bird sits up straight, suddenly, as if the thought has just occurred to them. "You . . . you could still have a family. If the Caravan took you, if they thought you were missing, if . . ."

Cal's jaw clenches and clenches and she worries she might break a tooth. Whatever Bird sees on her face, their voice trails off.

When they start up again, it's to say, "You already thought of that."

"If I was a human baby that the Caravan kidnapped and experimented on, and I have a family out there who've spent the last sixteen years missing me—yeah. It's probably for the best that they just keep thinking I'm dead. As far as I'm concerned, to them, I am."

Bird doesn't ask why. Cal looks into their face, the firelight casting a mask of dancing shadows along their jaw and mouth, and sees the unspoken question hanging like an unloosed arrow from their Cupid's bow.

"Whatever I am now, if that family actually exists, I think seeing me like this would just hurt them worse."

"You . . ." Bird frowns, biting at their lower lip. Their hands twist in their lap, like they're trying to make a Rubik's Cube from their knuckles. "You can still get close to people. You don't have to go put your mouth on everyone who cares about you."

Cal's eyes follow Bird's lips as they shape each word one

by one. When they press their tongue to the corner of their mouth in thought, her own parts.

Hm. She swallows and gives an internal shake. "Sure. No, I know. Obviously. But it feels a lot like walking around with a loaded gun in my hand. I'm pretty sure that's how everyone else feels, too. You wouldn't want me getting too close, would you?"

Bird's eyes slowly lower from Cal's to land on her mouth. They swallow this time. Cal can see their pulse bouncing in their throat. "Define too close."

She doesn't. Instead, she leans in.

Inches separate them now. Cal's mouth hovers close enough to Bird's skin that she can convince herself she *hears* their heartbeat, too. Maybe that's just the whooshing of the ocean.

She isn't sure what she expects to happen. If she had guessed beforehand, maybe she would've pictured Bird pushing her away, or at least scrambling back themself. Maybe she would've expected to get yelled at. Or at least for the personified will-o'-the-wisp to flinch at their new proximity.

None of that happens, though. Instead, Bird sways even closer, as if pulled forward by some force outside their own body.

Quietly, they say, "Okay. Okay, sure. It would be a *very* bad idea for us to get too close."

"Yes. Obviously." Cal is going to fucking puke. Her whole entire body trembles with a want so palpable she believes it would wreck her forever if she let herself look at it directly. "Because I could kill you."

"And I could break your heart," Bird counters, in a tone

which implies that outcome would be even worse than their own murder by envenoming.

"We are both fucked up beyond repair," Cal whispers. Has she edged in closer? Can she feel the warmth of Bird's mouth on hers already, or is she imagining it? "It would be so toxic."

"Irresponsibly so . . ." Bird agrees.

Cal is going to kiss them. She isn't sure she makes her mind up about it so much as she realizes there's no stopping what's going to happen. She tilts her head forward, her lips parting, searching, desperate to know what Bird tastes like, and—

A shadow in the shape of a boy appears beside them. His black hand moves silently between their mouths, curling over Cal's, his thumb pressing into the center of her tongue to keep it in her mouth.

Directly on the other side of the shadow's wrist, his hand covering Cal's mouth like a muzzle, she hears Bird *whimper*. The air punches out of her until she's panting.

She doesn't know what she's doing, not in any part of her operated by logical thought, but she wraps her lips around the shadow's thumb. Her blunt front teeth pin the digit down into the warm, wet cage of her mouth, and offer it like a sacrifice for her throbbing fangs. This time, Cal doesn't hesitate—she bites, hard.

The shadow does not pull away or try to stop her. But from somewhere to the side, someone groans.

Cal and Bird look at the same moment, staring across the fire, where Eamon has returned and is watching them. No, not only watching them—*protecting them* from themselves. His shadow is immovable and unkillable, and it cups Cal's jaw while she savors the cold, soft feeling of its hand in her mouth.

Shuddering, Bird presses their forehead to the back of the shadow's hand. They struggle to catch their breath but still say, "Thank you."

"Anytime," Eamon offers.

Cal does not know what deeply disturbed part of her is electrified by that word. But she growls and bites even harder.

Before

"It's done." A senior member of the Caravan hovered on the doorstep of Basil and Cassandra's RV. In the still predawn light, the world hovering on the blade's edge between star-scattered black and the powdery cornflower of a new day, his face appeared pale and half-shadowed. "The pyre is prepared."

"Thank you." The serpents making up Cassandra's scalp hissed and slithered as she pressed her fingertips tenderly to her parishioner's cheek. "The ceremony will be held as soon as the sun rises. You will let the others know?"

"Of course, miss." He swallowed, eyes twitching toward her shoulder. Despite his obvious curiosity, he did not dare to shift his weight and crane his neck, did not make any blatant attempt at investigating the goings-on inside. Still, he could not seem to help himself but to ask, "What about the child? What will you do with her?"

Cassandra's hand slipped from his face, and the man flinched in response to her antonymous strike. "We will do precisely what we always do. We will take care of our people. Have I given you any reason at all to doubt that?"

"Of course not. No, no, of course not. It's just that—"

"Do you believe exiling the child will undo what has already been done? An eye for an eye, and we lose another of our kind—is that what you would like to see happen?"

"I would never suggest that. But she's—"

"It has been a long night, and neither of us has slept. Perhaps we are both susceptible to speaking rashly in this moment." Cassandra curled her fingers around her doorknob, teeth gnashing as she began to pull it closed. "Goodbye."

The chickadees and mourning doves began their chorus just as the Caravan's leader, with the slam of a door, banished the outside world from her presence. Head throbbing—from exhaustion or stress or a likely combination of the two and more—she turned to make her way toward the camper's back bedroom.

Cassandra and her husband kept their makeshift home less cluttered than many of their followers. Their RV was still in much of its original state, clean and well organized. They did not need the embellishments that the others enjoyed, or the accommodation the members of their group so often wanted. To live this life at all was an embellishment—to breathe every day was an accommodation that had once not been promised.

Still, there were scattered, if subtle, indications of who lived in the portable house. A very old doll, tattered and dirty, slumped over on top of their refrigerator, watching everything that happened with its button eyes. A few feathers had fallen to the ground, making homes for themselves in well-tucked corners of the linoleum floor. Cassandra's journal, a compilation of her findings, a study in magic which may as well have been the Caravan's sacred text, was the only book. It sat in the center of the very clean kitchenette table, its black binding standing out against the white with a near violent demand to be noticed.

She pushed aside the accordion door and stepped into her bedroom—each of Cassandra's movements were as silent as death, a second-nature fact of her existence now, a consequence of years spent practicing to be a ghost. The room beyond the door was not much different than the rest of the camper, its decor practical and clean. A single black wardrobe, locked with a padlock, was the only suggestion that something might be peculiar here. But there was nothing of too much interest in the wardrobe, only the collection of knives the couple used in their sacrificial rituals.

Basil sat at the edge of the bed, slumped over with his head in his hands, wings drooping listlessly at his sides. So lost in whatever misery had taken hold of him, he didn't even stir when Cassandra entered. When she approached and pressed one soft hand to his collar, he only swayed closer to the touch, still not raising his gaze to meet her wondering stare.

"Are you thinking about Miriam?" she asked, thumb petting back and forth against his throat, careful not to cut him with her nail. Her crown of snakes squirmed in a quiet, watchful anticipation.

"What?" Basil raised his head, eyebrows tight with confusion. It took a moment for something to click into place, the name registering. "Oh. Miriam. Yes. That was unfortunate. She was a devoted member of our people."

She was, Cassandra supposed, and she had given her life for it tonight. But that was clearly not what was plaguing her husband.

Her eyes moved over him, brushing past the soft expanse of his wings to search the bed beyond. It did not take long for her to find what she was hunting. Tucked between two pillows, the baby girl was fast asleep, her brown curls tousled, her mouth puckered in a pout and her little fists clenched, even in sleep. She was a beautiful child, and somehow that made her even more tragic. Cassandra wished this little one had never existed in the first place, and, if she had answered the earlier question with any honesty, she had no idea what to do with her now that she did.

This girl, far more likely than their freshly deceased disciple, was causing Basil's distress.

As if sensing the dilemma hanging in the air with them, her husband offered, his mouth twisting to press against her wrist, "We could exalt her."

To hold communion with this child? It was not as if the idea had not occurred to Cassandra. But this girl was not a savior. Through no fault of her own, she was one of their most tainted. They could not punish her for that, not in fairness. But they could not embrace her, either, lest all of the Caravan succumb to her venom.

"No." Cassandra shook her head, serpents hissing. A forked tongue tickled against the shell of her ear. "She's unfit for such a fate."

"She is a danger to all of our kind," Basil warned, without necessity. Cassandra was aware of the problem this child posed.

Still, she said, "We are all a danger to each other, in one way or another. We cannot cast her out. She will stay with us. We will keep her safe. But we must always be watchful, now that we know what she is capable of."

Her husband turned his head to gaze on the sleeping toddler, pain etched into every crook of his expression. He need not say what permeated every inch of this moment. They both understood. This child's life was a tragedy.

It was cruel and deeply unfair, whatever circumstances had led to her becoming what she was. Cassandra's heart ached. She couldn't help but wonder if it had been the child's own mother who had done this, the same way *Cassandra's* mother had been the one to turn her into the monster she'd become.

A true death would have been kinder, in some ways. When Cassandra's mother, overwhelmed and at the end of her rope, deteriorating within her own mind and without anyone to rescue her, had gripped the once soft curls of her daughter's hair and held her beneath the bath water until her breathing stopped—in so many ways, it would have been kinder if Cassandra had simply died that day. At least the universe was benevolent enough to take away the memory of her own torture, tucking it somewhere on a shelf just out of reach. Cassandra knew her origin only from her mother's pleas for forgiveness; knew she had once been a happy child only from the evidence of her life scattered around the home she was forced to hide in. Her first true memory was waking in the walls, a phantom, a somehow still flesh-and-bone reminder of the worst thing her mother had ever done.

This child can never know she was made victim to the most unforgivable sin before she was even able to speak; that she was ruined and then abandoned, left to rot in her own damnation if the Caravan had never swept her up. None of their followers can ever know the truth of where they come from, lest it lead them to searching for answers in the human world, the world that slaughtered them in the first place—or worse, should they realize not *all* of their parishioners were gathered so serendipitously.

Some tragedies occur by the cruel hand of fate. Others

need to be manufactured. A community needs numbers, after all, however one can proselytize them.

But for her part, Cassandra would hold the truth. She would grieve what could have been. And she would give the girl a new life—whether it would be worth living or not.

Chapter 27

Felix

Ever since this began, Felix has been worried about getting to Port Haven. There's just so much he isn't sure of. That uncertainty is devastating for a boy building on faith.

What if things aren't right? What if everything goes badly? What if someone gets hurt?

Today, though, on the last leg of the drive, rapidly approaching the settlement that can only be ten, maybe fifteen minutes away now, he feels better. Things in the RV just feel . . . better. The tension and fighting, all of it seems to have expanded to the point of bursting, expanding until it couldn't anymore, and now they're all falling into a rhythm together.

Of course, Hugo is . . . taking some time to adjust to things, but that's okay and it makes sense and Felix isn't upset with him. He knows his brother will come around. There's nothing that could happen between them that would make things not okay anymore. Not even this.

And everyone else . . . yeah. They're all going to be okay. He knows it. They'll figure it out together, all of them. They'll get to Port Haven and they'll face whatever they find there as a family and then it'll just—it'll all be okay.

It's okay. Everything is okay. Felix knows this. Felix believes this, he *does*, and so he knows that it *will be*. Yes. Yeah. Yes.

The problem, of course, is that Felix is a liar.

You and I both know that, don't we, reader? And he can try his hardest to convince himself he believes it's all going to work out in the end, but faith isn't something a person can fake until it's real. And somewhere in the overflowing landscape of his head, Felix *knows* a black seed of doubt has already started to take root. He knows he's been outrunning it this entire time.

He can lie to himself all he wants and say he believes there's still a shot at a happy ending. But you and I can see there aren't that many pages left in this book.

They have to leave the RV half a mile from their destination, when the road gets too bumpy—nothing but rocks and sand in any direction—and narrow to continue, and walk the rest of the way. They make the walk in relative silence, none of them speaking to the others. Felix wonders if they're nervous. Maybe they're just tired. *He's* tired. Definitely.

Besides, it's nice, right? That they can enjoy companionable quiet together?

Right?

Port Haven is marked by a rickety, weatherworn wooden sign, almost hidden in the overgrown stalks of green and gold beach grass. Cal and Bird exchange a look, then start heading down a path just beyond, marked with pieces of driftwood and sparkling agate, like a witchy, coastal breadcrumb trail. Eamon trails after them, but stops a couple of yards in to look back at the brothers.

His eyes move slowly and carefully over Hugo, as if he's trying to memorize every line. He doesn't address him, though, and looks to Felix before he says, "What are you waiting for?"

Felix wants to reassure him. He tries to smile, and it feels weird on his face. Like maybe, by accident, he's grimacing instead. Why would he do that? Why would he do that when everything is fine?

"Yeah, Felix," Hugo drawls, putting a hand on the center of his brother's back. "Is something wrong?"

Eamon frowns.

"No!" Felix tries again at a smile. He's not sure if he succeeds this time, but he does manage to convince his feet to move. He surges forward, heading down the path, motioning for Eamon and Hugo to follow behind him. "Of course not. Everything is totally fine. Come on!"

Everything is totally fine.

Everything is totally fine.

Everything is totally fine.

Everything is—

Oh.

At the end of the path, Cal and Bird stand in a massive clearing, a stretch of nothing but sand as far as anyone can see. They're standing on a beach, he knows they are, but there's no ocean here. It's as if the sea forgot it was supposed to meet the shore, and all that was left was the sand, on and on and on like desert dunes. And nothing else. No RVs or campers. No tents. No campfires or sleeping bags or any signs of life at all.

There is no Port Haven.

Chapter

Eamon

He had not intended to get into a staring contest with Bird. They had just been there, and his eyes had just fallen on them, and he had decided not to look away.

Of all the confusing, conflicting, upsetting, and now nude pieces of the Caravan, all he was trying to piece together both in and out of his own head, Bird was a piece which did not frighten him. He was certain they had never met before, but something about them felt familiar anyway. Not in the way Hugo felt familiar, the way Hugo felt like a haunting in Eamon's memory, but in a way that told him, maybe, whoever he was before, Bird was someone he would have liked.

When they finally looked away, breaking his stare to stomp off in the same direction they'd arrived from, Eamon continued his initial search for the ghost himself.

There you are.

Hugo was doing a stomping of his own, on the outskirts of the celebration, pushing his way through throngs of dancing partygoers to head in the direction of the woods. When he disappeared into the embrace of the trees, Eamon got itchy.

He did not like when Hugo left the supervision of his stare; he did not like not knowing exactly what the boy was doing. Especially if he was in the woods.

And so, quietly, he slipped out of Mister Basil and Miss Cassandra's RV and followed after him.

Chapter 28

Bird

By the time Bird makes a full circle with their eyes, slowly spinning to examine every direction of the wasteland that was meant to be a haven, the path that led them here has already disappeared. There is no more trail lined with corvid trinkets. It is possible, and they must consider, there never was one to begin with.

"I don't understand."

The words feel foolish as soon as they've left their mouth. Sometimes when Bird speaks, they feel as if they're setting their ill-behaved problem children loose on a playground, where they will inevitably play poorly with others and force them to, embarrassed, apologize to someone's parents.

Bird was *never* a problem child. They were, however, dumped at many public parks. They did have many parents apologize directly to them when their shitty kids pushed the weird girl off the swing. Somehow, that always felt even more humiliating than being pushed in the first place.

"What happened here?" They try again, asking a question

this time in the hopes of more accurately getting their point across.

Felix walks forward, toward the vast expanse of nothing. Forever and ever and ever, the sand dunes stretch and stretch. How did they get here? Where did the *trees* go? With his back to them, staring out at nothing, nothing, he asks, "Do you think . . . do you think everyone here disappeared, too? What if it . . . what if it wasn't just the Caravan that went missing—maybe it was anyone nonhuman. Maybe we're the only ones left."

"Or maybe we're the ones who disappeared," Calliope corrects.

Bird turns toward her. The girl has her arms crossed tightly, nails digging into her own biceps as if she might keep herself tethered into her own body. "What do you mean?"

"Think about it." She shakes her head, looking up at the sky—the strange yellow sky, the same shade of golden fawn as the sand. Forever and ever and ever. "No one's cell phone has been working for days. The thing with the card readers. I . . . sometimes it's felt like I'm losing chunks of time. Like one second, it's day and the next it's night and I don't have any idea how I got from one to the other."

Ugly pieces begin clicking themselves into place in Bird's head, but they don't want to look at them. How long have they been on the road, really? How many days? How many nights? How is it possible that this time together has stretched on forever and passed in the blink of an eye? And is that a work of some grim magic, or just the fear of their family's disappearance and the monotony of an endless road?

Eamon crouches down and sifts a handful of sand between his fingers. When he speaks, his voice is quiet, a question meant for himself. "Where are we?"

Bird looks again at the sky. The endlessness of the sky, uninterrupted by stars or—

"The moon," they say, gaze jerking back to the others, eyes widening. "I . . . I haven't seen the moon in days. It's like we're . . . we're . . ."

"Still having a new moon." Calliope nods. "Yeah. You're right. You're totally right. And . . . you guys . . . have any of you actually seen another person? Any other person? Since the Caravan disappeared?"

That is ridiculous. Of course they've seen other people. They've seen campers at campsites and cars in parking lots and . . . and those things aren't actually people.

Have they seen a single car driving on the highway at the same time as them?

Bird's knees sway, threatening to go out from under them. "Are we . . . are we dead?"

"I saw someone." Eamon stands up, brushing sand from his fingertips against the thigh of his jeans. "There was a girl—I ran into her twice."

"Where was she? What was her name?"

"What'd she look like?"

He holds his palms up, fingers splayed. "Uh—okay. I saw her once after the truck broke down in Utah, and then . . . somehow, she was there again, in Oregon. She was working at the gas station."

"And you didn't think this was important to tell anyone?" Calliope demands. "That's fucking bizarre and you just—let it go?"

Eamon stares at her for a too-long moment, and Bird can see the way he writes his next line in his head before he says it. "I realize how this sounds. But until just now, I forgot it happened."

Calliope narrows her eyes but doesn't accuse him of lying.

Bird doesn't think he is. They do think they're going to vibrate right out of their fucking body.

"She was pretty," he continues. "Big green eyes. Lots of freckles. Her name was . . . She didn't tell me her name. She had a name tag, though. I saw it, it was . . . Oh. Charlotte. The name on her name tag was Charlotte."

Bird's body goes so cold they can no longer feel their hands. A wind begins to pick up, kicking sand around their legs. Their head turns, slowly, toward Hugo.

He hasn't said anything since they arrived. He'd walked in behind Felix and Eamon, expression stony and sour and far away, and he'd been silent the entire time they tried to figure out what the hell was going on. Now he continues to say nothing. He just glares, some malevolent twist to his features Bird can't remember ever seeing before. It makes them want to cry, or throw up, or both.

Slowly, Bird follows the line of his glare until their eyes land on Felix.

He's just beginning to turn his head away from the sky, looking toward the rest of them. Tears have filled his eyes. When he speaks, it comes out sharp and unpredictably shaky, like the jagged edges of a torn-open whisper.

"Please understand . . . I didn't have any other choice."

Chapter 24

Felix, Continued

He was just beginning to talk himself down from his panic attack, his shaking finally easing up and his chest loosening bit by bit, when the shadow crept up and stretched over him. Felix jumped and made a pitiful sound of surprise, his eyes widening as he whipped around.

"Oh. Hey."

Eamon tilted his head at him. "I am sorry. I did not mean to scare you."

"No, no, it's okay. I—um. I scare easily." Felix smiled. That wasn't entirely true, he had a pretty high tolerance for just about everything. But it made people feel better, sometimes, when he played into the idea they had of him. "Is everything okay?"

"Ah." Eamon glanced around him, looking deeper into the woods, as if trying to find someone with his eyes. "I am not sure. I watched Hugo run off alone. I was going to follow him."

Felix appreciated that Eamon couldn't seem to bring himself to lie. As weird as it sounded to admit he was just stalking someone into the forest, he just . . . admitted it. It was one of the weird little quirks Felix had noticed ever since Eamon stumbled into the Caravan campground when he did. He wished he knew if Eamon had always been like this, or if this was something Hugo and Felix did to him.

"I'm sure he's probably okay." Felix did not share Eamon's desire not to lie. Felix loved to lie. Felix lied as often as he could, because, he knew, most people vastly preferred being lied to. It was part of why he found Eamon so charming. They couldn't possibly have been more different. "Did you need something from him?"

"I . . . do not think so." Eamon rubbed his thumb across his lower lip, occasionally looking up and into the distance, as if still hoping to get a glimpse of the other Beránek brother. "I think there is something unwell about him."

That was such an interesting and fun way for Eamon to say he thought Hugo was off-putting as fuck. Felix smiled, placing a hand on Eamon's arm. He gave it a little squeeze. "Hey. I know the last few weeks have been . . . so confusing. And hard. But you don't need to worry about Hugo. He's not a threat to you."

Not anymore, anyway.

Eamon swallowed, paused, and eventually nodded. "Perhaps you are right. I think . . . perhaps the last few weeks have been too much for me. The strain may be affecting my ability to see things clearly."

"Everyone's new at one point. You're doing really great."

"I appreciate you saying that. But . . ." Eamon shook his head. Felix frowned at his expression, letting his hand fall away. "I do not feel as if this is where I belong. I am incredibly grateful to the help the Caravan has given me, but . . . I do not think this is where I should stay."

"Wait . . . no, you don't—you can't mean—" No, that was simply not an acceptable outcome. That wasn't what Felix was planning. That wasn't supposed to happen. It didn't make any sense. It was just—that was not right. No. Try again. "You have to stay with us. Where else would you go?"

"I am not sure. But I am sure I will figure it out with a map and some time."

Felix's jaw twitched. His hands balled at his sides into two small, vicious fists. "No. You can't go."

Eamon frowned. "What do you mean by that?"

"I mean you cannot leave. I won't let you."

Felix was so fucking tired of people leaving. Everybody always wanted to leave; everybody was always so eager for something better. Or else they got taken away. They got cut away from him, or cut open, and the result was still the same.

Felix's entire life was a graveyard for people who were supposed to love him. He was so tired of reading tombstones and pretending they were bedtime stories.

"Felix . . ." Eamon began, holding out his hands in a gesture as if to say, "Easy now."

Whatever he might have wanted to say, Felix didn't give him the chance. He reached up to clasp his hands on either side of Eamon's face, holding his skull between his palms. And for one brief, terrifying moment, Felix *believed* Eamon would never be able to leave him.

And in that moment, there was a stillness. Maybe it felt longer in Felix's head, just long enough for him to begin to wonder if he'd made a mistake and it hadn't worked.

And then—

Eamon's eyes rolled back into his head until they were nothing but whites. His body crumpled to the forest floor.

And the real meat of him, the *thing* that made Eamon whoever he was and whatever he had once been, was pulled directly into Felix's head.

It was eerily similar to the astral projecting, only played out in reverse. It was . . . easy. All it took was him believing he could do it. And Felix could *feel* Eamon. He could *feel him* inside his head.

What a fitting resting place, after all they'd been through together. Now they never had to be apart again.

A smile tugged at Felix's mouth. He never had to be apart from anyone again. Not from anyone he didn't want to lose.

He could keep them *all* safe.

And he believed that was exactly what he was going to do.

Chapter 29

Hugo

When Felix starts to cry, the light brown sky opens up like a zipper coming undone to reveal the shimmering, endless black beneath, and rain begins to pour into the valley.

No—not a valley. Not a desert anymore. Woods. They don't transform from one shape to another; they simply *were* sand dunes, and now they're trees.

Around him, the others are beginning to feel their feelings. Cal's breathing quickens as panic starts to flood her system. Eamon's face drains of blood, shell-shocked as he watches the world come apart. Bird's skin begins to flicker off and on and off and on like every old, broken light bulb along their road trip through Felix's imagination.

Hugo has felt his feelings.

He watches Felix's shoulders shake as his brother sobs, and he feels the way the earth rattles underneath them in response.

"You had other choices," Hugo reminds him, unwilling to let Felix get away with his lie. Not this time.

"Not good ones!" the other boy shrieks, and a bolt of lightning jettisons itself across the unzipped sky.

"Felix, what did you do?" Bird demands, voice cracking.

"I protected you . . . I just . . . I had to protect you . . ." He shakes his head, lower lip trembling. "I'm always protecting you. You didn't understand how bad the outside world was, but I believed you would come home. And you did."

"You . . . what?" He can't make himself look away from Felix's face to study Bird's expression, but their tone is shaky enough he worries they might pass out. "What did you *do*?"

"I doubt he *did* anything." Hugo shakes his head. His heart feels like a love letter crushed in an ungrateful palm. Maybe it's always felt that way. Or maybe he doesn't have a heart at all and this is just indigestion. "He's convinced himself his magic doesn't have limits, and now he sees proof of that in everything."

"Confirmation bias," Cal mumbles.

"LOOK AT WHAT I MADE US!" Felix screams, throwing out his arms.

The tapestry changes again. They're standing at the top of a cliff overlooking the ocean. It's so real, Hugo can taste the salt when the wind brushes his mouth.

"Look at what I made us," he repeats, softer this time, and the scene changes once more.

Now they're all standing together in a mass grave. A fawn with her throat slit stumbles toward him and nuzzles her bloody maw against Hugo's hand.

He winces, closing his eyes, and that hand curls into a fist. "Get her away from me."

When he opens his eyes again, they're back in the woods.

These woods are different than the last. Aspen and pine. Colorado.

The last place any of them were seen alive.

Good. This is where he needs them to be for what's going to happen next. He's been thinking about it for a while now.

Hugo has been putting the pieces together from the very beginning, the morning of the disappearance, but he hadn't wanted to believe it. And he hadn't let himself *really* entertain the idea until Eamon's shadow tried to kill him.

Up until then, Hugo had already managed to piece together that *they* were the ones who were missing. They were the ones being hunted. They were the ones who were in danger. But he still hoped, against all fucking hope, it was Eamon who was behind it.

See, he needed it to be Eamon who was behind it. He needed Eamon's power to run that deep and stretch that far. He needed it, because there was only one other option, and that option wasn't something he knew how to live with.

Besides—it would've been nice for Eamon to be the villain. It would've made it a lot easier for Hugo to deal with all his weird, complicated feelings about having been the one to kill him.

Before

The brothers were in the woods when they were seen by a human.

That had never happened before. They'd been so well hidden their whole lives, so tucked out of sight, kept off the beaten paths so anyone who might stumble across them had to have been looking. And no one ever came looking.

But then there was this human. Walking alone, chunky headphones on, eyes down, minding their own business. Maybe they were trying to get away from their family back at their own campsite. Maybe they'd gotten lost, wandering too far off the trail. Maybe they hadn't even realized yet they were so deep in the woods.

Felix tried to slip away, ducking and fleeing into the trees.

Hugo would have done the same. But he took a step back, then another, and then—

The human raised their head. Their eyes latched on to the antlers, sprawled like fruitless boughs from Hugo's skull. The cell phone fell from their hand, headphones yanked away, both disappearing into leaves and branches.

"Huey—" Felix whispered at his back.

But Hugo stared into the human's wide, unblinking eyes, unmoving for a moment that stretched and stretched until it couldn't anymore. Until snapping was the only option.

Don't do it, he thought. *Please don't make me do this.*

The human turned and started to race away.

Fine.

If anyone could stomach doing the horrible and unavoidable thing, it was Hugo. It always was.

He was faster and stronger and even when the human fought back, desperately trying to claw him off, he still managed to get his hands around their neck. When their hazel eyes turned red from the popping of blood vessels, he still managed to keep them pressed to the ground with one knee on their chest. Eventually, its rise and fall became slower and slower and then stopped entirely.

From a distance, Felix watched the whole thing.

Before

"Felix . . . what did you do?"

Hugo stared at the no-longer-human half-buried in the woods.

"Do you see that?" Felix whispered, a smile in his voice. "He's breathing."

The *human* was dead. But something new was living in its body. Something that would soon wake up.

"How did you . . . how did you do this?"

"It was easy," Felix answered. "I just believed I could save him, and I did."

Chapter 30

Hugo

Over their heads, the inky nothing of the ruined sky whispers in the same voice as the deer that wasn't. Hugo understands what he's hearing now. This unending void is where Felix pours every truth he can't look at—this is his devoted brother's shameful doubt finally come to call.

His inner world is coming undone. And that means they are running out of time.

"Felix." Hugo takes a step toward his brother. "You have to let them go now."

"No." Felix shakes his head. When he whimpers, thunder rumbles in the distance. "I can't. I'm *protecting* them. I'm keeping them alive. Don't you understand? That's what I do, Huey. I keep people alive—no matter what."

"I know. I know, but . . . you can't make people stay." Hugo shakes his head. "If you have to make them, it isn't real."

"I can make it real," Felix whimpers.

"I can make you a deal," Hugo counters.

Felix twists his hands, anxiously, over his belly. He worries his lower lip between his teeth. But the border of his curiosity has been breached. "What kind of deal?"

"Let them go."

"No, I—"

"Let them go, and I'll stay here with you." He's had time to think about this now. In the back of his mind, ever since the first inkling of possibility started to lift its head, Hugo has had time to turn it over and over again. He's already seen this ending through. He isn't going to back out. "Send them back home, Felix, and I will stay here with you forever."

"No!" Bird shouts, wheeling on him.

He pretends not to hear them, because that is the kindest thing he can do.

The black sky begins to fall, the shimmering nothing dripping from the split-open seam. It spills like oil, beginning to coat the tops of the trees, slicking down the branches like some awful toxic molasses.

In his periphery, new shadows begin to emerge from the nothing. In the whispers, growing louder and louder, *you will never go home again* and *i will eat you i promise* and *don't forgive me i am going to kill again*, stacking on top of one another until they could make a chorus that bellows throughout whatever plane they're trapped in, he thinks he hears a girl laugh.

Felix's inner world is unraveling, and every dark and awful thing he's ever seen, or thought, or wanted, is about to spill out over the elaborate fantasy he has created in his own mind. And when it does, Hugo knows how that's going to end, too. He just needs to make sure they're the only two around to see it.

"Send them home," he repeats, "and I will stay here with you and Charlotte forever."

Felix is a wretched little thing made of hope and fallacy and he trembles as he scrubs tears from his cheeks with the back of his wrist. "You're just saying that so I'll send them away. You don't want to stay with me, you want to save *them*."

"I do want to save them," Hugo agrees. His voice breaks when something in his chest overgrows and snaps free. "But there is no world, not the ones we've come from or the ones we've built or the ones we'll never even get to see, where I would ever abandon you. When everything else is gone, I stay. If we die, we die together. Do you understand? I will never leave you."

Felix gives a pathetic cry and throws himself into Hugo's arms. He wraps himself around his older brother, burying his face in his chest and squeezing tight. "I'm so sorry, I'm so sorry."

Hugo could pretend it's the tightness of the hug that makes it difficult to breathe. He wraps his own arms around his little brother and kisses the top of his head and tells him, "I know you are. I know you didn't mean to scare anyone."

"Um . . ." Cal sniffs, stepping toward them. "Felix? I would really—I would really love it if I didn't have to die here. Can you . . . can you please . . . ?"

Felix pulls back and sniffs, shifting on his heels. He can barely meet her eye, shame like a cloak over his face. "Okay . . . yeah. Okay. I am sorry, you know. I love you so much, I thought—I just wanted to keep you safe."

Cal shakes her head. When she speaks, her voice lacks the bravado he was expecting. She's had all of it bled out of her—what's left is the soft pink underbelly of who Cal could've been. "I'm sorry, too. I am . . . I am really sorry this happened to you. We both deserved better."

They all did. But that doesn't matter. Deserving something has never mattered.

One hand still on Felix's back, Hugo tilts his head to Eamon. The walking shadow has been silent for a while now. But Hugo knows he sees everything. Maybe even more than Hugo himself does.

"When you get back to the campsite—there's a wallet and a cell phone hidden under my mattress. I could never figure out the code to get into the phone, but . . ." He swallows. "But there are missing posters of you all over the country. Your family never stopped trying to find you. And I don't have enough time left to tell you how much I wish you never met me."

Eamon's eyes widen a fraction. Otherwise, he gives no indication of surprise. As if this was information he'd known all along, and he was just waiting for someone to acknowledge it.

And maybe it is. Hugo doesn't know if the others are on to something, with their theories about the Caravan making monsters out of humans. He doesn't know how they'd do it, if they did, or how they'd get rid of their memories. But he knows whatever Felix did wasn't a perfect replica of their methods, if those methods exist. There were gaps left behind, holes Eamon could still look back and see through. And maybe he can get all of his memories back someday, because of them.

"I'm glad I met you," Felix mumbles. "Even if you hate me."

"I do not hate you," Eamon answers, because he is kind and good and all the things Hugo has wished so badly he wasn't. "But I am glad we will not see each other again."

"Okay." Hugo nods. "Do it now."

"Are you kidding me?" Bird demands. "You aren't even going

to look at me? Look at me! You can't do this! You cannot do this to me!"

They throw their hands up next to him, desperately trying to get him to face them. He doesn't. He flinches and stares at nothing and nothing stares back.

"You could stay with us, Birdie," Felix whispers. "You don't understand how unsafe it is out there. Especially for you . . ."

"No." Hugo gives one resolute shake of his head. His jaw tightens. "They don't get to stay."

Felix makes a soft, miserable noise in the back of his throat. He doesn't argue.

"I thought you said staying was only real if it was a decision someone made." Their voice scratches against itself like sandpaper. "You're not letting me decide, so this isn't real. It isn't *fair*."

"Yeah." Hugo sniff and looks around them, to the others. "Please."

Cal nods, stepping forward and wrapping a hand around Bird's elbow. She tugs them back. "Come on. We can't—"

"Let go of me!" Bird thrashes in Cal's grip, screaming to rival the onslaught of whispers still reverberating through every inch of this should-be-impossible world. "Don't touch me."

For a split second, Cal hesitates. Hugo thinks she's going to let them go. Instead, she straightens her spine and tightens her grip. Over her shoulder, she says to Eamon, "Help."

The shadow steps forward and takes Bird's other arm. Together, the two of them drag them away, even as Bird's violent protests grow wilder. On either side of their anguish, the executioner and the apparition stand guard, witnesses to their grief.

With a little distance between them—and because he is selfish and stupid and knows how this is going to end, no matter what he does next—Hugo lets himself look at Bird. He meets the eyes he would know anywhere, in any world, alive or dead, and prays someday, in a lifetime so far away from this one, they might find each other again.

Because they're soulmates. It's the worst truth he's ever known. "It isn't fair," he agrees. "But *this* is the way I love you without ruining you."

Bird shudders, finally going still between their captors.

"And I hope you still love me enough to forgive me."

Their knees go out from under them, but Cal and Eamon keep them standing.

Hugo looks away.

"Now, Felix."

"Goodbye. I love you."

His little brother blows a kiss. There's a flutter of light in Hugo's periphery. And when he turns his head to look at the spot where they'd just stood, the other three are gone.

Everything hurts so badly he's certain he'll never be able to think again. And still, he breathes a sigh of relief.

"It's just us now," Felix whimpers through his tears, looking around at the black-soaked world around them. Slowly, the woods have begun to flood, a pool of that dripping ink gathering at their feet. "Well—almost."

From inside the roar of frenzied whispers, Hugo hears the girl's laughter again. A moment later, she steps free of the trees. And she isn't real, Hugo knows this, but she is exactly how he would have summoned her himself. Big green eyes. Freckles and freckles and freckles.

Today, though, the thick, black nothing of Felix's decaying mind coats her hair, making it stick to her back. It bubbles over her perfect face and down her shoulders, coating the dead girl in the secret shame of her twin.

Still, it doesn't deter her from running to them. Charlotte throws her arms around them both, dragging her brothers in for a group hug. "Oh, you're finally here! I've been waiting for so long!"

Felix curls one arm around them both. And Hugo knows it doesn't matter anymore anyway, so he does the same. He pulls his siblings in closer, holding them tightly against his chest. He listens to the sounds of their hearts beating alongside his own and he imagines he could memorize that sound and save it for later. Even though he knows there is no later.

When Felix finally pulls back, his tears have turned into the black goo. They slide down his face, leaving trails behind them that streak over his cheeks. And still, he smiles. "What are we going to do now? We can do anything we want. The whole world is ours."

The twins are both looking at him. Their smiles are identical, he realizes.

Their denial is almost infectious. He knows they cannot see their world is drowning, because they don't want to. They *believe* everything is okay, and so it must be.

There is a part of Hugo that envies them for it.

He touches his face to the top of Charlotte's head and breathes in deep. The sludge in her hair smells, as he knew it would, of gasoline.

Hugo reaches up to cup a hand over Felix's cheek. He brushes one black tear, smearing the opaque naught beneath his thumb.

"Right now . . . we're just going to keep believing everything is okay." He smiles, too. "I love you both so much."

In his palm, a spark ignites. Immediately, Hugo's furious fire meets the fuel of Felix's ignorant abyss.

And the whole wide world in his little brother's mind goes up in flames.

After

Bird

The night the unthinkable happens, Bird wakes screaming in the woods with Calliope's and Eamon's arms still wrapped around them.

"NO!" They nearly choke around the wail, desperately clawing their way free. They force themself to their hands and knees, scrambling through the sticks and dirt. "Where are they? Where are they, where—"

Whatever state Hugo and Felix's bodies were in before, they are no longer. Bird stares, horrified and confused, as their hands fall on bones hidden beneath the fallen leaves. With trembling fingers, they run their palms along the ivory, unbelieving what they're seeing even when they can touch it with their hands.

"Are those . . ." Calliope's voice floats toward the back of their head.

"Yes," Eamon answers. "They are exactly what you think they are."

The bones where their friends' bodies once laid are not human. The skeletal remains of two deer lie together in the woods—one stag curled around one fawn.

The sound Bird makes is inhuman, pulled up from the deepest pit inside them. They want to curl up and waste to nothing, right alongside them.

Calliope rubs their back, and Eamon watches, and neither of them say anything because there is nothing to say.

How are they supposed to move on in a world where Hugo doesn't exist? At least in a world where he hated them, they knew he was still *out there.* Without that, without the counterweight of his life holding theirs in check, Bird thinks they might just spend the rest of their time on Earth walking around off balance.

Because life is cruel, they aren't given any time to mourn.

There's a shuffling in the woods behind them. Bird doesn't sit up to look at who's approaching until they hear the voice of their mother.

"Oh! Sweetheart, there you are!" Holly Stieber slurs her words only a little, tipsy but not drunk. "I've been looking everywhere for you."

Slowly, slowly, Bird sits. They twist their torso to face her, not bothering to conceal whatever animal thing is living on their face. Calliope keeps an arm draped over their lap, a physical barrier between Bird and their mother. Eamon moves, subtly, a little closer.

By the looks of Holly's outfit, it's still the night of the new moon. If Bird listened closely, they could still make out celebratory shouting nearby.

Everything, everything, everything has changed and yet no time has actually passed at all.

If Holly notices Bird doesn't seem well, she gives no indication. "Come on, darling, you have to join the party. We have a surprise for you."

"No." Bird does not extrapolate on their response.

"But—" Holly pouts. "But we have a surprise!"

"This isn't a good time," Calliope growls.

"Well, it's the only time, actually. At least for another month." Holly huffs, straining to keep up her smile. It makes her look as inhuman as Bird feels. "Come on, you. Get up. *Now.*"

"Excuse me." Eamon stands, sliding his hands into his pockets. "What sort of surprise is it?"

Holly glances between Cal and Eamon and finally Bird, eyes narrowed like she's attempting mental math. When she looks back at her only child, her smile has stretched into something even more forced—there is nothing happy about the way her cracked lips peel back over her teeth, her mouth parted as if her jaw is thinking of coming unhinged.

"We're just so happy you're back, sweetheart. You . . . you have always been such a gift to the Caravan. We always knew you were special, and we knew someday, we needed to show you how much you really meant to everyone here. Now that you're home, we finally have our chance." Holly holds out her hand. "Come on. Come to the fire with me. It's a night for making wishes, and you're our best one yet."

Bird stares at their mother's hand. From beyond the cover of trees, they can smell the smoke coming off the campfire. And it could be their imagination, but they swear they smell roasting meat.

"Bird . . ." Calliope's voice is a warning.

"I know," they answer.

Maybe it's their own subconscious. Maybe it's Hugo, reaching through the veil across worlds and lives, one half of a soul stretching out to brush against its missing limbs.

Maybe it's Charlotte's voice, crawling up through time, an echo of a wound that never healed.

Maybe it doesn't matter who it is, as long as Bird gets the message.

Run.

Acknowledgments

This book was conceived and written on the traditional home-land of the Puyallup Tribe, and no location in this story could exist today without being stewarded by its ancestral caretakers. I am committed to a future where all land is returned to Indigenous peoples. I encourage readers to educate themselves on the Land Back movement and on whose homes they have built their own lives.

Thank you to my team at Wednesday for their work behind the scenes, including my editor, Tiffany Shelton. Multiple health crises and natural disasters attempted to stop us from making this book happen, but we did it—somehow.

As always, I owe so much of my career to my agents, Lee O'Brien and Victoria Marini.

Whatever I don't owe my agents, I owe to my partner, Westley, who had to quite literally *be* my hands on more than one occasion this past year. I know damn well everything would've fallen apart without you. I hope you know that, too. Thank you for giving me the kind of love that lets me tell people they should never settle for anything less than someone who's obsessed with them.

Finally, this book is for survivors of religious abuse—especially those still struggling to call it abuse, to dismantle dangerous beliefs, to claw their way to a new self in the aftermath of their world splitting open and swallowing them whole. This book is for those who are still stuck in those places of isolation and shame, who can't yet see a way out. For Izzy and Grey. For Katja. I love you.

About the Author

Westley Vega

H.E. EDGMON did not sleep for several years and is now the author of copious novels and short works for tweens, teens, and adults. Their lineup includes The Witch King duology, the Ouroboros duology, and *The Flicker*, and their writing has been described as "monstrously thrilling, deeply emotional" by *School Library Journal*. Across genres, H.E. hopes to find readers in their darkest moments and help them start a fire. In their laughably limited free time, they're likely hosting themed parties for no reason or trying to predict the future. They live in the Pacific Northwest, surrounded by chosen family and giant dogs.